DEEPLY ROOTED DREAMS

THE REWIRED SERIES
BOOK 2

ALEXANDER MUKTE

Three to Five Publishing, LLC
2107 N. Decatur Rd., Ste 438
Decatur, GA 30033
www.threetofivepublishing.com

Names: Mukte, Alexander.
Title: Deeply Rooted Dreams / Alexander Mukte.
Series: The Rewired Series.
Identifiers:
ISBN 978-1-952030-02-4 (paperback)
ISBN 978-1-952030-03-1 (ebook)
ISBN 978-1-952030-07-9 (library audiobook)
ISBN 978-1-952030-05-5 (retail audiobook)
Subjects:
BISAC: FICTION / Visionary & Metaphysical. |
FICTION / Nature & the Environment. |
FICTION / Magical Realism. |
FICTION / Own Voices.

For our sons, who provided the inspiration to write this book,

and

to my roots. I'm not as good as I can be, but I'm better than I was. Thank you for the sacrifices you've made, so that future generations may progress.

PROLOGUE

Excerpt from *The Recruiter*

"We don't have very much time, and speaking right now goes against protocol. But, since I am here under extraordinary circumstances, I get to bend a few rules. First, thank you for accepting my invitation."

I don't know that I'd call it an invitation, Jessica thought to herself.

"Oh, but it was, designed specifically for you," Ori said out loud.

Jessica gasped, "Can you—"

"Read your thoughts? Yes, not that it's difficult at the moment, but we will get into that at another time," Ori said. "We have a grave request for you. We need someone to do unbiased reporting on the trial."

"Trial, what trial?" Jessica asked.

Ori continued, "There is a trial underway now, at the very highest of levels. Evelyn and I have been on a mission to prove that these people are worth saving. I believe that if we can bring this trial and the progress being made out into the light, for the public to witness, then there is a chance that we will win."

"Who are *these people* in this scenario?" Jessica asked.

Evelyn placed her hand on Ori's forearm. "Jessica," she said, her voice calm, "this is a trial unlike any before and will be unlike any after. This is a trial that could determine the fate and future of all you know."

"What?" Jessica exclaimed. "This sounds extreme."

"I know this may be a lot to digest." Ori looked back at Jessica. "Think about it like this: the universe is a living thing, and just like any other living thing, its objective is to grow and expand. The Earth is meant to play a critical role in this universal expansion, but can only do that when human beings do what they are meant to do. There was a time when Earth was marvelous. However . . .," Ori paused, "let's just say that, currently, there is a lot of room for improvement. And what happens on Earth can cause a ripple effect throughout the universe."

"I suppose that sounds like it could be true," Jessica said thoughtfully. "Things have been getting better over the past few years though."

"And you've already started to write about these changes, which is exactly what we need," Ori said. "Things were bleak for so long that a total reset was being considered. Fear, violence, ego, and war were running rampant. An advocate proposed that if we were able to confine those negative forces, then Earth and its people could get back on the right track. We," Ori motioned to his group of friends, "have been charged with carrying out this task."

"And what is the right track?" asked Jessica, her head swimming.

"Every individual has greatness in him. The right track is when people are pursuing that greatness and not allowing these destructive energies and efforts to derail them."

"Okay . . ." Jessica thought for a moment. "Let's say that what you are telling me is true. Who will be the judge? How do you win a trial with the universe?"

"You collect as much consistent evidence as possible to support that Earth is still a beacon of light," Ori said.

"What does that kind of evidence look like?" Jessica asked.

"The only evidence that the universe cares about is people like you: people doing what they are meant to do, what they were built to do." Ori looked at his watch. "My job is to recruit as many people as possible, people who want to do the right thing with the gifts that they've been granted. The more people we have, the greater the chances of winning. All I ask of you is to simply document what you witness. That's it."

"That's it?" Jessica asked skeptically. "Document what I witness?"

Ori raised an eyebrow and gave a lopsided smile. "Are you in?"

"Well, it just kind of sounds like my job. But tell me this," Jessica paused. "Who are you, really?"

"It's a bit complicated, but in the flesh, I'm the Ori that you see. But my soul, or my spirit, is . . ." Ori searched for the right words, then smiled. "It's something very different. Something older than time."

"So," Ori extended his hand, "if you choose to shake my hand, you're making a choice to document only what you witness. Nothing more, nothing less. And by shaking my hand, I will grant you the gift of sight. This will allow you to see what is at stake. Do you agree? Will you join us?"

"Oh, why not!" Jessica firmly grabbed and shook Ori's hand.

"Great," Evelyn said, clapping her hands. "We've got the record keeper."

1

THE BAR FIGHT

urinal. No water flowed. The bathroom was not well lit, yet he could still see the dirty floor. Water trickled from the sink faucet, and the handles did nothing to affect the flow of water. All that remained where the soap dispenser had once been was a build-up of dirt. *My hands are probably cleaner if I don't use this water.* He tried to make out his reflection between the smudges and smears in the mirror. As he opened the door to head back upstairs, he felt the return of the rhythmic thump in his chest from the bass of the speakers.

There was no one else waiting in line to use the bathroom, which was odd for this time of night. The bar was popular with college students, who were typically from across the border, and anyone else who was drinking on a budget. The local patrons referred to the college student club-goers as outsiders. The locals appreciated the dive bar feel and the many secrets it held. These secrets are what brought Zach to Coco Locos.

He walked past the club entrance, where security guards assumed their post. A large crowd gathered in the streets, but before he could focus on that, something else caught his attention. Three other security guards were standing inside the doorway talking to a couple of Policía. *Odd.* The Policía were never in these types of bars. He slowly walked past, trying to read the expression on their faces. The security guards and the police officers were all on alert. *Why do they seem anxious?* He went up the stairs toward the dance floor.

Before the guards and officers disappeared from his view, Zach noticed something else: another man was pacing behind them—a tall, lean black man. He was wearing a white shirt, which had a dark stain on it, possibly from a spilled drink. As Zach took in the scene, he recognized that the three guards all had their backs to the man in the white shirt. It was as if they were protecting him. Zach inspected the man being shielded. With one hand he was holding a drink, and with the other, he was gripping his face. The stain on the man's shirt, Zach realized, wasn't a drink. It was blood.

He turned to continue upstairs. *I hope this guy Carlos shows up soon. Something doesn't feel right.* He had learned to live by his intuition, and right now, it was telling him there was not a lot of time before things at this bar got out of hand. If he wanted to get out of there unmarked, he needed to immediately find Carlos and complete their transaction.

Zach reached the dance floor just as the DJ played some classic DMX, which would typically have had this crowd going wild. He noticed that only the outsiders were dancing. The locals were just staring at them with a level of intensity that he had not witnessed before. One local gave him a slight head nod as they crossed paths. Zach noted that she was the last of the local women to leave the dance floor, yet the bar was almost at capacity. *Where did all of the local women go?* He hesitated for a second until he realized that it didn't matter. He had traveled this far. His contact said he would be here, so he just needed to wait.

Zach eyed the stairs, waiting to see someone who might be Carlos emerge. His problem was that he had no idea what Carlos or his representative looked like. He used old connections and contacted La Tiniebla Cartel's boss. It had been a long time since he had knowingly made a business deal with anyone allegedly on the wrong side of the law, but Carlos had critical information.

Zach stood at the end of the bar and glanced down at his watch. His contact was late. Just as he took his first step back toward the stairs, he heard a voice from behind the bar.

"Leaving so soon?"

Zach turned around to find a cleanly shaven man wearing a nice dress shirt and a blazer.

"It looks like it," Zach said warily. "I was waiting for someone, but he is late."

"Better late than never, don't you think, Zach?" the man asked.

"Carlos?"

The man gave a single patient nod and made the type of calm, direct eye contact that led Zach to believe him.

Zach checked his immediate surroundings and then reached under his shirt and pulled out a small waist pack. "As agreed, there are a hundred SIM cards in here, all programmed to be untraceable."

Carlos opened the pack and examined its contents.

Zach pulled out a cell phone. "We can test a chip if you'd like."

"We trust you, Zach," Carlos said before handing him a thick manila envelope. "And we appreciate it."

Zach stared at the envelope.

"Do you want to take a quick look?" Carlos asked. "All the information you requested is inside."

Movement in the periphery pulled Zach's attention to the dance floor. The group of local men was now standing around the edge of the floor. The men were squared up, ready for action. Simultaneously, the drunken outsiders remained oblivious to their offenses and the inevitable consequences.

"Now would be the time, Zach." Carlos's voice brought him back to the moment.

Zach opened the envelope and pressed the thick stack of papers against the edge. He could see a small bag of memory chips at the bottom. He read a few lines of the document. He nodded his head.

"Does this meet your expectations?" Carlos asked.

"You know, I don't typically do things like this," Zach said, looking back up.

"That's great to hear." Carlos smiled. "And who's to say that you did this at all?" Carlos paused. "You are playing a perilous game here though."

Zach's brows knitted together in an earnest expression. "I'm not playing a game. I'm doing what's right."

The two men stood in silence until the sound of a bottle crashing on the floor broke the moment. "I appreciate this," Zach said as he patted the envelope.

Carlos leaned forward. "So that you may rest easy, this is not a game for us either. The right thing in this situation is where our interests lie as well."

Zach gave a nod of understanding.

"It's time for you to go," Carlos said.

As Zach walked down the stairs, he noticed that more young men were coming into the bar and walking upstairs. Downstairs, he saw that the man in the white shirt was still standing behind the guards, pacing side to side like a caged animal awaiting his chance to strike a blow. As he approached the entrance, he found that the security guards had closed the door, even though the bar wasn't scheduled to close for a few more hours. Perhaps it had already reached capacity. *I'm sure that they'll be happy I'm leaving so they can allow one more paying person in.* The guard at the entrance looked at him for a moment before opening the door. Zach smiled widely, showing his teeth. "Thank you, gracias," he said.

When Zach reemerged onto the street, he was met with a swarm of angry locals, all clothed in red. The gravity of the situation set in, and he realized he was wrong about the man in the white shirt. He wasn't ready to attack; he was ready to take flight. Though they examined him closely, the crowd did not seem to object to Zach, allowing him to make his way through. Zach focused his gaze ahead and relaxed his hands. *I'm not a threat, I'm not a threat, I'm not a threat.* Just as Zach made it past the red sea, someone stepped in front of him —a man wearing a black suit and tie.

"Hi Zach," the man said. "You've been a very busy bee."

2

———

JESSICA AND HER SOURCE

Jessica looked up from her phone's glowing screen and stared off in a daze as her breath fogged the windshield. She hadn't seen any movement on the street, and she realized that she shouldn't expect to either. *It's doubtful that anyone will see me.* She glanced at her watch: 3:09 AM. She took one final look up and down the dark vacant street. She was meeting her source at a house in North Druid Hills, not far from where she was staying.

Jessica's boss had wanted someone willing to cover the Centers for Disease Control and Prevention's Global Viral Mitigation Forum. As an investigative journalist, she wasn't particularly thrilled to cover the conference, but it afforded her an ideal opportunity to connect with her source and avoid suspicion. As per usual, her source held on to sensitive information until they could meet in person. Zach insisted that she come down as soon as possible, and this conference's timing worked out.

Jessica took another deep breath, then figured it was time to get inside. She checked to make sure that her car's interior light was turned off. She got out and softly closed the door. As she approached the house, she avoided the streetlights, moving among the shadows. The house was not overly remarkable, just a single-story, red brick home. However, the house had the potential to be worth a lot of money once renovated.

Jessica opened the fence and entered the property from the backyard. The back door had a digital door lock. She used the six-digit pin that Zach had given her, and she heard the mechanical sound of the deadbolt opening. Zach had been incredibly forthcoming and trustworthy to this point, not to mention principled. She did not expect things to change now. The lights were out, making it difficult to see where she was going. Something told her not to turn on the lights. Jessica moved through the house, pausing every few steps to listen for any strange sounds. She entered a bedroom, then a small office, and later a bathroom. Besides a half-used roll of toilet paper, there was no sign that anyone had been in this house. The hallway led from the back area where the bedrooms were and opened up to the living room. The kitchen was on her left. Jessica paused before entering the room.

Her eyes shifted as she scanned the area. *Did I hear something?* She froze in place and strained to hear as much as possible. The house was quiet. The only sound was the faint buzz of the refrigerator.

She slowly moved forward into the living room toward a flat-screen TV monitor with a small box attached to it. Surrounding the monitor were several bookshelves with hundreds of Blu-ray discs. Unprompted, the box opened suddenly and ejected a disc. She squinted and whispered, "What?" She approached the ejected panel and reached out her hand to retrieve the disc. Just then she heard a sound to her left. She quickly turned toward the foyer, and within a split second, she saw a flash of light, noticed a metallic taste in her mouth, and collapsed onto the floor.

3

JESSICA COMES TO

JESSICA TRIED TO OPEN HER EYES AND FELT HER HEART POUND WHEN HER eyelids wouldn't cooperate. She rubbed her eyes, removing dried tears. Slowly, she peeled her eyelashes apart, which allowed her to see.

She was lying on her side. She surveyed the area around her but didn't recognize anything. She expected to see the boring beige walls of her hotel room—Str8 Truth Media budgets only allowed journalists to stay in middle-of-the-road establishments—but what she saw wasn't her room.

Her senses returned as her brain embraced the coolness of the grass under her cheek. Puzzled, she rolled onto her knees in an attempt to get up, but the rhythmic throbbing on the side of her head shackled her knees to the ground.

She tried to look around to assess where she could be. She made out a tree-lined grassy meadow, but before she could take in more, everything began to spin. Jessica had an awful flashback to the time in middle school when a friend convinced her to go on the biggest roller coaster. She threw up for an hour afterward and swore to never go on anything like that again. *That's one promise to myself I've never broken.*

But this wasn't that. Jessica lay her head back down on the grass, hoping it would stop the spins and the pain. Much to her relief, as soon as she closed her eyes and took a deep breath, a soothing feeling came over her. She inhaled deeply and exhaled even more profoundly. *Now, what do I do?* She still had her eyes shut tightly as she began to notice the pleasant sound of water nearby, which helped her relax.

The sound came from above her head. She shifted her body toward it little by little and tried opening her eyes again. Jessica was lying at the edge of a clear blue pond. As she gazed at the pond's surface, amazed by the color and clarity, a koi fish the size of her leg popped its head up.

"Where am I?" she whispered before several other large koi fish appeared. Jessica now pushed herself up onto her knees to get a better view of the water. What started as one fish turned into hundreds, all with their heads out of the water, looking at her. They had the shape of large koi, but instead of their scales being the typical white, orange, and black colors, all of their scales were transparent. Jessica could see the organs working together inside, and contrary to the transparent scales, the fish's inner workings were radiant colors. The sight was beautiful and confusing. She felt panic rising in her chest, and her headache returned, bringing her back down onto the grass.

She shut her eyes as tightly as she could, hoping this odd dream would end, when a flashing light turned the inside of her eyelids from dark black to a fleshy red. She raised her hand out in front of her to shield her eyes from the blinding light and opened her eyes to a safe squint. She watched a figure approach and asked, "Can you lower that flashlight, please?" The light was a vibrant violet-blue. *It must be one of those new LED energy efficient flashlights.* Her head was still ringing, and the light had not yet dimmed. Jessica repeated her request, "Can you please lower that flashlight?"

"Are you okay?" a woman asked. "What are you doing out here?"

Jessica shook her head. As the light dimmed, Jessica's vision returned. She inhaled deeply and looked upward. *Are those stars in the sky? I haven't seen that many stars since I went camping at the Grand*

Canyon when I was a kid. "Where am I?" Jessica asked. "And what time is it?"

"You are in the middle of a field," the woman said. "Do you remember how you got here?"

Jessica looked around again. *I don't even know where here is.* "I'm not sure," she responded.

"Do you want some help up?" the stranger asked, extending a hand.

Jessica regarded the woman, evaluating her before accepting her hand. She seemed tall and lean, yet strong, with curly black hair and a kind smile. She was wearing a white linen dress that flowed down to her ankles, and she was barefoot. *I'm in some hippie commune.*

"Any idea where you were headed?" the woman asked.

As the woman helped Jessica to her feet, Jessica tried to remember, and then she noticed the pond move. Jessica watched, mesmerized, as the clear blue lake turned white and choppy, more like a river rapid. Koi fish were jumping out of the water like sharks fighting over fresh chum. Jessica fell back to the ground, and everything went black again.

4

JESSICA'S ARTICLE

Tap tap tap. The knocking on the door was just loud enough to wake Jessica. Groggy, she opened her eyes, and this time she saw what she expected. She was comforted by the beige walls of her hotel room. She slowly sat up as she looked around the room. *Tap, tap, tap,* the knocking continued.

"Give me a minute," Jessica called toward the door. She saw that her roller bag was in the corner on the luggage rack, still zipped. She looked down, realizing that she was still wearing the same clothes from the night before, and she had slept on top of the bed covers.

She heard the knocking again, which forced her to gather enough energy to get out of bed and answer the door. Her legs buckled slightly with the first few steps. *I must be exhausted.* She grabbed her transparent mask and quickly placed it over her nose and mouth before opening the door.

"Deputy Director Shikibu," Jessica said, "I didn't expect to see you here."

"Ms. Ifill," she said, her tone far from friendly. "May I come in?"

"Of course, please do." Jessica held the door open and stepped aside. "I guess I shouldn't be surprised that the FBI would send someone to the CDC's forum."

The Deputy Director came in and placed a black backpack on the table next to the coffee maker. She reached in and pulled out a small black case, which she sat on top of the dresser next to the television. "Do you mind?" she asked.

"Not at all," Jessica said as the Deputy Director retrieved two small cotton swabs. Jessica pulled her mask down slightly, only exposing her nose. She placed the cotton portion of the swab in her nostril and exhaled audibly. Jessica then pulled her mask back over her nose and handed the swab back to the Deputy Director, who then followed suit and ran the rapid test on each.

"We're both negative. Are you comfortable pulling these down?" the Deputy Director asked, indicating her mask. "I'd like this conversation to be a bit more… informal."

Jessica felt a little uneasy about what was to come. Her relationship with the Deputy Director had always been kind and professional, but never informal. "Sure, Mikiko," Jessica said as she slowly pulled down her mask.

Mikiko pulled her mask down and smiled.

"I found your latest article quite interesting," Mikiko said, as she pulled a rolled-up copy out of her bag. Jessica saw underlined and circled portions in her article, "Dark Energy, the Trillion-Dollar Market or Marketing Ploy?" "How did that go over with your friends at the Singularity Group?"

Jessica shrugged. "I told them I was going to write the truth. They knew what was coming, and Leslie didn't seem worried about it hurting their competitive advantage."

Jessica had received a lot of attention for her latest in-depth piece on the Singularity Group's dark energy product lines. Jessica thought it was important that people know that there's no "magic" behind their Dark Energy Smart Screen Technology. It's just the latest evolution of Electro Encephalography or EEG technology that reads the brain's electrical signals.

"Why did you write this one?" Mikiko asked.

"These screens are on every device in the world. The public should know that the technology embeds brain signal reading electrodes into each screen. People should understand that when their skin touches a screen, that technology can technically read their thoughts."

Mikiko nodded. "I agree with you. People should know this, although they don't seem to care as long as it makes their lives easier."

Jessica realized that she still had no idea why Mikiko was in Atlanta in her hotel room. "I can talk about my writing all day, but why are you here?"

"Well," Mikiko started, "as part of this trip, I was originally planning to speak to a person that I believe we both know, Zach Carver. I'm just curious about how well you know him."

"Why?" Jessica asked, becoming suspicious of this line of conversation. She crossed her arms.

Mikiko looked around the room. "Do you mind if we sit?"

The two sat at the small round table in the room. As Jessica settled in her seat, she rubbed both of her temples with her index and middle finger.

Mikiko leaned back in the chair and asked, "Are you all right?"

Jessica looked up, nodded, and tried to smile as she rested her hands in her lap.

Mikiko stared at Jessica, and then as if she had decided on something, she gave a sharp nod and said, "I suppose desperate times call for desperate measures."

This made Jessica sit up even straighter in her chair. "What's up?"

"I assume that you are familiar with Confidence Biotech?" Mikiko asked.

"Yes," Jessica said. She and her colleagues had done several hours of research on the company. "They operate a relatively successful company, but we received a tip to look deeper into their financials and business practices. We didn't find an angle at the time, so other stories took priority."

Mikiko said, "We, too, investigated them but didn't come up with anything solid enough to support some odd complaints. The investigation stalled, but then our interest was sparked again when we found out that they were going to partner with the Singularity Group to develop some technology."

"But then the Singularity Group pulled out of that partnership," said Jessica.

"Didn't you wonder why?" asked Mikiko.

"Of course."

"Well, us too," replied Mikiko. "We began to uncover some tidbits of information, but now with the announcement…"

"What announcement?" Jessica asked.

Mikiko laughed tentatively.

Jessica shook her head. "No. What announcement?"

Mikiko studied Jessica. "You're serious, aren't you?"

"Yes," was all that Jessica could say.

"On the first day of the conference, Confidence Biotech announced that they are launching a brand-new global system that can remotely trace and track viral infections. It's called Global Breadth, and it relies on a proprietary, private network. They're claiming it to be infallible. We believe it to have been a product of that partnership."

"Wh-what?" Jessica said, looking down at the table. *How did I miss that?* "The first day of the conference?" Jessica asked, looking back up for confirmation.

"Yes," Mikiko affirmed. "That's why I came to speak with you. I assumed that you had some form of connection with Zach through your writing on the Singularity Group. He's a savant and the key point person on any new technology."

Jessica still didn't say anything as Mikiko continued, "But then Zach went missing last Sunday night."

"What?" Jessica asked, genuinely alarmed. "That's impossible!" *I just talked to him last night.* She continued, "I got in last night; why didn't I hear about any of this?"

"Jessica," Mikiko said with a look of concern spreading across her face, "your flight landed a little over a week ago. I came to your hotel room because no one has seen you at the conference all week. I need your help to help Zach."

A week ago? She tried to think back to her last meeting with Zach, but her memory was so foggy. "Do you have any leads on where he could be?"

"We did find him." Mikiko paused before continuing. "He's been admitted into an assisted living home not far from here. Zach's been diagnosed with an early stage of dementia."

"What? He's way too young for that," Jessica said. *This is impossible.*

"That's what I said. I hope that he's been misdiagnosed, but..." Mikiko trailed off.

Jessica searched her mind for any explanation and tried not to freak out.

"Jessica."

Mikiko saying her name brought her mind back to the hotel room.

"There's one more thing."

5

———

WHY ZACH?

Jessica bounced her knee nonstop as the information set in. Questions raced through her head. *I never noticed anything in all my time with him. With my history of dementia, how could I not have seen any of the signs?*

"Jessica," Mikiko said, "I know that this is a lot to take in, but I need—"

Jessica cut her off. "Had Zach agreed to talk to you? He was very skeptical of," Jessica cleared her throat, "law enforcement."

"He had," Mikiko said. "Zach reached out to me a couple of months ago. He didn't say anything to you because he wanted to keep you out of it."

"Out of what?" Jessica prodded.

"He confirmed that the Singularity Group was working in partnership with Confidence Biotech to create an incredibly advanced virus contact tracing technology. Zach was leading the initiative on the Singularity Group side. He had figured out a way to write the code to integrate the virus tracing features into the EEG screens. The contact tracer technology wouldn't require doctors to test each individual anymore. The technology is capable of testing large groups of people at the same time and identifying who has a respiratory infection and what type of infection."

"Did he explain how?" Jessica asked.

"No one knew, and Zach kept that very close to him," Mikiko said. "We know that it was a new advancement evaluating the aerosolized particles exhaled by individuals. Zach and the Singularity Group began to have reservations once Confidence Biotech started hiring their fleet of contact tracers."

Jessica raised her eyebrows. "Definitely worrying."

"These Biotech tracers are tasked with identifying and quarantining potential contamination threats. Most, if not all, of the new hires have military or law enforcement backgrounds and little to no healthcare experience. We believe they were also spreading information to dampen faith in the government-funded contact tracers."

Jessica didn't respond. Her face must've said it all.

"Yeah, I know," Mikiko said. "Confidence Biotech and their Biotech tracers started bringing test subjects from developing countries into the lab. Zach grew suspicious and reached out to me when he saw online chatter that some of the previously quarantined people went missing shortly after returning home. Zach cross-referenced the contact tracer trial results with the missing people's data and came up with a theory. Zach noticed that the people disappearing all had one thing in common, they were all asymptomatic or had immunity to the virus."

"ASIMs," Jessica whispered.

"Exactly," Mikiko said. "Scary prospect, but my team couldn't pursue it."

"Why?" Jessica asked.

"Mostly, a jurisdictional nightmare. The other thing was that Zach didn't have enough proof that those people's disappearances were tied to the contact tracer initiative. Still, because of the various countries and governments involved, I had to pass the case to colleagues in other departments. Do you mind?" Mikiko asked, pointing to a bottle of water.

"Not at all," Jessica said.

Mikiko opened the bottle of water and took a sip. "Zach was understandably frustrated with the lack of progress in the case. Zach also told me that he found a way to get evidence. He was going down to Nogales, Mexico, to meet with a source to get proof, then he and I were going to connect during the CDC's forum. This was a little after the Singularity Group pulled out of the partnership with Confidence Biotech."

"So how is Confidence Biotech still announcing this new technology?"

"That's part of what I'm trying to figure out. The Singularity Group, of course, worked to exit the partnership while protecting their part of the technology and IP. There shouldn't be a way for Confidence Biotech to have rebuilt on its own. And now with Zach's change in circumstances..."

"What do you need from me?" Jessica asked.

"I was hoping to gain some insight into Zach, his background, his state of mind," Mikiko said.

"Okay, where did you want to start?"

"I'm sure you know about Zach's past, right?" Mikiko asked.

Jessica, still not showing her hand, pretended to be ignorant. "What do you mean?"

Mikiko smirked. "The hacking."

"He mentioned that he started young, doing some small system hacks." She paused. "He bragged about how he had developed a pretty impressive network of social media bots."

Mikiko stood up and went to her bag. She reached in and pulled out a thick folder. "Zach used to be a major force in the hacking world. He went by the alias Digital Snowflake."

Because he was one of a kind. Jessica thought back to the first time she heard his alias and how hard she laughed. She fought back a smile when Mikiko said it.

"By the time he was a teenager, he pulled off the largest electronic currency heist ever recorded."

"He gave the money back, though," Jessica said.

"So you do know."

"Bits and pieces."

"They still tried him as an adult, and since he was a kid who was raised in the foster care system, he didn't have any family rush to his rescue. That was probably a blessing in disguise. While serving time, Zach was accepted into the Singularity Group's recidivism program. He proved to be brilliant in all things technology-based. He thrived in the Research and Development division once released. I had a team look into his latest activities, and I couldn't find anything that seemed suspicious. Jessica, I think this guy is a good seed. I don't know what's happening to him, but my gut tells me that something is off."

"What you're saying lines up with what I know."

"Well, the problem now is his current mental state. It's impossible to get any information out of him. He's confused and paranoid."

"I'm still not sure how I can help," Jessica said.

"Zach must be a key contact of yours inside the Singularity Group. With the details you had on their technology, you must have spent time with him. Outside of work, Zach was a bit of a lone wolf, so we don't have a lot of people to help here. Did you ever notice anything off? Any lapse in memory?"

"No, nothing. He was always incredibly sharp."

"It's bizarre that a man in his thirties can one day be all there, then the next day has an advanced state of a mentally debilitating disease."

"I can't believe it. Zach was different, but he was not mentally ill. He had a real sense of clarity and did not forget a thing."

Mikiko reached into her jacket pocket and pulled out a small black recording device. "I've gotten my hands on something; don't ask me how." She took a deep breath, placed the device on the table, and pressed play.

6

____

ZACH'S CONVERSATION WITH THE DOCTOR

THE RECORDING HAD A LOT OF WHITE NOISE. MIKIKO APOLOGIZED, "The techs couldn't clean up the audio entirely for some reason."

Jessica heard, "Good morning, Zach. My name is Dr. Serrano. Do you remember who I am?"

"Hello, Dr. Serrano," Zach responded. "Where am I?"

"You are in a safe place. Do you remember me?"

There was a pause.

"No, I don't. I'm sorry."

"That's okay."

"Where am I?"

"You are in an assisted living home. We are here to help you get better."

"Who are they?"

"Oh," Dr. Serrano said, "These are physician's assistants who are observing and learning today."

"Do I know you? I don't seem to remember much."

"What is the last thing you remember?"

"I remember talking to my friend Jessica. She came to my house to pick up some things."

"Where is your friend Jessica now?"

"She had to go on a trip."

"What trip?"

There was a long silence until Dr. Serrano repeated his question. "Can you tell me more about this trip that your friend Jessica was going on?"

There was a pause again until Zach said, "Are you friends with—" There was loud static that interrupted the recording. Both Jessica and Mikiko turned their heads and grimaced at the harsh pitch.

"What did he say?" Jessica asked.

"I had a tech team run some analysis to clean up the audio," Mikiko said as she got up and walked back to her bag. She pulled out a small tablet. "They just sent me the updated version yesterday." Before pressing play, she warned Jessica, "Brace yourself."

Jessica was confused, but she nodded her head to show she was ready. Mikiko pressed play, and the two heard Dr. Serrano's voice again.

"Can you tell me more about this trip that your friend Jessica was going on?"

Zach paused, then said, "Are you friends with Evelyn?"

"Who's Evelyn?" Dr. Serrano asked.

"Did Ori send you?" Zach asked.

"Who are you talking to?" Dr. Serrano asked. "Please note that the patient is speaking to the physician's assistants who are sitting in the room with me."

"Zach," Dr. Serrano continued, "Can you tell us more about Ori and Evelyn?"

Mikiko stopped the recording. "There's nothing else after that. He doesn't respond to any further questions."

"Wonder why he was asking about them? And better yet, how he even knows who Evelyn is," Jessica said.

"Bizarre, right? Even if someone had told him about Evelyn, why would he bring them up then? And what's more bizarre to me is that when we listened to this, my team seemed to only have a vague knowledge of who Evelyn was," Mikiko said. "I thought that they were messing with me, but they weren't. Those who did have a faint memory of her failed to remember what she looked like, and I came to find that this was widespread. It's almost as if she only ever had minor involvement with the Bureau." Mikiko paused, shaking her head. "I don't know what's happening."

"That's more than bizarre," Jessica concurred.

"So then, I tried to pull up videos and news coverage of her last case and Ori Clayborn's mysterious disappearance. Have you looked lately? Gone from the internet."

Jessica pulled out her phone and searched for an article. "There's nothing," she said in disbelief. "Have you spoken to Leslie?"

"I have. I mean, she remembers Ori, and so do all of the employees who had direct interaction with him during his tenure. I couldn't press Leslie too much, especially after the investigation all those years ago." Mikiko appeared bashful. "Now I am the one who seems delusional."

After the investigation into Ori's disappearance and the entire incident, one of Leslie's statements to the FBI leaked. Some media outlets called her delusional and questioned whether she was fit to run the Singularity Group.

"If you're delusional, then so am I," Jessica said.

"That's a relief," Mikiko said with a smile. "Given that Zach clearly remembers you, is asking about Ori and Evelyn, and you remember who they are, I have a favor to ask."

"Okay," Jessica said, encouraging Mikiko to continue.

"I can get you access to Zach. Could you try to talk to him and see if he responds better to you? Perhaps seeing you will spark some memories." Mikiko slid an envelope to Jessica. "Here's a burner phone. Use this if you need to get in touch with me."

"I, of course, want to help Zach in any way I can," said Jessica before pausing momentarily. "But if you aren't able to actively investigate this, why does it matter so much to you?"

"If Zach does have evidence of what Confidence Biotech is doing, and any of that is on US soil, I need to know. Especially if they are vying to become the nation's point for contact tracing." Mikiko's face softened a bit, and she continued, "And if there's some link to Evelyn..."

"Understood," Jessica said empathetically. "I'll see what I can do."

7

JESSICA'S NEW ASSIGNMENT

Jessica pulled into the parking lot of the assisted living home on the corner of Clairmont Road and Scott Boulevard. The building was a light gray with white trim around the window frames. It had sea-green awnings and a couple of towers in the same color.

She pushed the button to turn the car off and took a deep breath. *You can do this.* She eyed the building in her rearview mirror. It had been a long time since she had entered one of these, and walking back into one now was not the easiest thing mentally or emotionally.

Jessica opened the front door and stepped into a floor-to-ceiling glass cylinder that scanned for viral infection symptoms. The door closed heavily, and the sound made Jessica jump. *Still not used to that.* After a few seconds, Jessica heard the receptionist say, "You're clear." The interior glass door slid open, allowing Jessica to enter the building's lobby, where she signed in. She was then allowed into a common area for the residents.

Zach was standing by a window, staring out into the courtyard. She could immediately see a difference in his demeanor. Usually, Zach was this ball of positive energy that couldn't sit still if you paid him. He had a treadmill set up at his workstation to stay active while he took calls. Now, he was so still, as if he was frozen in time.

"Zach?" Jessica said as she took slow steps toward him. Jessica reached her hand out to touch his shoulder but remembered that wasn't always a good idea in this situation and retracted her hand.

"Zach, it's me, Jessica," she said, her eyes searching his face. "Sorry I didn't check on you sooner. I would have, I just didn't know this had happened or where you were."

Zach didn't respond. He continued to stare out of the window.

Jessica stepped closer to the window and followed his gaze to get a better view of what was capturing Zach's attention. The courtyard had a garden with calla lilies and other lovely flowers, and a small koi pond. A bench sat under a cherry blossom tree, which was in bloom. The beautiful pinkish-white petals gave the courtyard an elegant, serene feel.

Jessica was now standing shoulder to shoulder with Zach. She tried again. "I'm sorry that I wasn't able to help you, but I'm still trying. I need you to give me something. What happened to you? Why are you here? This isn't you."

This was worse than she was anticipating from the recording. Jessica started to look at Zach's face again, but movement in the courtyard caught her attention. Her eyes quickly locked onto the culprit, a doctor dressed in the requisite long white coat. He had a lean, athletic build and a freshly shaven appearance, making his brown jawline glow bronze.

"Handsome doctor," Jessica said playfully, "but not that handsome." She looked at Zach, who still didn't respond. The doctor sat on the bench and crossed his legs. He interlaced his hands behind his head and reclined slightly. Something about this situation, this man's presence, didn't feel right, and not just because doctors so rarely seem to have leisure time during their days.

Jessica's focus on the doctor in the courtyard was broken when she heard Zach's breathing intensify. Just then, the doctor stood up and walked toward them as if he could hear it too.

"What's wrong?" Jessica asked Zach. She turned to face the nurse's station and tried to get someone's attention.

"You see him?" Zach responded, still staring at the courtyard.

"Yes, Zach, I do," Jessica said, thankful for the sound of his voice finally, though the tone was concerning.

"You have to save my godson," Zach said.

Jessica had grown close to Zach over the years. She had done extensive research on the Singularity Group's Research and Development division, of which Zach Carver was a key figure. Jessica had learned much about him. She knew that Zach was raised in the system. His parents were shot and killed by rogue militia while protesting at a Black Lives Matter rally. Zach didn't have any other family. He bounced around different foster homes until he was fifteen. When he was caught hacking into a digital currency exchange market, he was sentenced as an adult. He met people in prison who introduced him to the Singularity Group prisoner relief work program. Leslie had a legal team petition to have him released early. The parole board agreed since Zach was caught while hacking back into the exchange to return the digital currency he had stolen. In getting to know Zach, Jessica came to know his circle. She was sure that if Zach had a godson, she would have known about it.

"What godson?" Jessica asked. "You don't have a godson."

"I see it all, you know? I can see everything. They thought that I was naive, but," Zach leaned toward her and winked, "I'm not naive." He tapped his index finger against the side of his head. "They need me. They need what I have in here." He then waved his arm across the room. "They make me take the medicine that makes everything go foggy, but I still have my vision. I can still see everything. I see it all." He paused and seemed to watch Jessica's face. "What I have in here," he said while pressing his finger against his forehead, "you have too. You can never let them have it. Never."

"Zach," Jessica began, "I—I." She didn't know what to say. "Okay. What is it they want? And what godson?"

Zach laughed, and Jessica realized that none of her questions would likely be answered now. His laughter grew louder and louder, and his body trembled. The orderlies came rushing over to restrain Zach. It took three of them to get ahold of him. Once he was on the ground, tears rolled down his cheeks, and Jessica realized there were tears on her cheeks too. The veins in Zach's neck bulged from strain, and he screamed so loudly that his face turned purple, "Save him! Save him!"

Jessica quickly turned to look for the doctor in the courtyard and was surprised to find him on this side of the glass, staring at her. He shifted his vision from her to the restrained Zach.

"What seems to be the problem here?" the doctor asked as he approached the orderlies.

"We don't know, Dr. Serrano," one orderly replied. "He just got out of control after speaking to his visitor."

Dr. Serrano knelt next to Zach and pulled out a flashlight to check his eyes. While the orderlies were concentrating on Zach, Dr. Serrano looked up at Jessica. Time stood still as Jessica locked eyes with the man. Suddenly, his eyes seemed to disappear, and his eye sockets turned black. Jessica took a deep breath and, against her better judgment, took one step closer to get a better look. Dr. Serrano tilted his head, seemingly intrigued, and smiled. He glanced down at Zach, and when he looked back up at the orderlies, his eyes had returned to the brown color they were before. Jessica watched as the doctor and the orderlies took Zach away.

Jessica stood there staring at the doors through which Zach was just taken when she heard a voice coming from her right side. "Looks like you've puzzled the good doctor, haven't you?"

Jessica turned to see who was talking to her. "Pardon?"

"Oh, I just said that the doc doesn't know what to make of you," the old man said, grinning. "My name is George," he said, extending his hand. George was a black man, probably in his early eighties. He was around six feet tall and had a spry, healthy look about him.

"I'm Jessica," she said, as they shook hands.

"It's a pleasure to meet you, Jessica."

Jessica looked back toward the double doors.

"Oh, he'll take good care of your friend," George said.

Jessica tried to nod but had trouble pulling her thoughts away from Zach.

"You've got the vision," George said, more of a statement than a question.

"What did you say?" Jessica asked, her attention now fully on George.

George smiled. "You and I have a lot in common. Would you

mind going for a walk with an old man? I need some exercise and walking with a beautiful young woman gets my heart going in the right direction."

Jessica laughed, then her expression turned to a frown. "I actually can't—"

"I know you are here to see your friend," George said, "but I'm afraid you won't get much more out of him. You've seen the most important thing that he needed to show you, or person rather."

Jessica's eyes drifted back down the hall, trying to see beyond the doors. What George had just said started to sink in. "Person? You mean the doctor?"

"Am I correct in thinking you're no stranger to establishments like this?" George asked, changing the subject.

Jessica paused, deciding whether to follow this new course of conversation.

"I am, unfortunately, no stranger, and by necessity," Jessica said.

"Someone close to you?"

"My dad," she said, as they took a stroll.

"I'm sorry to hear that. Was he here?" George asked.

"No, in Florida."

"Is that where you're from?"

"No, I've bounced around quite a bit. But I grew up out west," Jessica said.

"Ah, that's lovely, a citizen of this universe."

"What was that?

"What was what?" George asked, his head tilted.

"You said a citizen of this universe?"

George smiled. "Did I? We don't have the time to talk about that today. That's not what you came here to learn about anyway, now is it?"

"Well, no, but I also didn't come here expecting to find a doctor with decaying eye sockets either. So, a girl has to prioritize."

George laughed. "That's fair. So you did see that, huh?"

Jessica tensed. *Did I say that out loud?*

"Typically only those who are in debt and those with the gift of sight see the collector in that form. You didn't fear him, which means that you don't have any outstanding debts. So your ability to see him means that you most likely know Ori or one of his associates."

"How do you know Ori?" Jessica asked in surprise.

George laughed. "You're not the only one he has recruited." His expression became more serious. "Your friend Zach knew him personally as well."

"Ori was recruiting Zach?"

"Something went wrong. Ori has checked in on Zach, but he's in rough shape, as you saw."

"Ori has been here?" Jessica asked, straightening up.

"Of course," George said.

Jessica's mind worked. She focused her gaze on the ground, trying to plan what she should do next.

"Now hold on." George interrupted her train of thought. "There are a couple of things I need to tell you, and we don't have much time." George gave her a piece of paper. "Go to this address. He'll find you at the park."

Jessica opened the piece of paper. It read "951 Scott Circle tomorrow 0500."

"Secondly," George continued, "your friend Zach was doing the right thing. He's caught up in something, and this road does not end here."

Jessica searched George's face and then nodded. "Thank you," she said, simply.

"Excuse me, miss." Jessica heard a voice from behind her. "What are you doing out here?"

Jessica realized that they were now in the courtyard. Jessica turned to face the woman. "I'm sorry, we're just having a chat."

The nurse smiled. "Bless your heart. He doesn't get visitors, so it's good of you to spend time with him."

Jessica said, "George? But he's so charming."

"How do you know his name?" the nurse asked.

Confused, Jessica furrowed her brow. "He introduced himself to me."

Jessica looked back at George, who was paying no attention to the exchange. His gaze was focused on the koi pond.

"In all my time here, George hasn't said a word to anyone."

Jessica reached in her pocket to pull out the piece of paper with the address written on it. She opened her mouth to speak but decided against it. She patted George on the arm and whispered, "Thank you. I'll see you next time."

8

MALIK'S LONG WALK

Malik gazed at the clear blue sky, taking a moment to enjoy the feeling of his dark skin absorbing the warm sunlight. The bubbling sound of water brought his eyes to the fountain. Malik stared at the stone figure sitting on top of four fish spitting water streams toward the four corners of the Earth. The sculptured man was leaning back, his face turned to the sky. One arm was by his side, his hand gripping a snake just under the jaw. The other arm was lifted higher but was broken off right below the shoulder. *What are you looking at?* Malik wondered as he inspected the nub. It appeared as though the statue was pointing at the object of his obsession in the sky. And rather than sharing the statue's secret, someone destroyed the only clue.

Malik tried to follow the angle of the missing arm to a spot in the sky but was unsuccessful. He then shifted his gaze to the cobblestone path that connected the fountain to the estate's beautiful building, Wortley Hall. This large two-story structure looked like most properties built by the British nobility of the time. It was made of sandstone, and the entrance was highlighted by massive pillars on each side and a large crest carved into the stone above the door.

A group of men were filing into the entranceway, shouting something that Malik couldn't make out. Some men wore hard hats and clothes covered in black dust, while others wore rubber coveralls and matching rubber boots. Malik followed the men inside. They all gathered in one room and had turned their attention to a man standing at the front. The man was yelling, and as Malik watched, the man's face turned red with passion and anger.

Malik stood back, intrigued by the rally until a flash of light in his periphery made him blink. He turned his head just in time to see the flowing tail of a dress vanish down the hall and around a corner. Malik pulled himself away from the workers' rally to see what kind of trick his mind was playing on him this time. He wandered down the hall, briefly glancing at the portraits of aristocrats who once called this place home. Unsure of his path, he found himself in the most extensive library he'd ever seen. Malik spun in a slow circle, trying to take in everything. "How is this possible?" he whispered to himself. The library was three stories high, with books on every bookshelf and other books sporadically stacked in piles up to eye level. A lover of books, Malik was captivated by the sight until he heard a voice from behind him.

"Pardon me, Sir, may I be of some service?"

Malik turned to see a woman with soft, pale skin in a silver, flowing gown, with a large rose gold bow wrapped around her waist. Her dark brown hair was pinned up in an intricately braided style.

Malik opened his mouth, but no words came out.

"They are amazing, aren't they?" the woman said as she motioned around the room toward the books. "Father insisted that I have as many books in this library as would fit. He was adamant that I feed my mind. It's not always easy as a woman in this world. These books and the knowledge they hold will help me be heard."

"Lady Mary," a second woman's voice came from the distance. They both turned to see who was coming. This woman had curly light brown hair, and she wore a less elegant dress, likely made of cotton and linen. "Who is your visitor?" the woman asked.

"Oh, Evelyn, that's a good question," Lady Mary said as she turned back to face Malik. This time, her face had changed. Her pale skin was now covered with large, bright red bumps. The skin around her eyes was red, and her eyebrows and eyelashes were gone.

Malik felt his heart rate and breath quicken. Lady Mary tilted her head and examined Malik. Evelyn, who was now standing next to Malik, said, "Why are you here?"

Malik couldn't take his eyes off of Lady Mary. He tried to answer Evelyn, but again, he was speechless.

"Why are you here?" he heard Evelyn say again as he felt Lady Mary grab his wrist. He looked down and saw that the large red bumps blotting Lady Mary's face also covered her arms and hands. Malik jerked back instinctively, but Lady Mary's grip was more powerful than he expected.

"Why are you here?" Evelyn asked again.

Malik turned to face Evelyn. "I—I don't know." He jerked backward again to break free, and everything went black.

MALIK OPENED his eyes and sat up in bed. He reached for his phone on the nightstand. It was just after three in the morning. *Time to get up.* He hated it when he couldn't get a great night's sleep, and his wild dreams were occurring much more frequently. Fortunately, today was a day he didn't mind an early wake-up call. At the far end of his room, his clothes were laid out, and his pack was loaded and ready to go.

Malik had learned to enjoy long walks at an early age. His earliest memories of going for walks in the woods were when he was three or four years old. Now, it was ingrained in his psyche. If you have something on your mind you need to sort out, go for a walk. Let your conscious mind focus on getting exercise, and let your subconscious mind work on a solution to your problem. The more complicated the problem, the longer and more challenging the walk should be. Malik's problem required a longer, more challenging hike than usual. He'd been working on an invention for most of his life, an innovation that could change the world and save billions of lives. Yet how was he going to be taken seriously? His innovation was unconventional. Without support and funding, Malik's creation would never have a chance to do what it was meant to do.

When Malik's subconscious mind needed time to sort out a problem, he would hike Springer Mountain in North Georgia.

Springer Mountain marked the southern point of the two-thousand-plus miles of Appalachian Trail that ended in Maine. The majestic watercolor views of the Blue Ridge Mountains in autumn reminded Malik to appreciate the moment and everything he has. The mountains' connection to the Appalachian Trail reminded him that it is his decision how far he will go. Malik packed enough essentials to spend a few days on the Appalachian Trail, just in case.

It was a beautiful day for a hike. Malik was surprised that he was the only one on the trail. He reached the campgrounds and shelter that marked the Southern Terminus when he noticed something strange. There was a large group of women wearing burkas and scarves, covering their faces. The crowd of women surrounded the shelter, and none of them had hiking packs or even water bottles. Malik navigated his way through the crowd and toward the wooden trail shelter. What used to be an open entrance to the shelter was now a large sheet that made a makeshift door. Malik pulled the sheet back. He was shocked to see that the log cabin he had expected had been replaced by stone walls. Each wall was designed with patterns of triangles, circles, stars, and other geometric figures that Malik had only seen in pictures or movie scenes of a mosque.

Malik didn't know much about Islam, but he was pretty sure that he wasn't supposed to be in a temple with just women. He waited for some backlash, but no one seemed to notice him, so he proceeded. *This must be a dream.* Then something familiar caught his eye. It was a silver, flowing dress. *Lady Mary.* He watched her walk through the mosque and out the back door. He followed her outside to a tent in the middle of a desert oasis, where she joined a large crowd of onlookers. Malik approached the woman. This time, she didn't acknowledge his presence.

Lady Mary appeared different. Her eyebrows and eyelashes still hadn't returned, but the large bumps that had covered her face were replaced with scars. Malik positioned himself next to Lady Mary, trying to see what she saw. On the stage, in front of the crowd, three women sat in a semicircle. One of the three had something in her hand. Malik moved closer and recognized a small needle.

To the side of the stage was a line with women holding young children. One at a time, each woman carried her child forward and knelt. She presented her child to two of the women, who held the child steady. The third woman turned her back to the crowd momentarily, then turned back to the child and looked at the mother expectantly. The mother touched her left forearm, and the woman poked the needle into the same place on the child's forearm, almost like an injection. The mother and child then left the stage. This process happened repeatedly.

Malik moved through the crowd to get closer. He wanted to see what the lady with the needle was doing. As he got close, a fourth person was revealed. She was sitting next to the woman with the needle. The fourth woman was not wearing a scarf. Her back was facing the crowd, and her shoulders were exposed. Malik saw that her back was covered with the large red bumps he had seen on Lady Mary. The woman with the needle would puncture a sore on the woman's back, then she would immediately puncture the skin of the child. *Was this early inoculation?*

"What are you doing here?" Malik heard a voice from behind him. He turned to see the woman with the curly light brown hair, now slightly longer than before.

"Evelyn," Lady Mary said, rushing up and grabbing her shoulder. "Evelyn, are you seeing this? It's unconventional, but brilliant. This could change the way we approach treatment if I can just help people see."

Evelyn didn't respond to Lady Mary. She continued to look at Malik. "You've seen enough!" Evelyn tugged Malik's arm with force, and everything went black.

MALIK OPENED his eyes again and found himself in his bedroom.

9

MALIK'S INTRODUCTION

MALIK GOT DRESSED AND TIPTOED DOWNSTAIRS, MINIMIZING THE SOUND of the creaking wood floor next to his parents' bedroom. In the basement, Malik gathered his equipment, including air quality sensors he had modified to collect and store more particles. He carried the equipment to the backyard, climbed the ladder leaning against the three-hundred-year-old white oak tree, and fastened the air quality devices in different positions on the great oak.

"*Hoot, hoot.*" The owl was bold.

"Good morning to you too," Malik said as he climbed down the ladder and sat on the stump of the old pecan tree that his dad had cut down. The pecan tree never had a chance at sunlight between the tall pines and the white oaks. So, it grew in the only direction it could— an odd curve right over the neighbor's fence. It had been clear that the tree would not survive and that it was only a matter of time before it fell, causing damage. So, Dad did what he needed to do, but Malik knew he felt a little bad about cutting down life before it was ready.

Malik powered up his laptop and turned on his speakers. The benefit of his dad cutting down the pecan tree was that he left the stump. A hole at the top of the stump gave him direct access to the vast root and fungi network connecting the trees in his yard. He placed his cylinder speaker and a long metal rod into the hole and typed a few commands on his laptop. While his program ran its course, he lay back, closed his eyes, and inhaled deeply, counting to himself: one Mississippi, two Mississippi, three Mississippi. Up to seven Mississippi. He exhaled, following the same pattern. He did this until he completely lost track of time and was only focused on his breath.

"Maliiiiik."

His mom's voice brought him back to the backyard. Malik opened his eyes and turned his face to her. The sun had now forced the stars into hiding, but the moon was still hanging on.

"Are you going to work today?" his mom asked.

"Yes, why?" Malik asked.

"Well, you need to get up and shower. You don't need to go into the office smelling like outside," she said. "If you don't start moving now, you're going to be late."

Malik got up and collected the storage container from the air quality box hanging from the tree and his other equipment.

His mother, still observing, asked, "How's it going?"

"Good," Malik said. "With the last modifications, the antenna has been able to identify more distinct frequencies."

"That's great news. What's next?"

"What do you mean?" Malik asked.

"Do you think you have enough data to—"

Malik interrupted, "I'd like to get a little more information first, then we'll see how it goes."

Malik went upstairs, showered, and put on his dress slacks and a button-down shirt. While brushing his teeth, he paused and stared at his reflection in the mirror.

C'mon, man, don't be scared. You've got this. It's gonna work. It has to.

But what if it doesn't?

Malik shook his head. "Don't think like that," he whispered before spitting out the toothpaste.

Two knocks on the door made him jump. "Yeah?"

"Don't forget that after work, your dad and I are going to visit a few places and will probably eat dinner out. So you'll have to fend for yourself."

"Okay, Mom."

"Also, once you get a chance, you need to go get a haircut."

"What are you talking about? I love my hair," Malik said in a playful tone, as he opened the door.

"I know, I know. At least put some moisturizer in it." She smiled and pointed to a jar of cream on the bathroom counter.

She started to walk away, then turned back. "Also, Malik, be careful. More people have gone missing in the city. There's a community meeting tomorrow to discuss it. More petitions against the CB tracers' tactics are appearing..."

"Mom, I'm always careful," he assured her.

"I know, baby."

Malik glanced at his watch. "Gotta go!"

Downstairs, he grabbed his mask, picked up his car keys from the top of a pile of retirement community brochures, and put on his sports coat. He pulled out a pen from the inside pocket of the coat. He enjoyed the feeling of the grooves that ran along the length of the half-white, half-black pen, as if it was carved from wood. "There you are," he said softly.

10

CALLIE NEEDS A RIDE

MALIK TURNED THE KEY AND FELT THE DEADBOLT OF HIS FRONT DOOR lock into place. He turned to walk toward his car and saw Callie leaning on the driver's side door.

"Can I ride with you today?" she asked.

"Shouldn't you be done with tests?" Malik asked.

"Shouldn't you be done getting up at the crack of dawn?" Callie shot back. "Less attitude and more driving."

Callie was of average height and had a thin, frail frame. Her long, jet-black hair and hazel eyes attracted a lot of unwanted attention.

Malik rolled his eyes. "How's your mom doing?" he asked as he unlocked the door.

"Eh… not well. She's drinking more. It's impossible to get through to her."

"I'm sorry to hear that," Malik said as he took off his sports coat and was prepared to place it in the back seat, only to see Callie there. "What am I, Lyft?"

Callie only smiled as Malik placed his sports coat in the front passenger seat, then started the engine.

"Have you talked to Aunt Lily yet?" Callie asked.

"Not yet."

"Why not? She said that she was more than willing to help out in any way. And you know that she means it."

"I know. But I'm just—"

"You're just what?" Callie interrupted. "Collecting more data?"

"Exactly. We need to be certain before we file any paperwork. I don't want anyone to steal our idea."

"Sure. I'm glad that Dr. Patel likes you enough to give you a job, but c'mon, man. You're sitting on the golden ticket. You just need to cash it in."

"Whatever," he said. "Why are you going to the office today anyway? You don't have an appointment."

"I'm not going to his office; I'm going to the hospital."

"Why?"

"I'm going to mind my own business," Callie said with a smile.

"Baaahhh! Why do I put up with you?"

"That's easy, boy genius. You don't have any other friends who expect great things from you. Well, you don't have any other friends for that matter."

"You mean, I don't have any other friends who get on my nerves as much as you do?"

"Well, what are friends for, if not to annoy you?" She smiled. "In all seriousness, are you coming to volunteer at Mason Mill Park this weekend?"

"I—"

Before Malik could get a word out, Callie continued, "Before you give me some lame excuse, remember that I know that you have absolutely nothing else to do."

"That's not true," Malik said. "I could have a date or something."

"Oh really?" Malik saw Callie staring at him in the rearview mirror. "You asked her out?"

"Maybe. What if I did?"

"I'm calling bull. So, as I was saying, Ronnie's going to be there, and I'm sure he'd be happy to have your help. My parents will also be there, of course, and so will Aunt Lily."

"I don't think that's a good idea, Callie."

"Why not?"

"Your mom isn't my biggest fan." As soon as the words came out of his mouth, Malik felt how untrue they were. Malik and Callie had been the closest of friends ever since they were little.

"You know that's not true," Callie snapped. "My parents think of you as a son."

"I know." Malik focused hard on the road. "I don't know why I said that."

"I do. And you need to stop. Just let it go. No one is blaming you, so stop trying to carry a burden that's not yours to carry. I got sick. People get sick every day."

"But I—"

"Get over it, please," Callie said.

The two rode in silence for a few minutes until Callie let out a laugh. "I can't believe you said that. If my mom heard you say that, she'd tackle you and smother you with hugs and kisses. Then I'd be forced to choke on my dry heave."

"Don't be gross," Malik said as they both laughed.

"Your dad's going to be in town Saturday?" Malik asked. "That's surprising."

"I know, right? He's been buried in work, but he's finding a way to make it happen."

"That'll be nice. My mom hasn't mentioned anything, but I'm sure my parents will be there too."

"Dude, your mom doesn't miss anything." Callie paused and then said, "So…"

"What?" Malik said.

"Are we going to talk about the elephant in the…" Callie motioned around her. "Car?"

"What now?"

"This car. It's like the first-generation electric vehicle."

"That's right; it's a classic."

"I don't think that's the word I'd use." Callie brushed her hand against the ceiling of the vehicle. The cloth that lined the car's ceiling was detaching and hanging down. "You should do something about this before it gets worse and blocks your visibility."

"I've got it under control." He opened the glove box and pulled out a box of thumbtacks. "Here," he said as he handed the box to Callie, "put a couple of these up."

"Ha." Callie laughed. "No way will I support your stubbornness. I maintain that you need to fix it properly or get a new car."

"You're the only one complaining about it." At the next stoplight, Malik turned around, pushed a couple of thumbtacks in the ceiling, and secured the material in place. "See, all better."

"That's a shame," Callie said. "If this were Lyft, you'd be getting a one-star rating for having a hazard for a vehicle."

"You know I can't afford anything else right now."

"My dad told you that you can—"

"I said no, Callie," Malik snapped. "I don't want your old car."

"Okay, okay." Callie crossed her arms.

"What are you doing at the hospital?" Malik tried again.

"Mindya," Callie said.

"What?"

"Mind ya business," she said with a smirk.

"You're so shady these days. Are you going to see Ronnie?"

Callie's expression changed, the smirk fading away. "I'm just worried about him."

Malik heard the concern in Callie's voice.

Callie continued, "You know, this isn't easy, and he goes out a lot." Then the look in her eyes changed, and a smile returned as she sought eye contact with Malik in the rearview.

"Oh no," Malik said, "I know that look."

"What?" Callie asked as she raised her eyebrows in a weak attempt to look innocent.

"That's the look you get when you want to ask for something," Malik said. "Out with it."

"Can you keep an eye on Ronnie?"

"I see Ronnie all the time," Malik said, knowing that's not what she meant.

"No, I mean, spend time with him. Make sure he's okay. He's trying to carry too much."

"I am keeping an eye on him. He'll be okay. Promise."

Callie smiled.

"You, on the other hand," Malik said, "I'm not so sure about. When are you gonna tell me where you've been sneaking off to?"

With a sigh, Callie said, "Okay, I'll tell you, but you have to promise not to say anything."

Malik nodded in agreement.

"I've been interviewing for a new job. It will be a pretty big deal if I get it. I'll get to travel all over the place. I want it so badly."

"That's awesome. Why didn't you tell me? I could have helped you with interview prep."

"It's a secret, so you can't tell anyone."

"I won't."

Callie stared at him in the rearview mirror.

"I swear."

"Good," Callie said. "Besides, how can you have time to help me prepare for my interviews when you need to figure out what you need to do to take your invention to the next level."

"Our invention," Malik corrected as he pulled into the parking lot.

"No, Malik," Callie said in a calm, sincere tone. "It's your invention now."

11

MALIK AND THE DOCTOR'S OFFICE

Malik parked his car behind the doctor's office. He made it a point to try to be the first one in the office every morning so he could go through his routine setup without interruption.

He opened the back door and turned on the power to the building and then walked to the front of the office to inspect the two waiting rooms to ensure they were ready for patients. As per medical guidelines, the office had two waiting areas, one for those who have tested positive for the virus and one for those who have tested negative.

Malik then turned on the virus detection machine, which he could access from his tablet he had grabbed from his office. The machine took fifteen minutes to warm up.

Meanwhile, Malik accessed the patient list for the day. He confirmed that the appropriate medical records and notes were pulled for the doctor's reference. One long-time patient was coming in today with a hold on his account. Malik checked the files to understand the issue. He clicked his tongue and sighed. *Unpaid medical bills.* Malik then noticed the bright green light flashing from the virus detection machine.

The machine that Dr. Patel's office used was built by Confidence Biotech. Its design was based on the full-body x-ray machines that the

Transportation Security Administration introduced in American airports after the attacks on September 11th of 2001. It had modifications, of course. When a patient entered the cylindrical scanner, the glass door closed to seal the person in. The container was airtight but had a reserve oxygen tank, just in case the machine malfunctioned and the person was trapped inside. Two footprints indicated where the person should stand and what direction he needed to face. Once in the appropriate position, an image of a handprint appeared, indicating where the patient should place his palm. As soon as the person's hand was in place, the associated medical file was activated, and the virus detection test began. The machine gave audible and visual instructions. The person must inhale deeply and exhale through the mouth. Next, the person must inhale deeply and exhale through the nose. The machine picked up all exhaled particles. It analyzed the droplets within a matter of seconds and added the test results to the medical records. Once the test was complete, one of two sliding glass doors opened. One door led to the waiting area for patients with negative results; the other door led to the waiting room for patients who tested positive.

The two waiting rooms were adjacent and separated by a thick floor-to-ceiling glass wall. Anyone entering the office through the front had to come through the virus detection machine. Only the waiting area for patients with negative results had direct physical access to the receptionist area, though there was also a vestibule inside the front door in which visitors could speak to reception through the glass.

Malik walked into the machine, and the glass doors sealed him in. He faced the wall and placed his hand on the mark, as indicated. He inhaled and exhaled, as instructed. A green light flashed the word "Negative," and Malik viewed the tablet to ensure that the data flowed correctly. He then stepped out of the machine and watched the door seal shut again and a mist fill the space, performing the automatic sanitization process.

He tested the machine every day before they opened the office for their first patient.

As he finished, he heard Dr. Patel and the staff come in for the morning. Malik walked to the kitchen area and saw everyone conducting the daily throat and nose swab tests.

"Good morning, ladies," Malik said with a smile. In response, there was a collection of grumbles and a couple of "It's too early" replies. Malik laughed.

"Good morning, Malik," Christine said with her big signature smile. Christine was one of the office's longest-standing employees. She'd been hired as the receptionist back when one of the founders, Dr. Wen Shen, first brought on Dr. Patel. "Once you are finished getting settled in, I have something to show you," she said.

"I'll be right there," Malik said, and then chased down Dr. Patel. "Hey, Doc," he said, trying to keep pace.

"Good morning, Malik. How are you doing? How is your project going?" Dr. Patel was a kind man. When he discovered that Malik was out of work, Dr. Patel offered him a job at the office until he could find something else. Malik enjoyed working at the office so much he briefly entertained going to medical school. After watching Dr. Patel and his team of medical assistants and nurse practitioners perform their magic, Malik realized that working in the medical field was a calling. A call that he hadn't received in quite the same way.

"It's going well; thanks for asking," Malik said.

"So, what's up?" Dr. Patel stopped mid-stride and gave Malik his undivided attention.

"Well," Malik said, "your ten o'clock appointment has been flagged for unpaid medical bills. What do you want to do?"

"Oh, don't worry about that," Dr. Patel said.

"But—"

"I'll take care of it."

"I'm sorry, Doc, but I need to enter the billing code today."

"I'll eat the cost."

Malik shook his head. "Doc, if Devina were here, she'd tell you that you can't keep covering these costs."

Dr. Patel laughed. "She would say that, and I'd tell her that I can." Dr. Patel gently patted Malik on the shoulder and then walked into his office.

Malik laughed and walked back to the front desk to meet with

Christine.

Christine looked up and said, "Let me guess, he's covering someone else's costs."

"Yep," Malik said with a sigh.

"He's a good man, that one."

"Yep," Malik agreed. "So, what did you want to show me?"

"Oh, my goodness." Christine threw her hands in the air. "Look at this. She bought horses and a Harley."

"What?" Malik asked, leaning in to look at Christine's monitor.

"Devina bought land with horses and a Harley Davidson, a nice one at that. And according to this, she's going to buy a villa in Mexico. I think it's safe to say that Devina's not going to want her old job back."

"You just never know what people will do with their lottery winnings," Malik said.

"Especially winnings that big," Christine added.

"Lucky her," Malik said.

"Lucky both of you, in different ways," Christine said. "You get to work on that project of yours with one of the best internal medicine physicians in the nation. Everything works out for a reason. Most patients have signed the waiver. They like you and are comfortable with you using their data. This is a good opportunity."

Malik smiled. "Good point."

"All right," Christine said, snapping back to the moment. "Look at this." She motioned to her phone, which was aglow with little red flashing lights. "My phone is blowing up. I'm sure lots of people need to get in to see the doctor on this glorious Monday morning. I'd better get to it."

"Expecting a busy day?" Malik asked.

"There are rumors of a new virus strain. Anyone feeling slightly different will try to come in to see the doctor. Did you know that he has patients who live in other countries who fly all the way here just to see him?"

"I didn't know that."

"Yeah, we're a pretty big deal." Christine winked and picked up the phone. "Dr. Patel's office. What can I do for you today?"

12

A SMALL CRUSH

MALIK LOOKED DOWN AT HIS WATCH. IT WAS A LITTLE AFTER ELEVEN o'clock. He had finished with the stack of insurance claims to follow up on. Now it was time to emerge from his office to check on things. As soon as he opened the office door, one of the medical assistants zoomed by, just barely avoiding a collision with him.

"How behind is he?" Malik called after him.

"He just went in to see his ten o'clock appointment," the MA replied. "I'm bringing his eleven o'clock appointment back now."

"Has Magaly come in?" Malik asked.

The MA smiled. "Your not-so-secret office crush got here a little while ago. She's in room five with a patient."

Malik felt embarrassed. "What? No, I was just curious."

The MA had already turned the corner to retrieve the next patient.

Even a regular Monday was the busiest day in the office. The patients who had issues over the weekend tried to get in to see the doctor first thing Monday. Dr. Patel tried to accommodate everyone. Magaly had started as a medical assistant at the office and realized that helping the sick was her calling. She worked full-time and took classes to get her nursing degree. She got a job at Emory Hospital but still worked in Dr. Patel's practice now and then. Magaly was planning to become a nurse practitioner, and Dr. Patel was always willing to let people shadow him.

BEFORE MALIK KNEW IT, the end of the day had arrived. The last patient of the day was waiting on her prescription and scheduling her next appointment. The staff was busy sanitizing the patient and waiting rooms. Magaly was at the front desk talking to Christine. Now was as good of a time as any.

Malik walked to the front desk, rehearsing the lines in his head. *Hey, Magaly, how's it going? So, if you have some free time, I'd love to—*

Malik shook his head. "Love" was too strong. *It would be great to grab a coffee or a drink or some—*

The second he saw her curly black hair and bright eyes, his mind went blank. He felt the beads of sweat collect on his forehead.

"Uh, hi, Magaly!" was all he could say.

"Hey, Malik," she said. Her smile directed his way made it hard for Malik to think. "Busy day, huh?"

"Yeah," Malik said. "The only good thing about Mondays is…" the words came out of his mouth too fast, but he cleared his throat, "hearing a lot of good weekend stories."

Christine said, "Well, I'm heading home." As she walked past Malik, she whispered, "Nice save."

Magaly smiled, and Malik looked down at his feet.

"So," Magaly said in a light-hearted tone, "What are we going to do with you?"

Her tone made Malik look up, feeling hopeful. "It's funny you say that." Malik's stomach tightened. *If there was ever a good time, this is it.* "I was thinking that we could—"

"Excuse me," a familiar voice interrupted.

Startled, Malik turned to find a man in the vestibule.

"Is Dr. Patel still in the office?" the man asked.

The man was dressed in a crisp navy-blue suit. He was of average height, thin, and balding, with a well-groomed goatee. Malik recognized him but didn't let on.

"Do you have an appointment?" Malik asked.

"The doctor is expecting us," the man said. "We're from Confidence Biotech." This was Chance Domagk, the Chief of Staff to the CEO of Confidence Biotech. He continued, "Our CEO is on a tour meeting with a range of our key clients. Our head of sales spoke with Dr. Patel a few weeks ago about coming in and discussing our latest respiratory viral infection medication. He said that today would be a good day."

"I'll go ask him," Magaly said before heading to the back.

"You'll need to still go through the detection machine," Malik said. He logged into the receptionist's computer and set the scan for a non-patient visitor. He looked up, and his heart sank into his stomach. Standing before him was none other than Roy Mengele, President and CEO of Confidence Biotech. Roy was a large man, standing over six feet tall, and looked like he could bench press two hundred pounds on an easy day. He was immaculately dressed in a navy-blue suit and a bright red tie. *The Confidence Biotech uniform.*

"How do you like it?" Roy asked, nodding toward the machine.

"It's… it's great," Malik said.

"You ready for us?" Chance asked, stepping toward the opening of the machine.

"Yes, go ahead," Malik said.

Each of the men had come through the machine into the waiting area when Dr. Patel walked up to reception.

"Hello, gentlemen," Dr. Patel said. "We can meet in my office. Malik, you should come too."

Once in Dr. Patel's office, Roy said, "Thanks for seeing us, Dr. Patel. We understand how busy you are, so we appreciate you taking the time out of your day."

"It's my pleasure. How may I be of service?"

The sales lead jumped in. "Atlanta has seen a high rate of patients testing positive for the virus, as one would expect, yet I've noticed that you're not prescribing our latest antibody. We wanted to get a better understanding of why."

"I do prescribe it to any patient who requests it," Dr. Patel said. "But a lot of our patients can manage the symptoms with other methods. We try that first, and if they are unsuccessful, then I'll prescribe your medication."

"We are well aware that you're one of the best internal medicine doctors in the nation," Roy said. "I'm sure that the data from our latest research will give you confidence that our antibody will reduce the harmful symptoms faster than any other method." Roy turned the floor over to his sales lead. "Hank, if you don't mind."

Hank pulled out some marketing materials. He handed a brochure to Dr. Patel and one to Malik. "Your endorsement of this drug would be a huge benefit. I would be happy to walk you through some details."

Malik opened his notebook and pulled his lucky pen out of his jacket pocket. He listened intently as Hank rattled off statistics.

"Excuse me," Roy interrupted Hank's well-rehearsed presentation. Malik and Dr. Patel turned their attention to the CEO, who was now staring at Malik.

"You look familiar. Do I know you from somewhere?" he asked.

Chance chimed in, "You were an intern with us, weren't you?"

"I was." Malik nodded.

"That's right," Roy said. "I used to see you in our New York office." Roy seemed to stare at Malik's notebook. "That's an incredible pen. They don't make 'em like that anymore."

"It's my lucky pen," Malik said.

"I'd be willing to pay—"

"Malik," Dr. Patel interrupted, "you've had a long day. Why don't you head on home? I think we slowed you down on your way out of here."

"Well, I can stick around if you need me—"

"No, it's fine. Go get some rest."

Malik stood up, shook the men's hands, and walked toward the door.

"I hope to see you soon, Malik," Roy said as Malik closed the door behind him.

13

THE PARK

WHY WOULD ORI WANT TO MEET HERE? JESSICA PARKED HER ROYAL BLUE rental car in the near-empty parking lot of Medlock Park. She hadn't met up with Ori since their encounter in Nicaragua. However, Jessica couldn't help but question if that interaction counted as a meeting.

The empty baseball fields at the park were frosted with white from the early morning dew. Jessica imagined how packed this park must get during baseball season. She looked at the dashboard clock. It was four forty-five. *I'm a little early.* She got out of the car and walked around the park grounds to explore and stretch her legs. As she walked, she saw the first signs of activity. A woman was wearing a bright yellow reflective vest, walking her two dogs along the path. Jessica also saw an elderly couple making their way to a bench in front of the playground. The morning had a pleasant mist, and it was surprisingly warm for an autumn morning.

Jessica walked down the concrete path toward the largest baseball field. She saw a figure sitting on a green bench in the distance. *Could that be him?* As she got closer, she saw that it was not. She slowed her pace when she saw another man emerge from the thick fog around the wooded path on the opposite side of the field. She could tell by his walk, even from a distance, that it was Ori. The man on the bench stood up, and he and Ori had a short exchange. As Jessica approached, the man shook Ori's hand and continued onto the path, eventually disappearing around the corner.

"Good morning, Jessica," Ori said with a smile as he walked toward her. "How are you?"

"I'm fine," Jessica replied. "Is this real this time?"

Ori laughed. "As opposed to what?"

"I don't know, a dream," Jessica suggested. "Basically, should I expect to wake up on my couch or something?"

Ori laughed again. "No, you won't wake up on your couch. And even if you did, it doesn't necessarily mean that something isn't real. But…" Ori paused. "We'll get into that later."

Ori's clothes were not what Jessica expected. He was wearing a long-sleeved T-shirt with a hood, black joggers, and a pair of black-and-white running shoes. He also had on a baseball cap.

"This is a new look for you," Jessica commented.

"Is that what you want to talk about today?" Ori asked, bemused.

Jessica smiled and shrugged but remained quiet as the elderly couple from earlier walked by them, each with a walking stick. Ori and the couple exchanged friendly nods. Jessica followed them with her eyes as she wondered where they were going.

"This path." Ori pointed to the cement walkway in front of the bench. "It curves around the baseball fields and leads into a nature preserve of sorts called Mason Mill. It's a pleasant five-mile walk if you are ever interested."

"So, who are you exactly," Jessica asked, "and how is it that you are sitting out in the public as if the world doesn't think that you are dead?"

"Mmm." Ori nodded as if this was the thread of conversation he was anticipating. "Why don't we take a walk? I think better while moving."

They headed in the same direction as the elderly couple. The concrete path converted to wood as soon as they were under the tree canopy.

"You know my name," Ori said. "I can sit in public because the world thinks that I don't exist. Most people didn't know I existed in the first place, and many of those who did know of me think that I died."

"And yet, you are here, walking around as if everything is normal. How is that possible?" Jessica asked.

"It's not so difficult. People's memories are short. And otherwise, society, for the most part, lives completely online. If you remove all trace of yourself from the internet, voila!" Ori motioned as if he had just performed a magic trick. "You essentially cease to exist."

"Why did you fake your death?" Jessica asked.

"That, I did not do. Well, I didn't orchestrate the whole thing. Someone else plotted it. My team identified the culprits and handled the situation. We just let the world think that the conspirators were successful." Ori stopped, and Jessica instinctively did as well. They stood at a three-way crosswalk. Ori looked straight, to the left, and then to the right, before crossing.

We are the only ones out here.

"You should always be careful," Ori said.

"What?" Jessica asked. *Did he just read my mind?* She shook her head almost imperceptibly. *Impossible.* "Why would you create one of the most successful enterprises the world has ever seen, then just walk away?"

"Running that company was never my end goal," Ori said. "I did it out of necessity. We needed the Singularity Group because it granted us more access, and it provided a much-needed boost to innovation."

"Access to what?"

"Access to everything," Ori said. "People, ideas."

"But why go through all of this?" she pressed.

"The short answer is that we needed to jump-start a series of initiatives to get you back on a sustainable development plan."

"What are you talking about? And who is 'we'?"

"You've met the team—Evelyn, Jordan, Tony, and Vau. They are the main ones, but there are other key members."

"What do you mean by development plan?" Jessica said.

Ori didn't reply immediately. He led her off the path onto a dirt trail that led up a hill. After climbing for a few minutes, he stopped, tilted his head straight up toward the trees, and inhaled deeply. Then his attention shifted to his wrist where he adjusted dials on his watch.

Jessica repeated her question, "What do you mean by a development plan? I don't understand. And what are you? You haven't aged a bit." Jessica lowered her voice. "You're not some type of vampire, are you?"

Ori laughed and shook his head. "No, I'm not. Hey, how's your head?"

"It's fine. Why?" she asked before rubbing it. At that moment, Jessica realized that she had forgotten about the incident at Zach's house. "Don't avoid the question," Jessica said. "What are you?"

A fog rolled in through the trees. Jessica watched, wondering whether they should head back.

"That wasn't an attempt to avoid the question. I paused because I'm concerned for you," Ori said.

"Why?" Jessica asked.

"Because, Jessica," Ori said, "we've had this conversation before. You know everything about us."

"Wha—" Jessica said, then she laughed. "You're joking, right?" *How am I supposed to know these things? I haven't seen you in years.*

Ori regarded her for a moment, and then said, "You know what, change of plans." He made more adjustments to his wristwatch, and oddly enough, the fog cleared. "Let's go," Ori said and walked back the way they had just come, back toward the baseball fields. "Your memory lapse is a real cause for concern, especially considering that you are my scribe. More importantly, what is in your brain is the key to saving civilization as you know it."

"Wait, but—"

Ori cut her off. "You are going to be confused for a bit, and that's understandable. We need to see someone so that we can start sorting all of this out."

"Where are we going?"

"Buckhead."

14

ORI NEEDS A RIDE

"This seems ridiculous to ask, but are you somehow able to control the fog?" Jessica asked as she hurried to keep stride with Ori.

Ori looked back at her as if deciding whether to answer. Then he said, "Not all fog. But we do utilize fog and mist as needed."

"How so?" she asked.

"With this," Ori said, pointing to the device on his wrist. It was a black, likely Swiss-made timepiece with a rubber wristband.

"You did that with a watch?" Jessica was intrigued. "How is that possible?"

Ori stopped at the crosswalk. "It looks like a standard watch, but if you just..." he pressed and held his finger against the face. As he did that, the face transformed into the most intricate skeleton watch that Jessica had ever seen. "This allows us to modify and tap into various frequencies."

Ori surveyed the street. No cars were coming, so he crossed. "We use these if we want to communicate with nature, trees, move through frequencies. But we disguise them a bit," Ori held up his wrist, "so we don't attract unwanted attention." Ori tapped his finger on the watch's face, and it turned back into the black wristwatch.

"So, did you just say that you communicate with trees?" Jessica asked. *Not to mention move through frequencies, but one thing at a time.*

Ori looked at Jessica and shook his head, his face turning slightly sad. "What did they do to you?" He continued, "The science is quite simple, and people have known about plants' ability to understand humans for years."

"What do you mean understand humans?" Jessica asked.

"It can mean many things. I'm assuming you're loosely familiar with lie-detector technology, from movies, if nothing else?"

Jessica nodded.

"The approach is to use electrodes to send electrical currents through your finger or chest to measure heart rate, blood pressure, and breath, all to gauge whether there's an emotional response to questions or situations."

"Okay, I'm tracking with you."

"Well, there was a CIA interrogator and lie-detector expert named Cleve Backster who tested this approach on plants as well. He noticed that plants had an electrical reaction to stimulants in their environment, similar to that of human beings. Plants had even emitted energy that made them look like they were dead when they thought someone would kill them."

"Wow, to what extent is this understood?" Jessica asked.

"Plants, trees, nature have a physical reaction to their environment, including to humans. They can read your energy, your vibes, your actions. And these plants and trees are part of a network more massive than you can fathom. This energy gets absorbed into the Earth, aggregated, and projected back out again. The energy and light that Earth reflects is a combination of the collective energy from everything that lives on it." Ori walked over to a tree, breathed deeply, and placed his hand on the bark. Jessica felt a misty breeze and saw the branches sway delicately. "It's part of our responsibility to observe and listen. Communicating with and through trees is a hard concept to wrap your head around, especially if you think that a plant's role is simply to clean the air and allow you to breathe. Everything has a purpose beyond what you think. And every element, including human beings, is tightly interconnected."

"Why can't more people communicate with trees?" Jessica asked.

"People do. People communicate with nature all the time, many unconsciously, but many consciously as well. You just don't pay attention to the stories."

Jessica started to object but stopped short. "I guess that's possible. It'd be a little hard to believe."

"Exactly. Imagine that you've never met me, and we've never had this conversation. What would you think?"

Jessica thought about it and sighed. "I'd probably think that there was something a little off with those claiming conscious communication."

"And that's the problem. People who know these things, this ancient wisdom, aren't in hiding. They are just incredibly selective about with whom they share their wisdom."

"Yet you're sharing this wisdom with me?"

"Because if you are going to come to the Point, I need you to open your mind to a new universe of possibilities. You will learn things that will shake the very foundation of your existence. Suspend your disbelief, and everything will become clear. But first," Ori pulled on the door handle of her rental car, "we need to go see someone."

15

LORD GABRIEL

"So what's in Buckhead?" Jessica asked.

"We've got to see Gabriel," Ori said. "Someone is interfering with my plan, and I need him to correct it."

"What plan?" Jessica asked as she tried to pay attention to the road.

"This virus that's crippling the world. Its impacts aren't supposed to be this severe." Ori gazed out of the window. "Not in this reality."

"You're losing me again."

"Events were set in motion that would provide solutions to allow you to coexist with the virus while minimizing the harmful symptoms that come with it. And you are privy to all of it, but you can't remember it, for some reason." Jessica felt Ori glance over at her. "Everything will be explained in time, I promise. For now, we talk to Gabriel, or Lord Gabriel as he likes to go by these days. He claims that he descended from the House of Capet with a long lineage of nobility. It allows him a cover as an incredibly wealthy man."

"And he lives in Buckhead?"

"He's here for the CDC forum on the virus," he said. "Everyone wants to know what will be done."

Jessica programmed the West Paces Ferry address into the rental car's navigation system. After about a thirty-minute drive, she parked in front of a massive twenty-plus-story sandstone building. "He rented a room at St. Regis?"

Ori let out a laugh. "Nothing short of the penthouse."

Jessica pulled up to the valet stand and placed her mask over her mouth and nose. As she got out of the car, she looked over at Ori to see that his outfit was completely different. His look now consisted of a sleek silver suit, oxblood dress shoes, and a black mask covering his nose and mouth. He lifted his arms to adjust his cuff links. Jessica noticed that his watchband changed from black rubber to metallic gold.

Ori noticed Jessica staring at him and winked. "Walking into the St. Regis penthouse in joggers and a T-shirt would attract attention, wouldn't you say?"

The two walked to the elevator and rode it to the top. They were met by security guards as they exited the elevator. Ori walked by, not acknowledging their presence. To her surprise, no one said a word to him until they got to the door. A large man in a black suit held his hand up, motioning for Ori to stop.

"My name is Ori. Lord Gabriel is expecting me." The man nodded and stepped out of the way as the door opened.

The penthouse was one of the most elegant things Jessica had ever seen. There were floor-to-ceiling windows everywhere, with beautiful views of the city skyline popping out of the trees off in the distance. They were escorted through a foyer, past a sitting room with a grand piano, and into a living room. The living room entrance was bordered by four pillars, two on each side, and had a marble fireplace almost Jessica's height.

A man in white linen pants and a matching linen shirt, half unbuttoned, was sitting on the couch reading the newspaper. He set the paper down, then stood up and inspected Ori head to toe. "Ori." He put his palms together and slightly bowed. "Thank you for dressing for the occasion."

Ori glanced back at Jessica. "See, I knew he'd appreciate it."

"Ah, Ms. Ifill, it's lovely to see you." The man extended his hand.

"Yes," Ori interjected, "Jessica meet Lord Gabriel."

Gabriel shot Ori a puzzled look, and Ori raised his eyebrows in return.

"Ah, I see," Gabriel said, turning his attention back to Jessica, "but you can call me Gabriel. Please," Gabriel waved his hand to the pristine white chairs in the living room, "have a seat."

As they settled in, Gabriel said, "So…"

Ori tilted his head. "So…"

"Look, Ori, what can I say. These things happen."

"They shouldn't, not like this," Ori shot back. "Your folks are getting too reckless, and we don't have time to keep cleaning up their messes."

"You know that they aren't my folks any more than anyone else is," Gabriel said. "And it's not my job to control them."

"Here we go with that line," Ori said.

"That's not fair," Gabriel said. "We all have a role to play. You of all people should understand that."

"You're right." Ori took a deep breath. "I apologize."

"What is it that you were hoping for from me?"

"Answers."

Gabriel nodded in agreement.

"First, what happened to Zach?"

"The same thing that always happens," Gabriel said. "A healthy combination of greed, the need for power, and impatience."

"But he was our recruit and under our watch," Ori said. "So tell me, what happened to Zach?"

"He uncovered a plan to create an antibody from plasma harvested from people who were asymptomatic or who had immunity to the virus."

"And let me guess, these people weren't volunteering their blood, were they?" Ori asked.

"Ding, ding, ding. Come forward to claim your prize."

"Why would you allow this type of interference?"

"I didn't allow anything," Gabriel said. "If he had gone public with that information, it would have cost a lot of people a lot of money, and a lot of lives would be lost. The antibody works."

"That's foolish. He was my recruit, and we had a plan in place that would have been more effective and didn't require kidnapping and harvesting innocent people."

"Like I said, greed and impatience."

Ori stared out the window, rubbing his beard. After a moment of contemplation, he nodded to himself. "That's okay, there's another way. It can still work out."

"There's a difference between what I want to happen and what my job is. I can't understand why some of them request what they request, but we're bound to do what is asked of us. That's our role," said Gabriel, studying Ori's face.

Ori replied, "I know, but I think it's worth remembering that this mission is bigger than just them. As such, it's part of your role to ensure that there's no interference with sanctioned efforts on our side."

"Fair reminder," Gabriel said. "What do you suggest?"

"There's no way you can do something about these kidnappings?"

"It's out of my hands. They've convinced themselves that this is the only way to ensure survival."

"What would you say if I told you that I have another solution?"

"I'd tell you that unless the majority buy in, then there's nothing I can do."

"There's a kid, well, a young man. He's onto something and might be our last chance at solving this."

"Well, what do you need from me?"

"I need you to get Zach back."

"I don't see how that will be possible. I can't interfere." Gabriel eyed Jessica. "She's entangled, isn't she?"

"Correct."

"How viable of a candidate is this young prospect of yours? I'd hate to see them all moved back behind screens again."

"He's the best shot we have."

"You know what it would take to bring Zach back. That's a lot of potential exposure," Gabriel said.

"I understand."

"Here's the deal. If the boy comes through, then you can get Zach back."

"But?" Ori asked, anticipating some stipulation.

"But what?"

"There's always a 'but' with you."

Gabriel tilted his chin up. "But Jessica is out of play."

"I'd like to leave that up to Jessica. If she decides to sit out, then she comes with me."

"To the Point?" Gabriel asked, his eyebrows raised.

"Wouldn't be the first time. And when the kid does succeed, you have to ensure that they get back every second that they missed. Everything restored in full, in exchange for her sacrifice."

"Agreed," Gabriel said as he leaned back in his chair. "But you know the consequences if he fails. Does she?" Gabriel motioned his head at Jessica.

"Don't worry about that. I'll tell her."

"You better."

"One more thing. If anyone tries to interfere with the kid, our team will be there, and it'll be on you to clean up the mess."

Gabriel didn't reply and instead turned to Jessica. "Ms. Ifill, just out of curiosity, why did you go immediately to Zach's house after you arrived from the airport?"

Jessica was surprised by the question. How did he know that? How did she forget that?

"He told me that he had something important to share, something that needed to be done in person."

"*He* had something important that *he needed* to share?" Gabriel repeated back, gazing at her with a bemused expression. "You don't remember, do you?" Gabriel turned his attention back to Ori. "The universe and its mysteries, hmm?"

Ori checked his watch. "Time to go."

"Aren't you going to stay for tea?"

"Sorry, old friend, next time," Ori said as he stood up. Jessica followed his lead.

"Let me at least walk you out."

"Of course."

Once outside, the valet handed Jessica her keys. She noticed for the first time how young he looked. He was tall and skinny, but his face was that of a kid. The young valet held the door open for Jessica and closed it behind her. She watched as the boy ran around the car to open the door for Ori. After Ori exchanged goodbyes with Gabriel and the valet closed the door behind him, both Ori and Jessica reacted as the valet shouted, "Excuse me! Excuse me..." Jessica thought she had forgotten something and started to roll down the window when she realized that he was trying to get Gabriel's attention. Jessica heard the beginning of a conversation. "You're Lord Gabriel, aren't you? It's a real honor to meet you. My name is Roy," the boy said.

Ori caught Jessica's eye. "Let's head back to the park."

16

———————

WHAT'S THE CATCH?

ORI STARED OUT OF THE WINDOW, SILENT THE ENTIRE WAY BACK TO Medlock Park. Jessica, meanwhile, had been replaying that odd, cryptic conversation she just witnessed repeatedly in her mind. It's a strange thing to witness people talking about something that involves you and to understand so little of the meaning. Now parked, she saw more pedestrians walking their dogs. She looked at the clock in her car. It was almost nine o'clock. *It's still pretty early.*

Ori was intently focused on his watch, which he had reactivated to its fancy skeleton form. Jessica stared at it, seeing every internal gear working in unison. The watch had four detailed sub-dials and three bezels circling the face, which Ori was meticulously adjusting with his thumb and middle finger. After a moment, Ori pressed a button and nodded as if he had accomplished his task.

"Do you have a pen?" Ori asked.

"I should." Jessica reached into her bag in the back seat, pulled out a pen, and handed it to Ori.

Ori took a moment to admire the grooves of the pen that made it look as though it was carved from ivory or bone. "Lovely," he said as he scribbled something on the back of a white envelope.

"Gabriel asked if I was entangled," Jessica said, testing the waters.

Ori looked over at her, a little hesitant, before replying, "He was referencing quantum entanglement."

"Okay, and what is that exactly?" Jessica asked.

"Think of your mind and Zach's mind as two different systems that should operate completely independently. Somehow, your minds formed a deep bond and have become entangled. The disruption occurring in Zach's mind seems to have affected your mind as well. This is not unheard of. However, the human brain is resilient. Typically, your brain can revert to its independent system when necessary. In your case, we think that the incident at Zach's house, likely a blow to the head, left you more susceptible and less resilient. This is why you not only lost time but are having a hard time remembering things. If you come to the Point, there's a chance that we can help you get your memory back, which, if I'm correct, will ultimately help Zach."

"I'm liking this plan so far," Jessica said. "What's the catch?"

Ori was watching something out of the front windshield. Jessica followed his eyes toward the big baseball field off in the distance. Jessica saw a fog building in the woods that lined the outer edge of the park.

"If you come with me, and we aren't able to recover your memories, and if our mission isn't successful, then you may never return."

"And if I don't come?" Jessica asked.

"The likelihood of you recovering your memories is even slimmer. You'll still have some incredible years ahead, but they'll feel brief. And over time, you'll start to lose all of your mental faculties."

"Like Zach," Jessica said.

"Yes, unfortunately."

"But if I go and you're successful?"

"That means we'll have righted the course relative to managing the virus. Then we get to turn back time, in a sense, and Zach will be released."

"If going with you is the best way I can help Zach and regain my memory, then it's an easy decision to make."

Ori smiled and extended the envelope and pen toward her. "I

figured you'd say that. Here is everything you need to travel to the Point."

Jessica scanned the envelope to see *trust yourself* written on one side. She tucked it away. "So, what's next?"

"Now, I go back to make sure that things are still going according to plan."

The fog had thickened and was shifting closer and closer to the parking lot. Jessica watched as the people walking their dogs promptly got back into their cars. Ori chuckled and opened the door. "I should get going before people lose their minds."

Ori, now standing outside of the car, bent down and looked in at Jessica from the open passenger door. "See you soon." He closed the door and was instantly covered by the fog. Just moments after Jessica lost visibility of Ori, the fog dissipated, and so returned the clear blue skies.

17

JESSICA TRAVELS TO THE POINT

Jessica's flight landed at Vancouver International Airport. As the pilot turned on the light for everyone to get up, Jessica sat patiently in her window seat, reviewing the contents of the envelope that Ori gave her. She wondered if she was missing something. The contents were an old-school paper plane ticket to Vancouver, a handwritten-note in binary code, and a Singularity Group business card with small written instructions on the back: "Take the first ferry out at 4 AM, then follow R. Frost." Jessica raised her arm to look at her watch and realized she wasn't wearing one. Her phone said it was just after midnight. She had a few hours to kill, so she headed toward the ferry and found a twenty-four-hour diner.

Jessica sat down and studied the piece of paper with binary code.

01010000 01100001 01110011 01110011 01100001 01100111 01100101 00100000 01100110 01101111 01110010 00100000 01010100 01110111 01101111

She took out her phone and tried to pull up a search browser. Just as a binary code translator was appearing, she heard a friendly, energetic voice. "Hey there, welcome back."

Jessica looked up at the waitress, not sure what to say. "Good morning," was all she could muster.

"I'll get you some coffee while you take a look at the menu," the waitress said. "Oh, I know it looks different, but don't worry, we still have huevos rancheros." The waitress winked as she turned to go get the coffee.

Jessica scanned the menu. *I would love some huevos rancheros.* The waitress came back and filled Jessica's mug. "Do you want me to give you a little time before I put your order in?"

"Yes, please," Jessica said. "And hey, how did you know I'd want huevos rancheros?"

The waitress tilted her head at Jessica, then she laughed. "You only order it every time you come."

Every time I come? Jessica glanced at the waitress's name tag. "Thanks, Ruth."

"Anytime, hon."

A couple of hours later, Jessica sat at her table in front of an empty plate, sipping from her mug. Ruth came back by. "Is there anything else you need?"

Jessica shook her head and smiled. "All set, thank you."

After the waitress left, Jessica glanced out of the window. A green light in the distance caught Jessica's eye. She squinted slightly to get a better look. She could vaguely identify the rocky outline of land that the lighthouse was warning of. She inhaled deeply, softened her gaze, and allowed her shoulders to relax. As she exhaled, she felt a sense of peace come over her. She didn't know why. Someone important to her was sick, the world was being held hostage by a virus, yet that warm cup of coffee in a near-empty diner gave her a momentary sense of comfort. At that moment, she felt a flicker of hope that everything would be okay. As she sat present in the moment, she felt someone walk up behind her.

"Where are you heading?" The bass in the old man's voice sounded like a friendly, helpful character in a Western movie.

"Oh." Jessica turned around, slightly surprised that the man was there. "I'm waiting for the first ferry out."

The man was tall, rugged, with a thick white mustache and matching white hair sticking out from his mesh hat. "Well, Ms. Ifill, I didn't expect you to be here."

"You know me as well, I take it?"

The man gave her a confused look, exhaled through his nose, and smiled. "You could say that, seeing as I'm the captain of the first ferry out. You may want to get your check and grab your bag."

"May I have my check, please?" Jessica called over to Ruth.

Ruth walked over. "It'll be $7.95."

Jessica opened her wallet. She only had a ten- and a twenty-dollar bill. "Here," Jessica said, handing the woman the twenty.

"I'll be right back with your change," she said.

"That's okay." Jessica smiled. "Keep the change."

"Thank you." Ruth returned the smile.

"We ready to go?" the captain asked.

Jessica grabbed her bag. "I'm ready."

Jessica and the man walked to the door. The man paused, looking back one more time. "How about you? Are you ready?"

Jessica turned to see who he could be talking to. She looked back to see the waitress, standing alone behind the counter. Then, sitting at a table in the corner that was barely visible from the front door, Jessica saw a figure emerge. She was beautiful, in a striking red dress. The woman had ebony skin, jet-black curly hair, curving cheeks, and a smile so warm it felt like a hug. The woman stood and whispered, "I think so."

"They'll be okay," the captain said.

The woman nodded, grabbed a small bag, and walked to the front door.

The trio walked to the dock. The ferry was smaller than Jessica imagined. She expected to see a large vessel capable of carrying cars. This ferry, however, was no longer than one hundred feet. The main deck was covered, and underneath it had several rows of bolted down metal benches. The captain asked for and collected the coded paper from Jessica, then walked to the bridge and vanished as he boarded the boat. Shortly after, Jessica heard the engine of the vessel roar.

The captain reemerged. "You ladies can come aboard. We're just waiting on one more."

Jessica heard the roaring of a loud engine and even louder music speeding toward the dock. She watched as a car pulled up, windows down, blaring B.B. King's "Lucille." The driver's side door swung open, and a bald man with glasses stepped out. Jessica could see his smile from the boat.

"Y'all hold up!" he yelled, putting one finger in the air. He ran to the diner, and Jessica saw him toss the car keys to Ruth. "Take good care of her!" the man shouted before he trotted toward the boat.

"Whew, y'all just don't know," the man said as he boarded the ferry. The man had a sly smile and was wearing a sharp suit with a half-buttoned shirt. Jessica noticed bright red lipstick on the collar.

The man took a seat at the back of the ferry. The woman in the red sequined dress looked at Jessica and said, "You can't take him anywhere."

Overhearing the comment, the man, almost ready to fall asleep, said, "I still made it though."

The two laughed, and the woman said, "You sure did, but just barely."

As the ferry departed the dock and the sound of the motor and water drowned everything else out, Jessica couldn't help but stare at the woman's red dress.

"Hi, I'm Fey," the woman said.

"Nice to meet you. I'm Jessica."

"Nice to meet you too."

They rode in silence for a few moments.

"So," Jessica said, "where are you headed?"

"That crazy fool back there and I are getting off at the first stop."

Jessica nodded, processing this information.

Fey leaned back slightly. "You seem like the type of person who has a question. Go ahead and ask."

"The red is beautiful. I was just wondering why you're dressed so nicely? I mean, if we are going to the same island."

"Oh, we're celebrating. The end of one thing, the beginning of another."

Jessica smiled and nodded, not sure what to say next.

Fey took Jessica in. "I think your stop might be different, but that's okay too," Fey said with a big smile. She nodded at Jessica's tote bag. "You're going to have to hoof it, huh?"

"He said to bring a bag that I'm comfortable carrying and walking with for at least ten miles."

"Whoo, girl, that's not nothing!" Fey let out a hearty laugh. "Who is 'he'? Is that Ori?"

"You know Ori?" Jessica replied with surprise.

"I met him when I worked at an assisted living home. He visited from time to time. Girl, he was always in there crackin' jokes," Fey laughed, "and tryin' to dance. He's hard to forget."

"Doesn't quite sound like the Ori I know, but I'd love to see that."

Fey sat there enjoying her memory for a moment. Then she looked over at Jessica again. "Here's what I know about the last stop. When you dock, there will be only one path leading into the forest. Follow it until you reach a point where a single path becomes many. You won't know which to choose. You'll have to trust yourself."

"What does that mean?"

"Don't worry. The forest won't let you down."

"I think I'd rather come with you." Jessica grinned.

Fey's expression was one of empathy. "I think you have some other work to do. Everyone's journey is different. There are things on my path that are for me and things on your path that are meant for you."

JESSICA WASN'T sure how long she'd been on the ferry. She fell asleep at some point, and when she woke up, the ferry was docked, and the captain was standing nearby.

"Here's your stop," he said. "The end of the line for return visitors."

Return visitors?

Fey and the other man were nowhere in sight. They must have been off to their celebration a while ago. As Jessica disembarked, she wondered what time it was and glanced down at her wrist again. *Shoot, why do I keep thinking I'm wearing a watch?* Jessica looked around; there was no one in sight. Just as Fey said, one path led into the thick forest.

"Is there somewhere else where you can drop me off? Maybe someplace where there's someone who can help me?"

The captain shook his head. "That's not the way it works, unfortunately. You can only be shown the way once. After that, to return to the Point, you've got to get there on your own."

"Don't worry," the captain continued. "I'll be here in case you want to head back."

Jessica took a deep breath. "I won't need to do that." She reached in her bag. "But I do need to get you a tip." She found the single remaining ten-dollar bill and pulled it out to give to the captain. *I'm gonna need to stop for cash.*

"Keep it," he said. "One big tip for the day is enough. You'll be alright, young lady."

Jessica grabbed her bag, turned to the path, and started walking. She heard the captain shout, "Don't forget the instructions."

18

THE FOREST

THE TRAIL WAS NARROW, ONLY WIDE ENOUGH FOR ONE PERSON AT A TIME. Jessica couldn't help but pause and stare in awe at the trees. These were the largest and tallest trees she had ever seen. Their canopy protected her from the sun's rays. The sounds of birds chirping were comforting and pleasant. Undergrowth bordered the trail, and it was amusing to watch the squirrels chasing each other around, unconcerned with Jessica's presence. Their comfort level gave Jessica a sense of ease. *If they're out here playing, there aren't any large predators around.*

Jessica wasn't sure how long she'd been walking. The path wasn't nearly as confusing as she had feared. It was well worn and periodically alternated between dirt, gravel, and aged cobblestones. Parts were a little overgrown with shrubs and moss. She couldn't help but wonder who would have created this path and for what reason. *Was there ever a time when this was all cobblestone? If so, who built it, and why did they stop maintaining it?*

Jessica's mind flashed back to the wooded path connecting Medlock and Mason Mill Park. She had a vision of some men pulling up and replacing the rotten and broken wood planks with new wood. *"Hey, Mista Carver," Jessica could hear the Caribbean accent of the man who appeared to be the boss, overseeing the work.* Jessica shook the thought out of her head. *What was that?* She couldn't remember walking on that path before yesterday when she met with Ori.

The sun was now high overhead and did its best to seep through the treetops. Jessica's sweat-drenched shirt cooled her as it clung to her back. She walked past a marsh, where she stopped for a few minutes, captivated by large cranes. The trail looped around the marsh, and just as the path widened, Jessica found herself with three options. There was a gravel stone path to her left. She peeked down as far as she could, and it seemed like more sun was beating down on this path. *It looks like there's less shade that way.* The path to the right seemed like a continuation of the trail she had been on. Mossy cobblestone appeared to continue, with more canopy. The path straight ahead was intriguing. It was a dirt path that meshed with the surrounding nature and had a thick, dark tree canopy. Jessica peered down this path. She wasn't sure why, but this was the way she wanted to go. Jessica wondered what would happen if she walked down this path and turned back.

Jessica stood there, lost in thought, when the glint of something caught her eye. To her surprise, she spotted something lying on the path straight ahead. Jessica started down the dirt path to get close to the object. It was a half-full glass bottle partly buried in the mud. She pulled it out, twisted off the top, and took a sniff. "Gin?" Jessica said aloud. She emptied the contents on the ground, returned the cap, and placed it in her backpack. She was happy that she didn't completely stuff her pack. This left her room to store the bottle until she found a more appropriate place for it than the forest floor. She looked ahead down the dirt trail and hesitated.

"Let's check this out," she heard Zach's voice say, as her mind recaptured a vision of him leaving a wooden path and walking up a small trail on the neighboring hill.

"Why?" Jessica argued.

"If you want me to keep talking, then you better keep up. See," Zach said as he bent over to pick something up from the ground. He turned to Jessica, holding a small blue plastic bag that people use to clean up after their dogs in

his hands. "This doesn't need to be here and if we hadn't walked this way, we wouldn't have been able to take care of it. Let's keep on."

Jessica continued down the dirt path for a while until she heard water rushing. The farther she walked, the louder the water became until her path opened to a large meadow filled with shin-high grass and dotted with pink, purple, yellow, and white flowers.

Where is the water? She surveyed the massive open field, trying to identify where she should go next. Suddenly, Jessica saw movement in the corner of her eye. She turned her head and saw someone at the far edge of the field. She walked quickly in that direction, hoping to catch the person. She even ran for a bit to close the gap between them.

As Jessica got closer, she noticed a little girl chasing butterflies in the field. She slowed her pace and just observed her for a while. The little girl was walking with a slow and cautious tempo, trying not to startle the butterflies. There was something familiar about the little girl, but Jessica couldn't put her finger on what that was. It didn't seem like she had noticed Jessica. Jessica followed her into the woods, trying to keep a nonthreatening distance. The little girl lost interest in the butterflies and now seemed to be searching for something. *What could this child be doing out here?*

"Hello, little one," Jessica said.

"Hello," the little girl said. She was wearing blue jeans and a pink shirt, both covered in grass stains.

"What are you doing out here?" Jessica asked.

"I'm Nia, the Explorer!" The little girl puffed her chest out and put her fists on her hips like a superhero. "Wanna make some discoveries with me?"

"Uh, sure," Jessica said. "I'm Explorer Jessica."

Nia laughed. "I know who you are, silly. C'mon, let's follow the map." Nia ran off, and Jessica followed her.

She knows me? "Wait up, Nia," Jessica called after the girl. She was faster than Jessica had imagined. "Where are your parents?"

Nia turned to face Jessica and laughed again. "You're so silly," she said. "Now, let's go."

Nia disappeared deeper into the trees, and Jessica followed. The sound of water grew louder as Nia led her down a trail with willow trees providing an arch-like cover. The shrubs on both sides of the path reminded Jessica of a wall of defense. She lost sight of Nia for a moment. She stopped and looked around, hoping to see movement, then caught a glimpse. *There she is.* "Nia," Jessica called as she chased after her.

When Jessica caught up to Nia, she had stopped, almost frozen in place, staring at a statue several stories high of a bald man with a broad nose and large eyes. "This is a great discovery, wouldn't you say?"

Jessica nodded but couldn't manage a response as she tried to catch her breath. She took her pack off and set it down by her feet.

A deep voice came from behind them, "I'm sure you are pretty tired."

Jessica turned to see a mountain of a man with copper skin and long hair tied in a ponytail. He was wearing a T-shirt, and the parts of his arms that were visible were covered with tribal tattoos.

"Vau!" Nia shouted with joy as she ran over to him.

He bent down and scooped her up in his arms. "Hey, kid, you're getting big."

"I know," she said with a smile. Nia tilted her head toward Jessica. "We were making discoveries."

"I see that," Vau said. He looked up at the sky. The pinks and orange colors of the sunset were coming in. "You'd better get back," he said as he put Nia back down on the ground.

"But I want to come," Nia moaned.

"You're not that big," Vau said, "but someday."

"Ah man, you always say that," Nia said as she ran back out of the forest.

Vau extended his hand to Jessica. "I'm Vau. You must be Jessica."

"Hi," Jessica said as she shook his hand. She gestured back toward the stone figure. "What is this?"

"This," Vau said as he slapped the statue, "is an old mark of the travelers. It indicates that there's an entrance to the Point somewhere close by."

Jessica was studying the figure. "I've seen this before. I read about it...," she tapped her forehead, "in ancient history myths of Central and South America, I think. These were built by the Olmecs, right? How did it get here?"

Vau shrugged. "How did they get anywhere?" Vau looked up at the sky again. "It's getting late. We should get to town before we lose the sunlight."

19

BIRDS, BEES, AND PHYSICS

Jessica followed behind Vau as they exited the forest. The narrow trail then turned into a wide dirt road, lined with wooden fence posts that separated the dirt road from the surrounding fields of colorful wildflowers. Jessica watched as chickens darted across the dirt road, flapping their wings in a futile attempt to catch flight. "Welcome to the Archer's Point," Vau said. "But everyone here just calls it the Point." Every so often the dirt road split off, leading to homes in the distance.

"Where does the name come from?" Jessica asked.

"This place was going to be called the Point at Sagittarius A." Vau grinned and shook his head. "But who wants to say all that?" He continued walking. "The Point is much cooler."

"Uh, yeah, I guess," Jessica said.

"We're coming up to the center of town." A cluster of magnificent adobe and stone homes, in a variety of colors, appeared. Vau stopped in front of one red adobe home that seemed older than the rest. The window frames and door were made of wood. A small flower garden lined the walkways and the entrance to the house. "Professor Raziel asked that we stop by here before we head to where you'll be staying."

As they got within a few steps of the entrance, the front door swung open. "Jessica," an older gentleman with olive skin and a thick gray beard greeted her. "I'm glad you made it safely. I'm Professor Raziel," he said.

"Nice to meet you," she replied.

"Please come inside." The professor moved to the side, allowing Jessica and Vau to enter. The inside of the house was pristine. The floor appeared to be of polished pink stone or granite. The furnishings were simple—a couch, an armchair, a small table, and bookshelves. The large bookshelves were made of a dense wood and lined every wall. *It's like a library in here.*

"We take a lot of pride in seeking knowledge, everywhere," the professor said.

"We figured that it made sense for you two to meet each other. Jessica has a lot of unanswered questions, and we need to get her caught up quickly." Vau turned to Jessica. "Professor Raziel knows everything, about everything."

"Well, that sounds promising," Jessica said. "Is this your house?"

"No," a familiar voice answered, "it's mine."

Jessica turned to see a tall, strong, yet delicately built woman with braids down past her shoulders. She was wearing a beautifully colored dress that flowed down to the floor and beaded bracelets halfway up to her elbows.

"My name is Aja," the woman said. "My house is on the way to where Evelyn and the team are, so I asked Vau to bring you by so I could greet you."

"Have we met before?" Jessica asked.

"We have," Aja said. "How is your head?"

Jessica remembered. "You were there, by the pond that night."

"I was," Aja said. "You were in bad shape the last time we saw each other. Are you feeling better?"

"I am," Jessica said. "However, I'm having trouble remembering things."

"So I've been told. Well, I hope that spending some time here will help you recover what you've lost." Aja looked at Jessica with an expression somewhere between concern and kindness. "Jessica, you have had quite a long day already. Can I offer you some tea and something to eat?"

"That would be great."

"Today is so pleasant. Why don't we have tea on the back patio?" the professor said. He extended his arm, pointing to the door at the back of the house.

"Sounds lovely," Jessica said.

"Excuse me." Aja vanished further inside the house.

The professor addressed Vau, "Could you help her with the tea and honey?"

"Sure," Vau said before disappearing around the corner.

The patio was covered by a large pergola draped with orange flowers. Surrounding the courtyard was a larger flower garden than was in the front of the house.

"Oh my," Jessica said.

"Is everything all right, dear?" the professor asked.

"This is—it's breathtaking."

"It is, isn't it?"

Aja came back with a silver platter full of rice and bowls with different vegetables.

"How did you decide what to plant?" Jessica asked her.

"Oh, I can't take too much credit for any of it. The flower garden was already here. I just built the home around it," she said. "Now, my role is to maintain the garden for the birds and the bees." She smiled. "I also get to enjoy the honey."

As Jessica ate, the professor asked, "So you probably need a re-introduction to how it works?"

"How what works?" Jessica asked.

"How it *all* works," the professor said with a sly smile.

Jessica felt anxiety rise in her chest. *What am I doing here? I have no clue what I'm even supposed to be understanding.* Jessica gave a helpless expression. "You know, I'm still not quite sure what I need. Every time I think I know something, I learn something new, and I just get more confused."

"Wisdom is a funny thing like that," the professor said. "As you learn more things, you come to realize that there's so much that you truly don't know or understand. But, it's fantastic that you are here."

"Thank you." Jessica smiled as a warm feeling came over her body. It was a feeling of comfort.

"Have you seen Ori yet?" the professor asked.

"No, not yet."

Jessica's attention was drawn back to the vibrant flowers that surrounded the back patio. Her eyes caught sight of a bee flying from flower to flower. She imagined the bee at peace while it collected the sweet nectar.

"Do you teach somewhere here?" Jessica asked, turning back to the professor.

"Something like that," the professor said. "You can say that I'm retired. I just mentor people now."

"What was your area of expertise?"

"Why limit myself to one area of expertise?" The professor grinned.

"I like that." Jessica laughed. "Well, is there an area of study that draws you more than the others? I mean if you *had* to choose."

"Hmmm." The professor pondered this while he tapped his index finger between his upper lip and the bottom of his nose. "If I *had* to choose," Professor Raziel glanced back to Jessica, "then today I would say physics."

"Why physics?"

"It's the closest mankind has come, in these times, to understanding how the universe around them works. Don't you find it fascinating that mankind uses its relatively finite sets of symbols, numbers, and rules to try and explain that which is infinite? That's a great task, and I admire those who endeavor in it."

Jessica admitted, "My brain doesn't work that way."

"Oh, don't be so hard on yourself. You could understand some principles if you were introduced to them the proper way." The professor looked around like he was searching for something. "Ah," he said, "do you mind a quick lesson?"

"In *physics?*" Jessica laughed again, not sure she was up for this.

"It will be fun, and you'll learn how capable you are at learning," the professor said confidently. "Isn't that part of why you are here?"

He does have a point. "I mean, you are the professor, right?"

"Excellent," he said.

Just then, Vau returned, holding a shining silver tray. On the dish was a white porcelain teapot, decorated with a single line of small red flowers circling the pot's base. Jessica could see the steam coming out of the spout. There were four porcelain teacups with matching red floral patterns. Each cup also had a golden ring lining the rim. There was a small bowl filled with brown sugar cubes and a cup with milk. The tray also held a glass jar filled with amber-colored honey that shined in the sunlight.

"Perfect timing, Vau," the professor said.

"Are you about to teach a lesson?" Vau's eyes grew wide.

"I get the honor of teaching Jessica something new," the professor said.

"Don't let me interrupt," Vau replied, sounding eager.

"Okay, Jessica, I'm going to teach you two things, systems and state-space. They may seem simple, but they are incredibly complex. If you can understand the basics of these things, then you are that much closer to understanding how the universe works."

"Okay…" Jessica said.

"The first term is system. A system is a collection of things that work together for a common purpose. An example of a system could be your car. It's a collection of parts, energy, and other features that have a common goal of transporting riders from one place to another in relative comfort. Does that make sense so far?"

Jessica nodded.

"The next term is state-space or state of space. The state of space refers to all the possible states of the system. Think about the car example again and all the possible states. Is your car driving smoothly? Does it have gas? Does it have a flat tire? You get it."

Jessica nodded again.

"Okay, I'm going to use a different example of a system, one that's a bit more complex." Professor Raziel picked up the jar of honey from the table and held it up. "There is a system in place to create honey. A collection of bees, flowers, micro-organisms that all come together, and the result is honey. They all work in synergy to create something greater in combination."

"Working together," Jessica said.

"That's right. You can only have synergy when you have a system of things bringing their diverse characteristics together, and the sum is greater than the parts. The opposite of this is called interference," the professor continued.

Jessica's ears perked up at this. It rang a bell.

"Interference occurs when there is a lack of diversity in the system, and everything in the system is after the same goal. It results in crowding out, overpopulation, and destruction."

"Wait," Jessica said, "didn't you say that with honey, the bees, the flowers, and the micro-organisms all come together to make honey?"

"No." The professor smiled. "I said that their combined efforts result in honey. The flower wants to be pollinated, the bee wants to collect the nectar, the micro-organisms want to spread. Each member in this system does exactly what it was put on this earth to do. As a result, we get this delicious honey to enjoy."

"Okay, I think I understand what you are saying."

"Wonderful!" the professor said as he clasped his hands together. "And you questioned your ability to understand a little bit of classical physics. The challenge is to get people to understand that they are part of a complex system, and each one has a part to play. But these days, most people don't understand or seek to understand how they fit into their system."

Jessica let that sit with her, as she wondered what her part was in the system.

"Are we ready for some tea?" Vau asked, offering the steaming cups.

Aja offered more food as well. After a quick, delicious meal, Aja addressed Vau, "It's getting late. You should get her to the house."

All four of them stood up. Aja turned to Jessica and grabbed her hands. "We are so glad to have you here. Thank you for all that you have done for us. We truly appreciate it."

20

───────

THE ECONOMICS OF THE POINT

Professor Raziel, Jessica, and Vau walked through the center of town. The streets were paved, but aged.

"This is the main street," Vau said. He motioned around them. "You have the high school, the city hall."

As Vau spoke, Jessica took in the quiet street and downtown buildings. "Where are we, exactly?" Jessica pulled out her phone. "I tried to look at my smartphone map, but I don't have a signal. I don't believe I've seen Archer's Point on a map before."

"We work very hard to keep it that way," Vau said. "It's by invitation only."

Jessica kept looking around the downtown area, admiring the variety of shops. *This is pretty impressive.*

Vau interrupted Jessica's thinking. "We have a handful of restaurants, all excellent. We have an ice cream shop, a theater, two bars, and a coffee shop. And there's our bakery."

"We also have a fantastic dispensary," the professor said as both he and Vau smiled. "Pretty much everything you need."

"What do people do around here?" Jessica asked.

"Whatever they want," Vau said, looking confused by the question.

"Do you mean, what do they do for money?" the professor asked. Jessica nodded.

"This place built its wealth from the exportation of innovative ideas," the professor said.

"What kind of ideas?" she asked.

"This place started as a hub for people with ideas about technology, education, and energy sources," Vau said.

The professor picked up where Vau paused. "That evolved to developing more effective agricultural techniques, and then, of course, the arts."

"One of our many claims to fame is that we introduced the idea of polyculture farming," Vau said.

"What's that?" Jessica asked.

"Let's head on to the house," the professor said, "and we can show you."

At that moment, Jessica thought about how long she'd been on her feet. She'd flown to Vancouver late the night before. She'd spent all day walking through the forest and was now walking through even more of the village, yet her legs weren't tired. *What was in that tea?*

"At our peak," Vau continued, "we produced the largest number of musicians, painters, writers, and inventors the world had ever seen. Engineers were using our technology to create the greatest structures known to man. We were able to discover ways to cultivate soil that allowed people to farm in places like the Amazon rainforest."

"I thought that the soil in the Amazon rainforest was rich with nutrients. That's why it has such plant diversity."

"On the contrary," the professor said. "The rain washes all the nutrients away. So when very early settlers came to us with this problem, we had to figure out how to use the materials there to create a soil rich and healthy enough for farming."

"Do people still farm in the Amazon?" Jessica asked.

The professor appeared to daze off. "Not like they used to. Those were the times when you'd find great cities in the middle of the rainforest."

"Now the rainforest solely relies on the dust from the African deserts to provide its nutrients," Vau said.

"You guys are losing me," Jessica said.

"Oh, our bad. We forgot about…" Vau used his finger to point in a circular motion at Jessica's head. "We get carried away sometimes."

They left the downtown area and were now on a gravel road, once again surrounded by trees as high as she could see. Jessica wasn't sure what species they were. *I mean, they are red, so maybe redwoods?* She knew what pine trees looked like, and these were not them.

"Do you license ideas, like patents?" Jessica asked.

"Yeah, along those lines," the professor said. "I'm sure that you're familiar with the network effect. The more people who use what we create, the more we gain."

"You guys must be killing it if the Singularity Group's touch screens are an idea that you licensed," Jessica said.

"That product is doing incredibly well, but it still has room to do more," Professor Raziel said.

"What other technology are you developing? Or do I need to sign some sort of nondisclosure agreement?"

Vau said, "You can have access to anything that you want to learn."

"Our ideas are market driven," the professor said. "We try to create things that are needed. We try to prioritize other ideas over technological innovation, for the moment, that is."

"Why?" Jessica asked, surprised. "Technology is the future."

"Yes, technological advances are an important part of the future. However, people consistently break their agreements, and so we really must be cautious."

Vau chimed in as if he felt Jessica's confusion. "If you haven't realized it yet, you'll come to learn that this place, this town, is older than you can imagine. Long before your history books even began to think about documenting things, people used the technologies and processes that we developed to inhabit the most uninhabitable places. As time moved on and as mercantilism became more popular, businesses were doing anything to maximize their profits. We saw more people breaking their contracts, especially when it came to our technology and education."

"How so?" Jessica asked.

"How were they breaking their contracts?" Vau asked.

Jessica nodded.

"We licensed our technology to people for specific uses. We later found out that people were reverse engineering our technology and using it in ways that we never wanted it to be used," the professor said. "There was nothing we could do about it, so we decided to stop licensing our technology."

"What about education?" Jessica asked.

"We used to teach the teachers," the professor said. "The founders of the Point had a vision, that if everyone in the world were knowledgeable, then they would all live in a better world. So we brought the most promising leaders here and taught them everything we know. The thought was that they would teach their people, who would, in turn, educate and inform the rest of the population." The professor sighed deeply. "The reality was that more of our pupils kept the information for themselves. They would share some bits of it, but only with a select few."

Vau frowned. "Similar to technology, they reverse engineered what we gave them and used it for exploitation."

"Do you teach anyone now? I mean, anyone who's not from the Point?" Jessica asked.

"Yes, of course, we do. We just have changed our approach for finding and selecting pupils," the professor said. "In the past, we would proactively approach the leaders of different communities, those who had been selected by their people. Now, we only teach those who seek the information we have and find their way here. People like you."

"It's much more difficult to get here than it used to be," Vau added.

"We weren't getting the results that we wanted." The professor continued with a smile, "Fortunately, many people have become curious and want to question everything. Like, are we even farming the right way?"

The professor slowed to a stop and waved his hand in front of him as if he just pulled the sheet off a big reveal.

Jessica looked up to see a large stone structure that reminded her of a French chateau. The house was at the center of a garden, where each row yielded a different color plant. The berry bushes radiated against the pink and orange backdrop of the twilight sky.

21

MALIK'S FIRST RODEO

Honk, honk.

"Malik," his mom shouted, "get out there and tell Ronnie that he doesn't need to lay on that horn."

Malik opened the door and saw Ronnie impatiently waiting in his car.

"Hurry up, dude!" Ronnie shouted.

"Just give me a minute," Malik called as he quickly ducked back into the house. He grabbed his cowboy boots. He'd gotten them from an up-and-comer in the music scene while visiting a buddy in Nashville. There were few occasions in Atlanta for a black man to wear cowboy boots, so Malik jumped at any opportunity to strut around in them. Ronnie was plugged into the agriculture community. He said there would be a rodeo for the migrant workers. Malik wasn't sure what to expect, but he knew this was an opportunity to rock his boots.

Malik came out of the house and jumped into the white Silverado, instead of the two-door sports car he'd been expecting. Ronnie was a big dude. He had the build of a farmer and a buzz cut. His family came here to work the farms, but Ronnie had the opportunity to study finance. His grandpa still had a large crew of workers he contracted out to different farms. Ronnie helped Pop with the back office work.

"Your grandpop let you drive his truck?" Malik asked.

"I can't pull up to a rodeo in my car. Plus, we're going to need four-wheel drive where we're going."

"What are you talking about?"

"You'll see," Ronnie said. His smile was sly.

This was Malik's first rodeo. Trying to manage his expectations, he spent last night watching rodeo videos online. He kept prodding Ronnie with questions, "So what are we talking about here? Barrel racing? Pole bending? Bull riding? That mutton-busting thing where a kid rides a sheep?"

"I said you'll see," was all Ronnie would give him. They drove for so long, Malik fell asleep. He jumped awake when the truck hit a large pothole, and he banged his head against the passenger side window. He peered out the window. It was pitch black except for the full moon that illuminated the trees. But something was different. Malik wasn't seeing the Georgia pines he had grown accustomed to seeing when traveling outside the perimeter. He saw fields of banana plants with bright blue bags covering the large bunches of bananas.

"Where are we?" Malik asked.

"We're here," Ronnie said as he pointed to an arena built in a field. Ronnie parked, and they joined the people making their way to the stadium. Malik heard the cheers getting louder as they approached.

The scene in the arena was not what Malik expected. A few dozen spectators in plainclothes were standing inside the arena. Nothing seemed to be happening though.

"What's going on?" Malik asked.

"Just wait for it." Ronnie leaned forward.

Malik turned back to see that someone opened a gate where someone was attempting to ride a bull. The rider lasted for approximately three seconds. Once the bull successfully bucked the rider, he turned his attention to the other people in the ring. The bull chased the people around the circle. Some participants quickly climbed up the arena walls, barely missed by the horns. The brave ones side-stepped the bull's horns and tried to slap the bull on the forehead. Every time someone successfully touched the bull behind the horns, the crowd roared with cheers. This went on until the bull became tired or bored, then the next bull and rider came out.

"I've got a buddy from San Jose. He's always told me that I needed to see how the Costa Rican Ticos do rodeos," Ronnie said as he nudged Malik with his elbow. "How wild, right? I'll be right back. I'm going to buy us a couple of beers. Maybe if we drink enough, we'll have the liquid courage to jump in the ring."

"I doubt that," Malik shouted as Ronnie disappeared into the crowd.

Malik stood in the stands and watched as bull after bull tossed a rider and chased the crowd. When a lucky soul or two touched the bull, the spectators would go nuts.

A couple was standing next to him. The husband was more than a few drinks in, and his buddies were tugging on his arm, trying to get him to jump in the arena. The wife leaned toward Malik, pointing to the arena as she talked as if trying to explain things to him. Malik couldn't understand a word the woman was saying, but he smiled back at her anyway.

Several bulls had come and gone, and Malik licked his lips. He realized that Ronnie hadn't come back with his beer. Malik reached for his phone; it didn't have a signal. *Maybe there's a long line at the concession stand.* Malik left the stands to find the closest concession stand.

The area under the stands was empty. There wasn't a soul. No vendors, no Ronnie, not even a sign that the arena was even open. Plastic tarps and clothes were covering the ice chests next to the concession stand booth.

"What the…" Malik said. He listened for the crowd, and even they had gone silent. He went back out toward the arena. Everyone was lying on the ground, motionless. A bull walked around, sniffing at the bodies on the floor. It appeared to be confused. Malik turned his sights to the spectators in the crowd. All were lying down, motionless. Malik looked back at the couple he'd been standing next to. The woman had vanished, but her husband was lying there. He was now dramatically thinner. Dark lesions started to appear on him, covering his exposed skin in a matter of seconds. Malik instinctively touched his mask and backed up as he saw that the lesions were spreading to everyone now lying in the stands.

Suddenly, Ronnie walked up with two beers. He handed one to Malik and sat down nearby in the stands as if nothing had changed and the rodeo was still happening. However, Ronnie's muscular frame was now frail. He too was covered in lesions, but he didn't seem to notice.

"I like your buddy. That man's a fighter." Malik turned around and saw a thin man with a thick mustache wearing blue jeans, a T-shirt, and a cowboy hat.

"Who are you?" asked Malik.

"I'm just a cowboy. But that lady," the cowboy pointed across the arena, "she calls me a goddamned hero."

Malik looked across the arena. Standing on the opposite side and glowing was the woman with long, curly, light brown hair. "Evelyn," Malik whispered. *This is a dream.*

The cowboy continued, "Let me tell you something though. If those assholes aren't gonna help you, then you do it your damned self. Do you understand me? To hell with 'em."

Malik eyed the man, letting his words sink in. The next thing he knew, they were both standing behind a concession stand. Now a thick crowd surrounded the concession stand like it was halftime at a football game.

"Step right up, step right up," the man was shouting as he waved his hands in the air. "I've got what you need." The cowboy had metal shakers and was mixing drinks like a bartender. He poured the cocktails in various glasses laid out on the table in front of them.

The man glanced at Malik and said, "You've got to do what you've got to do sometimes, kid." Then the cowboy handed people the glasses. As soon as they threw back the cocktails, their dark lesions vanished, and they regained their weight and color in their skin.

Then the man grabbed the neck of Malik's shirt and jerked Malik within inches of his face. The man twisted the shirt with a solid grip, and with one hand, he lifted Malik off the ground. The cowboy stared at Malik. "Do you have what it takes to go all the way, kid?" Then he threw Malik backward. Malik closed his eyes and braced for impact…

He woke up in his bed.

22

A DELIVERY FOR THE DOC

THE NEXT MORNING, THE DOCTOR'S OFFICE WAS BUSIER THAN USUAL. A long line of patients hoped to grab an open slot with the doctor or one of his nurse practitioners. Malik was working with the front desk staff, frantically trying to get all the patients tested and sorted into the appropriate waiting areas.

"Malik." He heard his name being called from the delivery window.

He sighed and tilted his head back. "Not now."

"But I need to talk to you," Callie said.

"We're swamped. I don't have time right now."

"You want to hear this," she said. "I've discovered a clue."

Malik focused on the screen, checking people in, and resetting the virus detection machine. Still without looking at Callie, he said, "Come back when we are less busy."

"Excuse me?" The voice coming from the delivery counter wasn't Callie's.

Malik turned around and saw a boy with short black hair wearing a baseball cap and a plaid-patterned cloth mask. He was holding a white cardboard box with a matching cardboard lid.

"Hi, is Dr. Patel in?" he asked.

"Give me one minute," Malik said. "I'll be right with you."

"I don't have a minute," the delivery boy said. "Can you check to see if Dr. Patel is in? This will be quick."

"He's not available right now," Malik said while checking someone in on the computer. "He's busy with patients. Can I help you?"

"Sure." He slid the box to Malik. "Tell the doc that I've finished cleaning out the old storage unit. Let him know that I've finished shredding the obsolete files, but these looked different. I wasn't sure what he wanted me to do with them, so I figured I should bring them to him. These don't have any patient information or anything."

"Got it," Malik said as he took the box.

"Oh, hi, Jordan." Malik heard Dr. Patel's friendly voice from behind him. "How are you, young lady?"

Young lady? Malik thought, slightly embarrassed. *I'll blame it on the mask.*

"Are you all finished?" Dr. Patel asked.

"Hey, Doc," she said. "I was just telling him," she pointed at Malik, "I've shredded all of your and Dr. Wen Shen's obsolete files. There were some things in the storage unit that I didn't know what to do with though, so I boxed them up. You can decide what to do with them."

"What obsolete files?" Malik asked, now paying more attention.

"I asked Jordan here to clear out our storage unit. We had boxes of old paper records from thirty years ago, just sitting around. You have to wait until a patient hasn't seen you for ten years before you can shred the file. Jordan's been handling that for us."

"And this is the last box," Jordan said.

"Thank you, Jordan," Dr. Patel said. "What's next for you?"

"I'm not sure exactly, but other work will pop up. It always does."

"Well, if you ever need a recommendation or anything, please don't hesitate to reach out," Dr. Patel said as he pulled out his phone. "I just sent you the money. You should have it in your account now."

"Thanks, Doc," Jordan said as she checked her phone and left.

Malik turned to look at Dr. Patel. He was going to ask him what he should do with the box, but the doctor was off again, seeing patients. Malik set the box down under the front desk.

"Nope," Christine said. "You're not leaving that thing here." She smiled. "That's why you have your own office."

Malik scoffed and jokingly rolled his eyes. "Fine. Are you good up here?"

"Yeah," Christine said, "we should be able to handle it now."

Back in his office, Malik opened the box. There was an old magazine, some printed articles, a notebook, and an old map with circles drawn on them.

Malik set the box aside and started away at his daily list of things to do.

The hours were passing quickly when Dr. Patel poked his head into Malik's office. "Do you guys want lunch today? It's on me."

"Sure," Malik replied, as he stood up to walk around the office and collect everyone's orders. When he reached the front of the office, he was surprised to see Magaly standing there.

"Oh, hi," Malik said as he handed the notebook to Christine for her to write down her order. "What are you doing here today?"

"My shift ended early," she said. "I just stopped by before heading out to lunch."

"We're collecting orders," Christine said. "Dr. Patel's paying if you want to stick around."

"I don't know," Magaly said. "I should probably get some rest."

"You'll need lunch first anyway, right? Why not grab a bite with us?" Malik said.

Magaly smiled. "Why not?"

23

A CHANCE ENCOUNTER BEFORE LUNCH

Malik was walking to the patient waiting area to lock the door for lunch when the door opened and Chance Domagk from Confidence Biotech walked in.

"Dr. Patel is in with a patient right now," Christine said. "If you want to see him, then you'll have to come back at the end of the day."

"I'm here to see him." Chance pointed at Malik. "Do you have a minute?"

Malik looked at Magaly and shrugged. He locked the door and walked back around the receptionist desk to the glassed-off delivery window.

"How's it going?" Chance asked as Malik approached the window.

"I'm all right," Malik said. "What can I do for you?"

"My boss, he's a real fan of that pen of yours. He's a fan of antiques, and he wants that pen." Chance pulled out his phone. "He's willing to pay a lot of money for it. Name your price." Chance had his cell phone and fingers ready to make a transfer.

"My pen?" Malik asked. "It's not for sale. It's my lucky pen."

"One thousand?" Chance proposed.

"No, thanks." Malik shook his head.

"Okay, ten," Chance tried again.

"Ten thousand dollars?" Malik was floored. His heart raced. *It's my lucky pen, but…*

"What's so special about this pen?" Magaly asked as she pulled it out of Malik's jacket pocket. Malik felt chills when Magaly's hand brushed against his chest.

The smile left Chance's face momentarily, but he recovered quickly. "There weren't many of them made. It's an antique with intricate detailing, and it uniquely stores ink. My boss wants to own the entire collection."

"So is he willing to pay, say…" Magaly pretended like she was thinking hard. "I don't know, one hundred thousand dollars for it?"

"Tough negotiator," Chance said, and seemed to reassess the situation. He returned his attention to Malik. "Dr. Patel mentioned you were doing research here. You were an intern at Confidence Biotech. I know you wouldn't have been allowed to enter it, but I assume you remember our incubator program?"

"Sure, why?" Malik asked, wary of where this was going.

"In exchange for the pen, you could enter a project in our program for funding. If it passes the early assessment, then we could fund the development of it."

Malik's eyebrows shot up. *Was this for real?*

"Hello, Chance, what brings you here?" Dr. Patel interrupted.

"I was just talking with Malik here."

"Talking to Malik about what?"

Chance was silent. The smile left his face once more. This time, it didn't return.

Malik stepped in. "Mr. Domagk said that if I trade him my lucky pen, then Confidence Biotech would offer me a chance to submit a project for funding and development."

"Is that so?" Dr. Patel asked.

"That is, if Malik has a viable project," replied Chance. "It would have to go through the program like anything else. No promises, but it's a pretty good deal if you ask me."

"Malik," Dr. Patel said, "you can drive my car to pick up lunch if you'll put that box that Jordan brought in it."

The Jag? Malik couldn't hold back a big grin. "You got it."

Malik looked at Chance. "I appreciate the offer, but I'm going to have to pass." He turned and left to grab the box out of his office when he heard Magaly shout, "I'm coming too."

Malik and Magaly rode in silence to the restaurant. Malik thought hard about what to say, but nothing came to him as his sweaty palms gripped the steering wheel. He made brief eye contact with Magaly and then quickly looked away. Magaly motioned to the box in the backseat. "What's that?"

"It's some stuff that was left in a storage unit that Dr. Patel shared with another doctor," Malik said.

"What doctor?"

"I think he said it was Dr. Wen Shen."

"No way! That stuff must be from way back."

"You know who she is?"

"She's the one who started this practice a long time ago. She used to work for the CDC. She was a pulmonologist who was ahead of her time in the field of virology. Dr. Patel used to talk about her all the time. She taught him everything he knows about mitigating viral infections."

"What happened to her?" Malik asked.

"I'm not sure. Dr. Patel said that she traveled back to her village in China every year to offer free medical care. One year, she never came back."

24

MALIK'S TIME IN CORPORATE

The restaurant was packed, and the order that Malik had called in wasn't ready. He and Magaly grabbed seats at the bar to wait and ordered two waters.

"So," Magaly said as she was playing with her straw, "who was that guy trying to buy your pen?"

"He works for Confidence Biotech. He's the right hand to the CEO."

"And the CEO wants to buy your lucky pen?"

"Yeah, wild, right?"

"Why? What's so special about the pen?" she asked.

"Well…" Malik pulled the pen out of his pocket and held it up for their inspection. "This pen is made of something called mycelium. Think of mycelia as the root system for fungi, allowing the fungi to feed and get the needed nutrients. When mycelia connect with trees and other plants' roots, they create what's called a mycorrhizal network. This mycorrhizal network allows trees and plants to communicate with each other."

Malik paused. Magaly had an amused expression. He realized that he was nerding out. He cleared his throat. "Besides the fact that mycelium is just cool, I've also had this pen for pretty much my entire life, and it's never run out of ink."

"How is that possible?" Magaly looked skeptical.

"No, really," he said. "I found this pen when I was two or three years old. I used it to scribble all over my parents' antique coffee table. My dad tried to throw it out, and I cried until he dug it out of the trash."

"Really?" Magaly laughed.

"True story," Malik said. "My parents joke about it now. They figured that one day I'd lose it or it would run out of ink," Malik leaned toward Magaly a little, and with a triumphant expression told her, "and neither has happened yet." They both laughed.

"And now that guy was willing to give you ten thousand dollars for it, or fund your project," Magaly said. "I didn't know that you used to work at ConTech."

"Is that what the cool kids call it?" Malik smiled.

"You know it," she said, "and don't change the subject." She leaned in and gently nudged her shoulder against his before sipping from her straw.

"I didn't technically work there. I interned there while I was at college."

"I'd consider that working," she said.

"It was unpaid," Malik said.

"Ugh, yuck." Magaly stuck out her tongue like she got a bad taste from her drink.

"Exactly… I wanted to work for Roy Mengele. His rags-to-riches story was inspiring. He came from nothing, worked at a hotel, and then someone took a chance on him. Fast forward, and he became the CEO of a prominent biotech company."

"Was it a good experience?"

"In certain ways."

"So what's the deal with the incubator program?" Magaly asked.

"It's typically for full-time employees to enter business ideas or revenue streams. They give you time out of the week to work on the idea, and if company executives find it promising, they will help you launch it. The company funds it and helps set up and manage everything from testing through trials."

"That sounds great."

"It's great, except it becomes their intellectual property."

"Ah, okay. Self-interest."

"Of course."

The two sat silently for a moment.

"Can I see that lucky pen of yours again?" Magaly asked.

"Sure." Malik pulled it back out of his coat pocket. "But I don't know if you know this: it's worth ten, if not a hundred, thousand dollars."

"I could be interested. I'd just need to take out several loans first. But how do I know it's lucky?" Magaly asked with a twinkle of mischief in her eye. She reached across Malik and grabbed a white paper napkin. "I think I need a test." She wrote on the napkin, using her hand to shield it so Malik couldn't see what she was writing. Their order came just as Magaly finished writing her note. Magaly folded the message and placed both the paper and the pen inside Malik's jacket pocket. She gently patted his chest. "Let's see how lucky this pen is."

The rest of the day flew by so fast, Malik didn't remember the note in his pocket until he was in his car, getting ready to head home. Nervously, he pulled the note out of his pocket.

It read, "I'm off this weekend. Take me out Friday night."

25

MEETUP AT THE POND

Jessica opened her eyes and looked around. *Where am I?* She knew that she was far from her hotel room in Atlanta and even farther from her home in DC. Yet, as she took in the room and wrapped herself in the blankets, she felt comfortable and safe in this strange bed. Jessica had slept deeply, expecting to wake up to the bright morning sun, but it was still dark. She got out of bed and walked over to the window. She opened it, breathing in cool air from a star-filled night sky. She felt more rested than she had in a long time.

Although Jessica couldn't see the moon, it must have been a full one. Everything on the ground was illuminated. Her room had a perfect view of various trees planted in perfectly alternating rows that, from her view, formed a quarter of a circle. Jessica had a memory for each tree she recognized. The pomegranate trees were from her childhood in Arizona. The apple trees reminded her of time spent in New England, while the orange trees brought back a memory of the last time she spoke with her dad. He had been physically there, but his mind kept slipping away until it couldn't find its way back. When he was there with her, he was there. He had always been the most present father. However, when his mind took flight... Jessica shook her head. A tactic she'd learned to fight off negative, unproductive thoughts. *At least I had him when I did.*

After three rows of trees, there was a path that led from the house and disappeared into the forest. Jessica saw something move on the path and froze, as if she was somewhere she shouldn't be. Someone was walking toward the house from the forest. The person seemed small in stature, but that might have just been the distance. Jessica then saw two other people walking from the house to meet with the person: one was Vau, and the other was Evelyn. As the third person got closer, Jessica recognized it to be Jordan. She was Ori's former right hand at the Singularity Group, and Jessica believed she was still supporting Leslie there in some way.

They stopped a ways away, but Jessica could still hear their conversation.

"How'd it go?" Evelyn asked.

"It went well. I delivered the box," Jordan said. "He thought I was a boy."

Vau laughed loudly. "I told you the hat and baggy clothes would be a good cover."

"Whatever," Jordan said. "Is Jessica here?"

"She's upstairs in her room," Evelyn said.

"Can I go see her?"

"Not yet," Evelyn said. "You've got to debrief."

"Besides," Vau chimed in, "Jessica should be sleeping."

"Pffft. She's never slept through the night here," Jordan said.

"Still, her mind has to adjust on its own. Ori must see her next. She's his recruit," Evelyn said.

"Fine," Jordan said. "Where is Ori?"

"He and Tony are by the pond," Evelyn said. "If you go now, you can catch them before they head back. Have Tony do a sweep."

"You know," Vau said, "just in case you left a trail."

"I never leave a trail," Jordan said as she turned to walk down a path headed back into the woods.

Ori? The pond? Jessica's heart raced. She threw on her clothes, ran out of the room and down the stairs, and sprinted down the path in pursuit of Jordan. The woods were thick with large trees, but the moonlight provided enough light on the dirt trail for Jessica to see.

Jordan was out of sight, yet somehow Jessica's legs knew where to take her. The trail opened to a grassy meadow. Jessica knew this place, and not from long before. She had been here recently. This is where she came the night of the incident at Zach's house. She stopped and scanned the area. Jessica saw Jordan off to her right, just as she disappeared, walking down a slight hill. Jessica walked in the same direction. When she arrived at the top of the slope, she saw the outline of three bodies standing at the edge of the pond. Jessica knew who they were, but their forms appeared altered, more fluid somehow. Tony and Jordan walked off together along the other side of the pond. Ori saw Jessica and waited for her as she descended the hill. By the time she reached him, Jordan and Tony had vanished.

Ori was taller than usual and was more of an outline of himself. He had no defining features, and millions of tiny lights, like stars, had replaced his skin. She couldn't have fathomed this a day prior, but at this moment, all felt normal and quite familiar. *I've seen him this way before.*

"Welcome back, Jessica," Ori said.

"Am I dreaming?"

"No, you're not. Here at the Point, we can be ourselves. I'm glad you made it safely. Sorry that I couldn't bring you here. There are rules, one of which is that you only get an escort once. After that, you must be able to return here on your own. What are you doing out here?"

"I—I couldn't sleep,"

"Believe it or not, that's a good thing. That means your mind is trying to work something out. It's sometimes easier to find answers when everyone else is asleep."

"What are you doing out here?"

Ori studied the pond. Jessica followed his eyes to see a giant koi fish floating at the top. Its skin was opaque now, although Jessica could still see some of its internal system moving and working like she had the night of the incident at Zach's. It was moving slower than the ones she'd seen before.

"Is it dead?" she asked.

"Not yet, but it's in trouble."

"What's wrong with it?"

Ori inhaled deeply. "Many, many things," he said as he exhaled. "But that's not your worry, that's mine. C'mon, let's get you back."

"I overheard Evelyn say that you wanted to see me first thing. Since I couldn't sleep and knew that Jordan was coming to see you, I figured I'd see you now. I hope that's okay."

"It's all good," Ori said. "I'm glad you saw the pond… again." As they walked away from the pond, toward the house, Ori's skin, features, and typical appearance returned. "I'm sorry that we had to bring you back here under these conditions, but I didn't see any other way. The virus is growing out of control, and if a cure is to be discovered, we needed to get Gabriel's blessing to bring you back here."

"But," Jessica thought back to the conversation at St. Regis in Atlanta, "I thought that your deal with Gabriel was to get Zach's memory back."

"It is that too. But, my primary objective was to get you here. Zach has an important role to play, especially when it comes to this virus. But your role, what you'll do, what you've done, will buy humanity time."

"I thought that the dire situation is this pandemic, which seems to drag on."

"This pandemic is a challenge, one that you all could have solved by now if you were to get out of your own way. But that's not what we were activated to help prevent. We've placed several solutions for the virus on Earth with people who have the background to bring them to reality. But there's so much division and interference that it will be decades and millions of lives before you figure it out."

Jessica felt guilty without knowing why.

"Don't worry," Ori said, "and don't feel sad. People will learn to manage until they understand how to coexist."

Jessica realized they had already walked back to the house.

"Get some rest now. Tomorrow morning you and I will talk more."

Jessica walked toward the front door of the house.

"Wait," Ori shouted from behind her.

Jessica turned and watched Ori walk to one of the orange trees. He picked a beautiful large orange and tossed it to Jessica.

"What is this for?" she asked.

"Proof," he said. "I'll see you in the morning."

26

AN ORIGIN STORY

JESSICA PULLED THE COVERS OVER HER FACE, TRYING TO SHIELD HER EYES from the sunlight. She didn't remember falling asleep, but she felt rested. *I know I should get up, but this bed is so comfortable.* Her stomach rumbled as it stated its case. The smell of fresh biscuits did the trick. She sat up, her legs hanging over the side of the bed. The orange sitting on top of the wooden bookcase gave her a sense of assurance. As she picked up the orange, she noted what was on the shelves. The bookshelf was tall, up to her shoulders. A couple of shelves were filled with what appeared to be volumes of the same unmarked books. The spines of the books were a green color, and the covers were cream. There were no titles or even an author's name. Jessica was about to open one when her stomach grew more assertive. She placed the book back, grabbed the orange, and started downstairs.

The wall next to the stairs was covered with various art pieces. There was only one she recognized. She couldn't help but stop and stare.

"It's Salvador Dali's The Persistence of Memory," Zach said. "What do you think?"

"It looks like what would happen if you left a bunch of watches in Yuma during the summer," Jessica said as she stared at the pocket watches lying flaccid over the tree branch. "What else should we see?"

"I just want to see this," Zach said.

"Wait, you made me get on a train from DC to come to the MoMa in New York City just to look at this one painting?" Jessica asked.

"Well, there are paintings we can look at in my..."

Jessica's thoughts were interrupted by laughter. She continued down the stairs and saw walls covered with floor-to-ceiling bookshelves. Jessica pointed to the left of the bookshelves as if giving a tour "These are the religious texts. If you move to the right," she said, "you'll get into the diaries of some of the greatest thinkers." Jessica put her index fingers in the air. "These are written in their native tongues. The English translations are in the cellar." Jessica continued scanning the room and whispering to herself, "The history section is there, and of course, you have the best fiction and comics at the end."

"I'm glad your memory is starting to come back," Professor Raziel said. She wasn't sure how long he'd been there. "I was about to head out, but the team is outside. Please grab a bite to eat."

Jessica went outside to sit under the covered patio. "Jessica," Ori welcomed her, "you remember everyone?" Everyone gave her a smile and a wave.

"So, team," Ori said, "as I think you all know, Jessica has had some issues with her memory. She's going to be here for a few days until she gets it back. Humor her questions as she tries to remember. Each of us," Ori waved his hand around the table, "has a distinct role in the team based upon a gift, a specialty, that helps us pursue our purpose."

Ori then pointed to the different team members. "That's Vau, whom I know welcomed you yesterday. Vau is our anthropologist and subject matter expert. He's the longest-tenured person on the team, and he can form a personal connection with anyone. That's Tony," Ori continued. "He can understand the most complex of systems, in and out. Tony is overall programming. He takes research and insights from Vau to launch different simulations. He's also in charge of clean up."

"What's clean up?" Jessica asked.

"If we leave any evidence behind, Tony will sweep the place clean," Jordan said. "He's the reason people don't remember us."

"And I'm sure you remember Jordan," Ori said as Jessica and Jordan exchanged a friendly nod. "Jordan is over field operations. She can blend in absolutely anywhere. She makes sure that everything is coming together well and will intervene in our absence."

Then Evelyn came outside and sat in the available chair. Jessica remembered her well, with her fair skin and shoulder-length curly hair. "Perfect timing," Ori said. "And of course, Evelyn. She runs this team and the missions. She's also a master at reading the signs."

"You can think of it as data analytics," Jordan said.

"Evelyn's gift is analyzing information from the past along with what's happening now to accurately predict what will most likely happen in the future." Ori elaborated, "Evelyn can identify and interpret ripple effects through time based upon the knowledge and information she has access to." Ori gazed at her with a proud expression. "She's the best at it."

Evelyn gave a humble smile. "It's fascinating work."

"And you?" Jessica asked Ori.

"I help with planning, and I recruit the targets."

"Ori understands the consciousness of people," Evelyn said. "He knows your every thought, and more importantly, he understands events in your life that lead you to your thoughts."

"That's remarkable," Jessica said.

"It's an excellent skill when you need to be able to offer people choices," Ori said.

"It's a blessing and a curse," Vau said.

"Thanks for the reintroductions," Jessica said. "So I understand who you are. Could I get a reminder on what you are?"

"Well, this team takes on missions that help keep the relationship between humanity and Earth on course. But, I have a feeling that was intended to be a broader question," Ori said.

"We've been called a lot of things. Pick a culture," Jordan chimed in.

"Depending on the culture and the time period, we've been called different things," explained Vau. "The Celts called us druids, the First Nations called us spirits."

"The more logic-driven people have called us beings of light," Tony said. "And celestial beings for the stargazers."

"Angels?" Jessica posed, to which Jordan and Tony both had a physical and audible reaction. "Did I say something wrong?"

"That just boxes us in a little bit," Jordan said. "Everyone always—"

Ori interrupted Jordan, "There have been times when we've been called that too. There was a time when our presence wasn't so covert or mysterious, when we were able to enjoy every moment of a beautiful day as ourselves."

Jessica recognized the look of nostalgia in his eyes.

"Back then," Ori continued, "we were called things like muses, magisters, teachers. We've been here with you all since the very beginning. Everything on this Earth has a purpose." Ori made eye contact with Jessica. "Our purpose is to be the bridge between the physical world that you know and the nonphysical world that you seek to understand. Our purpose has been to teach men how to coexist with the world around them and to teach the Earth how to coexist with human beings. We taught man how to farm, fish, hunt."

Evelyn chimed in, "We helped you understand math, science, astrology..."

"How to sail, how to fly," Vau said, gazing off.

"The arts," Evelyn said with a radiant smile. Then she closed her eyes and raised her shoulders. "Oh, and such delicious foods."

Jessica saw them all nod and give a pleasant sigh in unison.

"Our original purpose was to bring these elements of civilization to the world," Evelyn said. "We've helped you make the most of your time here on Earth."

"We've also done our best to keep you out of trouble," Jordan said, in her typical straight-shooter style.

"In the early days," Ori said, "we took on these forms to live and work among people. They were so curious; they wanted to understand how everything worked. We gladly taught them everything we knew. Any question they had, we answered."

"Any question?" Jessica asked.

"Any question," Jordan confirmed.

"Why would you do that?" Jessica asked. "What about those who misused the information? Couldn't you anticipate that if you're all-knowing?"

"It wasn't our job to choose what you could and couldn't learn," Evelyn said. "If you were curious enough to come up with a question, it was our duty to answer it."

"Why would you do that?" Jessica asked again.

"Because that was our purpose," Jordan said.

"That was a long time ago," Ori said. "Once man's desire for conquest surpassed his desire for understanding and learning, it was decided that the knowledge we have could cause more harm than good. So, we pulled back and blended in."

"Some of us hoped that, one day, your lust for conquering others would subside, so they stayed," Evelyn said. "But you see, we are bound to give you, teach you, whatever it is that you want, even the greatest secret."

"What secret is that?" Jessica asked.

"The power of manifestation," Jordan said.

"You are incredibly unique. Human beings are the only creatures in existence that were made in the image of the creator," said Evelyn. "This has nothing to do with what's on the outside or on the inside. This is all about your ability to use your brain and your imagination to bring things to reality, to create something that never existed before. If your mind can imagine it, then you can bring it to life."

"In that vein, not only are we bound to teach you whatever you want," Ori said, "we are also bound to help you obtain whatever it is that you imagine."

"Genie," Tony blurted out. "I liked when people referred to us as genies. That was a fun period."

Ori stared at Tony.

"What?" Tony asked.

Ori waved his hand in a dismissive gesture and looked back at Jessica. "So, if discovered and asked, we do have the obligation to have a more active role. Now, this is wonderful when people envision a life surrounded by loved ones."

"Or when a young woman envisions being the President of the United States," Evelyn said.

"This is, of course, a problem though when people have selfish intentions. But many human beings are also very disconnected from their subconscious thoughts, and that presents problems as well," said Ori. "You can remember a time when the world was filled with war, not because the majority of people secretly wished for more war…"

"Although some did," Jordan said.

"Very few," Vau chimed in. "But many people can't seem to imagine a world without greed, hate, violence, oppression."

"And the collective thoughts of the many *can* create reality." Ori shook his head. "The world was filled with war because the majority of people could not imagine a world without it. Once most people can imagine a world without it, then it becomes possible."

"But what about people who were in war-torn places?" Jessica asked. "How would you expect anything else?"

"People just needed to question it," Jordan said. "For most of the world's problems, the question that enough people aren't asking is 'Why? Why does it have to be that way?'

"What about deep-rooted conflicts and complicated cultural differences that can't be overcome?" Jessica asked.

Ori leaned in. "The body, the soldiers, just want their lives back or a better version of life for them and their families. It's the heads of the serpents that are always the problem, especially if driven by ego, greed, or power."

"What about hate?" Jessica asked.

"Hate is also manifested; it has to be created," Ori said.

"Hate is a weapon," Jordan said.

"The first weapon," Tony interjected.

"That's right," Ori agreed. "Its blade has been sharpened to perfection over time. It cuts the fabric of man so cleanly that you would never know that you are all one."

While much of this was wild and hard to wrap her head around, that last comment rang true to Jessica. It got quiet for a moment.

"So then what is your purpose now? You still teach select people with honorable intentions who find their way here. Your team is trying to right the course for humanity in some way. How?" Jessica asked.

"The solution will not be easy. The right thing to do is always the hardest thing to do," Ori said.

27

ORI'S DEPARTURE

"Sadly, there are still people who think the only way to power is through greed, oppression, trickery." Ori continued Jessica's immersion, "That couldn't be further from the truth. Knowledge has always been and will always be the secret to empowerment. The more you know, truly know, about who you are, what you are, and how the world around you works, the more powerful you will be."

"Before we withdrew," Vau said, "mankind was at its pinnacle of innovation. They were able to create the most extraordinary things—the machinery, the artwork."

"The world moved on from that time," Evelyn said. "The age of Leo."

"The age of the lion, king of beasts," Vau said.

"What's the age of Leo?" Jessica asked.

"We all answer to someone, right?" Ori said. "It was decided that the people had learned enough to make the world the way they saw fit, so we would now be taking a more measured approach. We would teach those chosen by the people to be leaders. Ideally, the people would have been able to choose honorable, noble leaders of good character. From there, they would be our connection point, and they would disperse the knowledge."

"This was the beginning of the great shift," said Vau.

"A people who question things are people who cannot be controlled." Ori paused. "You began to see a concerted effort to obliterate anything that would cause people to question authority."

Evelyn spoke, "Ancient secrets, information that was in what you now know as Central America, were destroyed like it was nothing. Libraries of the greatest information known to man were burned without a second thought. Erased."

"We did see this coming," Ori said. "So we had great structures built, things that proved a highly civilized people once lived there. This is why the pyramids and other great ruins dot the Earth."

"I thought the pyramids were ancient burial sites or tombs or something," Jessica said.

"But what's inside is the least impressive part," Vau replied.

"The point with these great structures was to make them so intricate and complex that it would force future generations to question how they could ever have been built by a less advanced people," Ori said.

"The Pyramids of Giza, weren't those built by slaves?" Jessica asked.

"C'mon," Jordan said. "Common sense would tell you how unlikely that is, from the sheer size and weight of every stone to the precision of every angle. If simple unskilled labor could do it, then why hasn't anyone ever built anything even close to it?"

"So then what happened when the great shift started?" Jessica asked. "That's when you guys withdrew?"

Everyone was silent, and they looked at Evelyn. "That came in time."

"It was then that I saw the consciousness of man's chosen leaders," Ori said. "I saw corruption. Not only were they stifling knowledge among their people, but the thirst for power was growing. I decided that we should no longer trust the nature of man. My colleagues couldn't yet see what I saw, but I decided I had to leave. If my colleagues wanted to continue to give man knowledge, then that was their decision." Ori cast his gaze downward with what seemed like regret. "Things became worse than I ever imagined."

"So this team stayed to continue your work?" Jessica asked.

"That's right," said Ori.

Jessica looked at Evelyn. "But aren't you guys married, if that's even the word you use?"

Evelyn smiled. "Yes, our souls are bound to one another. But, you see, time works differently for us. And we each had what we thought was a separate responsibility for the time being."

"And so Ori left, and things got worse?" Jessica asked.

Evelyn said, "He warned us all of what he saw. Nothing was definite until mankind acted on it."

"We don't like to relive the past," Jordan said.

"No, it's okay," Ori said, looking at Jordan. "She needs to know. When I left, my team lost access to the consciousness of man. I see what mankind is thinking, consciously, or subconsciously. It was my job to advise my team. When I left, Evelyn could no longer understand what they were thinking or planning. She could only use their past and current behaviors to assess what they may do in the future. With the absence of their thoughts, this team was less able to carry out missions successfully and manage the course of events. Our kind was blindsided when men took some knowledge and committed grotesque crimes against their fellow man."

"And that's when it was decided that another change was needed for all of us," Vau said. "It was time to pull back from man."

"Our roles have evolved and adapted, but all are now more covert," Ori said. "You met Gabriel. He oversees the humanity side of the equation. Aja's oversight is Earth itself. And Professor Raziel and others share knowledge here at the Point, with those who are worthy."

"Where does this team fall?" Jessica asked.

"We don't fall in one particular place," Evelyn said. "Whenever a critical mission is needed for the greater balance, we answer the call."

"And you're back now, clearly," Jessica said, addressing this comment to Ori.

"Indeed."

"What is it that you are back to do?" Jessica asked.

"When you arrived, the professor talked to you about the concept of systems, correct?"

Jessica nodded.

Ori continued, "Man and the Earth are supposed to work together, in harmony. There's sadly a massive disconnect that has reached a tipping point. If you can't overcome that, then there could be mutual destruction."

"What gives you faith that the greater balance can still be achieved?" Jessica asked.

"While my abilities allow me to see a lot of bad," Ori replied thoughtfully, "I see hope in the consciousness and dreams of the young. If I can see that, we have to try."

Evelyn then cleared her throat and said, "And this is where we need you. This may seem cryptic for now, as you're trying to regain your memories, but your role as the scribe is an important part of our mission."

"I don't see how my articles can make much of an impact in this way," replied Jessica.

"But you're more than your articles," Evelyn said. "You've developed a strong reputation for speaking the truth. And you are helping to plant seeds. The right people will believe you."

"How are you so sure?" Jessica asked.

Ori picked up a biscuit. "Because people are pretty consistent. An honest person will always be honest."

As he took a bite, Evelyn stood up. "Speaking of being consistent," Evelyn said, "you've been consistently skipping the council meetings. There's one today, and you need to attend. We need to get started."

Everyone stood up from the table.

"Fine," Ori said with a sly smile. "I'll be there."

"It's also your turn to do the dishes," Jordan said, grabbing the biscuit out of his hand and walking off the porch down a path that led to the forest.

"Don't be too long," Evelyn said as she, Vau, and Tony followed Jordan.

"I'll stay back and help," Jessica said.

28

ORI GIVES JESSICA A QUICK OVERVIEW

Ori smiled. "I hope we haven't overwhelmed you yet."

"It's a lot, for sure," replied Jessica, "but I think I'm following. I'm starting to think of you guys as system administrators. You've got people on the ground, watching, observing behind the scenes. This is headquarters, where you can see the whole picture, and house the history and knowledge."

"Yep. And those of us on the ground can make a bunch of small impacts that have a ripple effect and add up over time. Maybe we plant an idea in a struggling farmer's head about a different way to farm. Or we encourage someone to go ahead and make that movie they've been dreaming up, which inspires countless other people to think about the world differently."

"How many of you exist?" Jessica asked.

"Oh, we're everywhere," Ori said. "You've had several interactions with us. You just haven't noticed."

"How is that possible?" Jessica asked.

"We are now meant to always stay in the background," Ori said. "Remember, this is your human experience. You are the main character of this narrative, and while you choose, more or less, who your supporting cast members are, you should only see what we allow you to see."

"Here's where I'm confused," Jessica confessed. "How is it that you were the CEO of a very successful company and Evelyn was an agent with the FBI? Those sound like main characters to me. On top of that, you both are believed to have been killed in some very dodgy operation gone wrong. That's not being in the background at all."

Ori sighed and shook his head. "You know when I decided to leave this work? Well, I went a bit rogue. I bounced around a bit through time, trying to make a bigger impact. In the scenario you're referring to, I chose to create a large business. In your world, commerce and money impact so many people's lives that it only made sense to focus my efforts there, trying to get more people to the fourth phase. But someone interfered with my version of reality, or they tried to at least."

Ori put the last dish away and looked around at the clean kitchen. "I think we are good here. We should get going. We don't want to be late for Evelyn's briefing."

"What do you mean someone interfered with your version of reality?" Jessica asked.

"The universal rules are pretty simple: you get in life what you put out. I was only putting out positive, constructive energy to help people grow and achieve their best. It shouldn't have led to destructive forces showing up at my door. By that time, our leaders and colleagues had seen the truth in my earlier visions about the nature of man. My team came to find me and bring me back. Once I showed them what I was pursuing, they stayed to help me. We didn't even realize at that point how much I would need them. And as you've noticed, Tony has cleaned up most of the traces left behind on that one."

Jessica and Ori now left the house and were walking down a path in the garden toward the forest. Jessica prompted Ori further, "You said something about a fourth phase?"

"There are five phases of awareness governing how human beings experience their world. Phase one involves just being aware that you exist and questioning things that pertain to your reality. Thoughts like, 'Why are we sleeping in an open field when we can hide in a cave?' Phase two began as people learned about different ways in which other people experienced life. Think of this as reading a book or watching a movie where you can imagine and see how other people live, though you haven't directly experienced it yourself. Phase three was the dawn of the three-dimensional form of living. People learned to travel and take part in the lives and realities of other cultures. This is a phase of exchanging ideas, philosophies, food, art." Ori showed a fleeting smile. "This is pretty much where most of you stopped."

Ori stopped walking for a moment. Jessica hadn't been paying attention to where they were walking. She looked up and saw they were on a cliff, staring at an enormous mountainside. Jessica tried to see the top, but it vanished in the clouds. "The next phase, the fourth, is when you all are meant to learn how to own your own time. That's why I started the Singularity Group. I needed to find a way to enable more entrepreneurship for those who sought it."

"But, entrepreneurs work more than most people who have a corporate job," Jessica said.

"That's true," Ori said. "But if their business aligns with something that they love, something that they are meant to do, then it's energizing. And they own their time. They don't answer to anyone but the market. When things are going well, they have time to learn and grow in different ways. They start to move into the fifth phase."

"What's the fifth phase?" Jessica asked.

"One's ability to master multiple things. And only in the fifth phase do you learn how to consciously manifest what you want in the universe."

"What's bad about people staying in the third phase?" Jessica asked. "It sounds like people are coming together and sharing ideas."

"This is true. It was good for a while. But as you can see with the virus, people are at risk of reverting to the second phase of existence, only experiencing other ways of living from the pages of a book or from behind a screen. This is very dangerous because if you can't experience something for yourself, you run the risk of accepting someone else's opinion as truth." Ori continued, "The third phase is also still heavily ego-driven. You aren't tightly tuned in to your intuition and your energy. It's about you and your experience. It's about what you can get from the world. Which is very important. But the fifth phase is more about what you can give to the world when you understand how powerful you are. You have the time and vision to solve some of the problems that threaten the world. And that's what we need."

"How do you get more people to move to that higher phase?" Jessica asked.

"People pursue a higher way of life because they receive various seemingly random cues from the universe telling them they are capable of doing and being more. A conversation with a random stranger on a plane. A book recommendation from your barber. A former friend who you respect pursuing a life that seems extraordinary. Those seemingly random interactions and instances can all take someone on an evolution of the mind, body, and spirit. And when a person is open to these cues, the brain rewires itself."

"And now there's more urgency for people to evolve to this phase?" Jessica asked.

"This period is almost coming to an end. Only those who are at the next level will survive," Ori said.

"What do you mean?" Jessica asked.

"Earth itself is part of a system that sheds, or stretches, or grows. To make matters more complicated, the version of Earth you know makes up one reality of many."

"The multiverse?" Jessica asked, half-jokingly.

"You know it?" Ori asked.

"Umm, there was this Spider-Man comic."

"Well then, you know what happens in your version of Earth has a direct impact on existences in alternate realities. Typically they are minor, but in this instance, it could shut down the entire existence. That's why we are so focused on getting as many people as possible to a level where they are capable of surviving and thriving in the next phase. The more people at the fifth phase of existence, the more likely you all can come together and create solutions that will save the planet."

"Like how to fully cure the virus that the world is struggling with?" Jessica asked.

"Exactly," Ori said. "Think of the virus as a stress test for humanity. What if it was triggered as a mechanism to test how able you are to set aside your perceived differences and come together to solve a problem? Humanity is so fractured that there's doubt among us. However, our team believes that you can still do this, and we've been tasked with proving it."

"Who is judging us?" Jessica asked.

"Well, Death is the one you need to worry about. Death is the final decision-maker."

Jessica couldn't help but ask, "Are we doomed?"

"No," Ori said. "This virus, it wants to survive as well. If humanity dies, so does it. You need to learn how to coexist before the big event that's the real threat. The reset."

"What was the last, um, big event that occurred?" Jessica asked.

"It was the great deluge," Ori said. "Let's go; Evelyn's about to start the briefing for another important recruit."

"Another recruit?" Jessica called after Ori as he walked down a path toward the side of the massive mountain.

They approached a cave-like entrance at the base of the mountain. Ori glanced back. "Are you ready to go even further down the rabbit hole?"

29

TRAVEL TO THE COMMAND CENTER

"So…" Jessica started to say, but hesitated. *I've done nothing but ask questions all morning.*

"So, what?" Ori encouraged her.

"So why did Evelyn infiltrate the FBI?"

"Each system has a defense mechanism, sometimes multiple defense mechanisms, meant to provide enough protection for the synergy to take place. Evelyn needed to understand how humanity's defense systems worked. The manmade systems that were intended to keep the population safe weren't functioning correctly. She had a theory that something was wrong. So she piggybacked into my reality so that she could have a safe place to make observations and perform tests. The Singularity Group is intentionally idealistic. I thought we needed to see what would happen if a company was created that pushed innovation boundaries while creating a healthy, financially independent middle class of people. When people have their basic needs met—shelter, safety, food, and health—they should pursue a higher purpose, if they so choose. It's a lot to ask, in western capitalist society, for someone to build an infrastructure like this and leave money on the table. So, I decided to do it, and when Evelyn joined, she was able to observe how the system reacted."

"Which wasn't well," Jessica said.

"Let's just say that there's a lot of room for improvement."

As they got to the bottom of the hill, Jessica asked, "Is this a cave?"

"Not quite. It's the exposed root structure."

At that moment, Jessica realized this wasn't the side of the mountain she was looking at, but the base of the biggest tree she had ever seen or even imagined. The earth surrounding the enormous tree was covered with white and yellow mushrooms. Jessica saw no light escaping the dark entrance as they approached. However, once they were inside, the mushrooms covering the floor glowed with a bright green light. As the two walked deeper into the root structure, the green light became bright enough for Jessica to see her surroundings.

"This is our command center," Ori said.

"It's an enormous tree."

"Not just an enormous tree, it's *the* tree."

Jessica knelt. The earth was soft and cool to the touch. It could have been her imagination, but it felt as though the ground was giving her positive energy. Her mind felt at ease. Her muscles felt fresh and relaxed. She stood back up, and as they continued walking, she couldn't help but inhale as deeply as she could. She filled her lungs. The air was cool, with a pleasantly sweet aroma. The glowing fungi seemed to change shapes and positions. Jessica's attention was pulled away when the feel of the ground changed beneath her feet.

Jessica's and Ori's footsteps now clicked along a solid floor. The bioluminescent walls were replaced by small, precisely organized light bulbs. They then entered what appeared to be an elevator made of all black glass paneling. As she and Ori turned to see the door close, Jessica watched with wonder as she now saw bright pink and white veins illuminate the walls, floor, and ceiling.

Jessica was captivated and simultaneously felt a familiar feeling. She hadn't even felt them move when the doors opened. She wasn't sure if they had gone up or down. Jessica felt frozen in place, her natural defenses kicking in. Then Evelyn walked by, glanced over, and said, "Perfect timing."

30

EVELYN'S REPORT

Jessica followed Evelyn and Ori down a long hall. "We are about to enter our briefing room," Ori said.

"This is where we prep the team on any major updates or special assignments," Evelyn added.

Two glass sliding doors opened automatically as the three approached. The briefing room was shaped like an octagon, and all walls were made of glass. At the center of the room was a large round table where Vau, Tony, and Jordan were seated, talking among themselves. Another person was standing next to Vau. He looked familiar, a Latino man with a goatee, wearing a nice charcoal suit. He walked over to them. "Hello Evelyn, Ori."

"Hi, Carlos." Ori shook the man's hand, and then said, "Please meet Jessica."

"Jessica, yes, it's a pleasure." Carlos looked back at Ori. "Is she who you were waiting for at the park?"

"She was," Ori said.

"Ori, speaking of our little chat," Carlos said, "do you mind if I speak with you in private? There's something that you need to know. A request has been made that you should be aware of."

Ori turned to Jessica. "Excuse me for one moment." Then he and Carlos vanished behind a glass sliding door.

As Jessica took in more of the briefing room, she saw a large screen covering one wall. The wall featured ten video feeds. One showed a beach where the water was turning red. One had a large map of the African continent covered in a black cloud. The image zoomed in, and Jessica realized that the ominous cloud was a swarm of locusts. Another featured beehives caving in over time. Others showed disease, protests, riots, and war. There were images of tall trees being cut down, massive hurricanes, wildfires, and flooding. Each video feed was equally alarming. There was also text along the bottom of the feeds with years and cities around the world.

"What are these?" Jessica asked.

"Those are your check engine lights," Evelyn said before she took her position in an open seat at the round table. "All right, listen up." Jessica noticed the team sit up straight in their seats. She took a chair next to Jordan.

Evelyn continued, "As you all know, through the Singularity operation we were able to contain war and ego and accelerate the proportion of humanity moving into GP4."

Jessica leaned toward Jordan and whispered, "GP4?"

"Growth phase four," Jordan explained.

"Oh right, people taking more ownership of their time," Jessica said. Jordan nodded.

"Of course, there's much more to contend with. We've been making some good headway on the next recruit," Evelyn continued. "We'll wait for Ori to get back to provide an update with that." Evelyn paused. "The other major update for this session is that we have confirmed that the next reset will be via solar flares."

"C'mon," Jordan said.

"Ugh," exclaimed Tony.

Vau, more calmly, asked, "Do we know a tighter window of time?"

"I'm trying to get as much information as possible but, like always, the timing is rough. We just need to stay focused on getting them as close to ready as possible."

"They are far, and I mean far, from ready," Jordan said.

"Then that means we have a lot of work to do, now doesn't it? Ori and I meet with the council later today, so I'd like for us to run through the state of the world. I'd like a very high-level overview of where we are and what that means now that we've confirmed the nature of the event. Vau, would you mind kicking us off?"

"Sure," he said. "There's still a significant amount of deforestation in some critical areas in Africa and the Amazon. It looks like they will hit the twenty-two-point-five percent mark."

"I'm guessing that's not a good mark to hit," Jessica said.

"No, it is not. Once the Amazon basin hits twenty-two-and-a-half percent of deforestation, it will not sustain its ecosystem. It will rapidly decline as will its biodiversity and protection."

"The Amazon is like the lungs of the planet. Imagine surviving with collapsed lungs," Jordan said.

"On a positive note," Vau added, "there's been a significant increase in the awareness and implementation of regenerative and polyculture farming. Not only in rural areas, but also in the cities."

"At what level?" Evelyn asked.

"On all levels," Vau said. "More universities are providing data to support these efforts, and governments are now pushing for and funding these farming methods. If regenerative farming speeds up and expands, then there's still hope."

"Good, thank you. Jordan, what do you have?"

"Well, the virus has significantly separated the haves from the have-nots. However, the increase in regenerative farming has led to a decrease in unemployment and an increase in healthy food security. With that, plus the impact of the Singularity mission, we're seeing more people become financially independent on a sustainable scale."

"Great," Evelyn said. "But..."

Jordan continued, "But the second and third wave of the virus keeps kicking humanity in the gut. We've got to get it under control if we are going to have a chance."

"We know, and we're working on it," Evelyn said. "That will be part of Ori's update, along with the Singularity Group transition to Zach."

Jessica sat up straight. This was the first time she'd heard Zach's name in a while.

"All right, Tony, you're up," Evelyn said as Ori walked back into the room. "What do you have?"

"Starting with some administration, we are completely clear from the Singularity mission. Only our recruits and our contacts know we were there. If anyone finds us, they will need help and a lot of it."

"Good," Evelyn said.

"Our screens are on all major devices around the world. This covers smartphones, mobile phones, tablets, TVs, and computers. The good news is that we see what everyone in the world is paying attention to. The bad news is that there's a lot of garbage being pumped into the minds of humanity." Tony looked at Ori. "If they start slipping back into GP2, they're in major trouble."

"Yeah." Ori sighed deeply. "We are working on it."

The room was silent for a minute. "Aja," Evelyn took command of the room. Everyone, including Ori, was focused.

Where does she come in?

"How's she doing?" Tony asked.

"Not well," Evelyn said. "I mean, her whole purpose is to protect all nonhuman life forms. She's pleased with the progress Vau shared earlier but is concerned with the outlook. Her resources are stressed and stretched to the limits. Between deforestation, desertification, pollution, and population growth, Mother Earth is in a tenuous position. Aja and her team are doing everything they can, but they need more help. She's worried that the forests can't do everything— heal themselves and mitigate the virus. Getting her approval won't be easy."

"But our recruit is the best way now," Ori said. "We can use him to jump-start things and put a couple of methods in play."

"That will be important," Evelyn said.

"We've got to go for it. There's no way he alone, in his lifetime, is going to be able to convince a very skeptical population and mass-produce enough what, atomizers?" Ori said.

Evelyn pursed her lips. "I've been giving him some inspiration."

"Even with that," Ori continued, "time is limited, and scale and reach are the name of the game."

"You're right," Evelyn said. "I'll keep working on her and see what I can do."

"Thank you," Ori said.

"All right, you're up," Evelyn replied. "Bring the full team up to speed on the latest with the Zach situation and this recruit."

Ori took a breath and looked around the table. "The bad news first. We weren't able to correct the interference with Zach…"

"Just great," Jordan interrupted, exasperated.

Tony almost simultaneously gave a sarcastic, "Fantastic."

"Yet," Ori looked at each of them as he finished his statement. "Gabriel and I have an arrangement that, once complete, should put all things back on track."

"So what's the plan with Zach out of play?" Vau asked.

"That's a great question and leads me to my good news." Ori turned his attention to the wall of screens that now together displayed one big image, a young black man with an earnest expression. "This is Malik. I've been priming him for a while now. Our sources close to him believe he has what it takes to go all the way." Ori looked over to Jordan expectantly.

"I've checked him out," she said. "He's pretty solid."

Evelyn spoke, "I've interacted with him a few times too. He's brave and has a big imagination."

Ori continued, "He has a solution at his fingertips, but some news just came in."

"What?" Tony asked.

"Carlos just informed me that there's been a request to make a move on him," Ori said.

"You've got to be kidding me," Tony said.

"What is wrong with Gabriel?" Jordan asked, her frown deepening.

"It's not his fault," Evelyn said.

Ori continued, "I made it clear when I spoke to him that we wouldn't allow anymore interference."

"Really?" Jordan's voice raised an octave or two, her eyebrows raising with hope.

"Don't get too excited," Evelyn said. "We'll address it in the council meeting first. We need to give Gabriel a chance to intervene."

"You know he never does," Vau said.

"We know," Evelyn said, "but it's a professional courtesy."

"For now," Ori looked at Tony, "you're up."

"Who am I?" Tony asked.

"You'll be a worker," Evelyn said. "Just keep eyes on him. Don't intervene."

"There will be plenty of eyes all around," Ori said.

"Sounds good," Tony said as he held up his wrist with his index finger and thumb in the ready position on the bezels. Jessica then realized that they all had the fancy skeleton watches with three bezels. "Where and when am I going?"

Jordan leaned over and pulled a business card out of her pocket. Jessica tried to read the details, but the numbers were too small. Jordan slid the card across the table to Tony. "That's a safe entry point close to a trail. If you go at that time, no one will spot you."

"Thanks," Tony said as he referenced the card while adjusting the dials on his watch. "All right," Tony said as he got up, "I'll keep you posted." Tony walked behind one of the sliding glass doors and out of sight.

31

___

CONTAIN OR CORRECT INTERFERENCE

"ALL RIGHT," EVELYN SAID, "I'VE GOT TO MEET WITH AJA. SHE'LL WANT an update before the council meeting."

"Ori," Vau said, "I've got to run some Match Day items by you."

"Let's do it." Ori looked at Jordan. "Can you hang out with Jessica for a while? Answer any questions that she has, and please, keep it optimistic?" Ori flashed her an oversized smile.

Jordan gave an innocent smile, which quickly fell as Ori and Vau left the room.

Jessica eyed Jordan. "What was all of that?"

Jordan studied Jessica for a beat or two, as if assessing what she was ready for. "So, the big event. Do you understand this fully?"

"I know the last one was a flood, and the next one is solar flares," Jessica said. "That's most of what's clear so far."

"Let's start there," Jordan said. "Every two thousand years or so, Earth moves through a procession of the equinox. An oversimplification is a change of the North and South poles' position, which changes the stars that you use to guide you. There are twelve ages of the procession. You call them your Zodiac symbols. Once Earth moves through each age, it completes a Great Year, which is around 26,000 of your years. At various points during the Great Year, Earth is very susceptible to a catastrophic existential event. Though we are working all the time, this is when our team is most vital." Jordan paused momentarily until Jessica nodded her understanding. "This is when the chips are down, and we have to take on what's still needed to save the planet and humanity."

"Why you all?" Jessica asked.

"Because we're the best," Jordan said with a wink. "More like it's just what we've been trained and equipped for. But for all of us, it's tricky. We help humanity help themselves. We have to get you to rewire your minds so that you think and behave a certain way. And that must align with the age of the procession. Right now, you are in the age of Pisces. Under the Procession of Pisces, the objective is simple, yet complex in execution." Jordan wavered, "Well, complex for this universe. Humanity, like a school of fish, must all swim in the same direction. The many must act and behave like one."

"What does that mean?" Jessica asked.

Jordan laughed and leaned in. "This means that first, you gotta stop interfering with someone else's flow. That means no killing or sabotaging someone else. Second, you have to be able to listen to diverse points of view. Imagine how a school of fish behaves. In a big body of water, you never know from which direction the threat is coming, whether it be from the sharks below or the birds above. You all have to trust and believe in one another. Third, you must work together as one to survive large threats. When needed, you have to be able to move in a coordinated fashion and change directions quickly. If we can get you behaving in this way, not only does the power to manifest hold the most potential impact, but it means that more of you will be tuned into the right frequency. The more people who are tuned in, the more who will receive the message that will allow you to survive. That message will be your role, something unique to you, that you are meant to carry out."

"Getting everyone on Earth to act as one is impossible," Jessica said.

Jordan scoffed. "I'll channel my inner Ori. Nothing is impossible. You have two things going for you."

"Which are?" Jessica asked.

"Number one, you have the internet. This is an incredibly

powerful tool. And number two," Jordan gave a little shrug, "Earth needs you. Well, for now at least. Oh… and don't forget that we are incredibly good at understanding enough about what motivates humanity to work the system discreetly. We want to save as many of you as possible."

"Okay, well what was Evelyn saying about having contained war and ego?" Jessica asked.

"You know how there are those of us who have stayed among men? While mostly our purpose is to help rewire your thinking and help you pursue your purpose, we can be used in less positive ways as well. Without our help, some people with negative intentions can cause minor interferences in the advancement of others. When we start to see people have an impact on significant portions of the population, we pursue whoever is behind that individual because they are usually one of us."

"And they would knowingly aid in something that negatively impacts masses of people?" asked Jessica.

"Not all things that seem bad are bad when used appropriately. Throughout history, disease, famine, war, and more have been tools to maintain balance. However, if any of these get out of control and are used too broadly, that throws off the balance. Well, there are those of us that embody these things to serve humanity or Earth or both."

"What would cause them to get out of control?"

Jessica could tell that Jordan was carefully considering her answer. "In most cases, because the humans who are tapping into them are going too far. In those cases, as we saw with Silas, it took both his awareness and our help to pull him back and calm war. In other rarer instances, as we experienced with ego, one of us was getting caught up in the impact he was having and the power he held. We had to contain him against his will."

"Silas was one of you?"

"Yes, he is one of us. You'll probably actually see him later," replied Jordan.

"And ego? What, or I guess who, do you mean by that?"

"In your investigation years ago, you probably knew of him as Agent Chivington," explained Jordan.

"So you guys have to keep tabs on all this?" Jessica asked.

"Yes. And what makes this even more complicated is that when one of us dies among men, we lose our memories. If we aren't quickly recovered, we are even more susceptible to the mal-intentioned."

"That would be scary, particularly for an embodiment of ego or war," Jessica said.

"Absolutely. We work to make sure our specialists know who they are and are in control. Carlos, for example, knows who he is."

"And just who is he?" Jessica asked.

"He's the one who receives the truly grotesque requests," Jordan said. "If there are those who are causing serious interference, Carlos knows about them. He will help us track them down because they must never know we're coming."

"Why not?" Jessica asked.

"Ori can read all the thoughts a man can and will ever have. You will never know that he was inside of your head. But he can't read the thoughts of those like me without them knowing. And if they sense him in their heads, they could intentionally cause other interference that creates a ripple of new future events that we haven't planned for. To get inside the head of one of us, we have to go through the minds of a human who's being impacted by them, one person per being of light. The catch is that, even then, the only time we can get through without them knowing is between the hours of three and five in the morning, when people are most deeply asleep. So we have to cast these incredibly complex webs. They must never know that they are trapped until it's too late. You see, we have seen the future, and we are working back into the past. If the interference creates many new futures, then it could take Ori and Evelyn too long to come up with another plan."

"I don't know what she's been telling you," Vau gave Jessica a conspiratorial look as he and Ori walked back into the room, "but use your judgment."

"You doubt me," Jordan replied playfully. "I gave her the facts. Now you're just messing with my flow."

Vau added, "In all seriousness, most of our kind in the field have spent lifetimes doing great work. They make up our network. We partner with them to set things in motion. We all work together to correct major interference. We use our network to identify recruits or to identify target interference. Since colleagues of our network are typically trusted, loved, and respected members of their community, we can access anything we need. All with discretion."

"It's our shared purpose," Ori said. "They want to fulfill their purpose and help both humanity and Earth."

"Plus, Earth is the only place in existence that we, too, can create new life," Vau said.

32

A SANITY TESTED

MALIK TOSSED AND TURNED IN BED. HE PEELED THE COMFORTER OFF HIS body, hoping that would cool him down enough to stop sweating. *Why is it so hot?* He covered his face with the pillow, shielding his eyes from the sun. *The sun.* "The sun!" Malik said as he sat up in his bed. Malik couldn't remember the last time he slept past sunrise. He looked at his phone. 8:03. The first patients should be arriving for virus screening in thirty minutes. He sent a text to let the office know he was running late, then he jumped out of bed, splashed water on his face, brushed his teeth, and hurriedly dressed.

Malik ran downstairs, but something was different. The house was quiet, which wasn't so much of a surprise. *Mom and Dad probably had an early start.* He went to grab a cup of coffee, but the pot was empty. The coffee maker was not only empty, but Malik could see streaks of dried coffee at the bottom of the glass. Coffee gets brewed daily in their household. Malik grabbed a bottle of water from the fridge and a couple of granola bars, threw them in his bag, and headed for the front door. He grabbed his mask and started to lock the door behind him when he remembered that it was Wednesday. He ran back inside the house and downstairs to the basement. He opened the freezer. *Only ten left.* "This will have to do," he said as he put the atomizers inside a cooler and placed several ice packs on top.

Once on the road, traffic was much lighter than usual. It had been a while since he had been driving in the morning rush-hour traffic, but this felt light. It was a sunny autumn day. There wasn't a cloud in the sky. With no traffic around, Malik got to appreciate the yellow, orange, and red leaves that painted Olmsted Linear and Shady Side Parks. Malik arrived at the doctor's office within ten minutes. He checked his watch. "Eight thirty-eight, nailed it." The parking lot was empty, and the doctor's office looked closed.

Malik got out of his car, walked to the window, and tried to peek inside, cupping his eyes to block the reflection from the sun. The inside of the office was empty. Malik backed up and noticed the For Sale sign out front. "What the…" he said to himself, but the sudden drop in temperature made him shiver. He looked up to see the clouds confidently roll in and push out the sun. Malik walked back toward his car, still staring at the doctor's office, looking for some sign of what had happened. Why didn't he recognize anything? *Where's the name of the practice? Why is the color of the building different? Where are the dogwoods?* His train of thought crashed when he felt a firm hand grip the back of his arm. He turned to see who it was but then felt someone else grab his other arm. Before he knew it, everything faded to black.

THE NEXT THING HE KNEW, the sound of trickling water made him open his eyes. He was sitting on a stone bench, looking at a small pond with koi fish. He tried to move his arms, but they wouldn't budge. He looked down and saw he was trapped in a straitjacket. Malik thrust his shoulders and arms as hard as he could from left to right, back and forth, up and down, until he conceded that whatever movie he saw when a character escaped from this jacket was a lie. Malik shouted, "Help, help!" until a nurse came.

"How's it going today?" the nurse asked. He seemed like a kind, older man.

"I'm not supposed to be here," Malik said.

"Oh, I know, Malik. But hey, once we get you all better, you'll be free to leave."

"I am all better," Malik said. "Nothing's wrong with me. I'm not supposed to be here."

"I know, I know," the nurse said. "Hey, there's some good news. A friend is here to see you."

Malik then saw Ronnie in the doorway. "Ronnie! Please tell this man that there's some mistake and that I'm not supposed to be here."

Ronnie patted the nurse on the back. "It's cool, George. I've got it from here."

George, Malik thought, noticing the familiarity between them. "Ronnie, you've got to help me. Can you get ahold of my parents? There's been a mix-up. I shouldn't be here."

"What are you talking about?" Ronnie asked.

"I was heading to work at…" Malik said, but Ronnie cut him off.

"At the doctor's office."

"That's right," Malik said, growing excited. "See, you remember. You've got to tell them."

"Bro," Ronnie said, "you've got to calm down and let them help you."

"Wh—what do you mean?" Malik said with a nervous laugh. "Is this a joke? Are you playing a joke on me?" Malik laughed again before looking around the room. "Where is everyone? Where's Dr. Patel? Christine? Who else was in on this? Did…"

"This isn't a joke." Ronnie's voice was quiet, and his face stoic. "It's hard to keep seeing you like this."

Malik felt something sink deep into his stomach as his smile fell away. "You're serious?"

"Yeah, Malik, I am."

Malik felt a tear fall out of the corner of his eye. "What happened?"

"After Callie got sick, you lost it. You kept saying all these crazy things. You quit your internship and dropped out of school. Your parents didn't know what to do, so they put you in here."

"What crazy things?" Malik asked.

"The same crazy things that you were starting to say now: That you work in some doctor's office. That you're working on some supersecret project, and you swear it will cure the virus."

"But..." Malik said. "That, that was all real. That all happened. That's all happening."

"Is it?" Ronnie asked. "Then who..."

"Who what?" Malik asked.

"Whooo?" Ronnie said again. This time he drew the word out longer.

Malik leaned back and closed his eyes. "This, this isn't real."

Hooooot. Malik opened his eyes and saw a large owl perched on a branch outside his window. It was dark, but the light from the moon was just enough for Malik to make eye contact with the owl before it flew off. Malik looked at his phone. 4:44.

33

THE ATOMIZERS

Malik was loading more atomizers into the cooler when he heard footsteps coming down the stairs. "Good morning, Mom."

"Remind me again how this is legal? And why I shouldn't worry about the FDA kicking down my door?" she asked.

"Because these are natural aerosols," Malik said, choosing his words precisely. "These atomizers are made of natural organic aerosol materials pulled directly from trees, and they help boost the immune system. As long as these," Malik held up an atomizer, "are not, and I quote, adulterated or misbranded, then the Food and Drug Administration doesn't have any reason to worry about me."

"Malik, you need to be careful. There are more and more people going missing, especially in the downtown area. I wish you wouldn't go."

"Mom, what other treatment do they have access to?" Malik asked.

"I know, I know," his mom said with a heavy sigh. "All right, don't be late for work," she said as she walked back upstairs.

Malik set the cooler down by the front door as he went to grab his mask and keys. He noticed the stack of brochures still piling up and just shook his head.

"Hey," his mom shouted to him, "hold up." She came out of the kitchen and handed him a small box of disposable masks. "There were extra from the community meeting."

"Thanks, Mom," he said, while he picked up a brochure. There was a photo of two couples, both with white hair, laughing while drinking wine. "Are we serious about this?"

"Your father and I have talked a lot about it, and I think it's time that we consider it. She hasn't been responsive in a very long time. We need to make sure that she has the best care possible."

"But," Malik said.

"I know," his mom cut him off. "I don't want it any more than you do."

She hugged him and pulled his head down to kiss him on the forehead. "Now go, boy, you better not be late."

Malik was loading the cooler and box of gloves in the car when a voice came from behind.

"How many atomizers do you have?" Callie asked.

"A little over a hundred," Malik said.

"That's not bad," she said.

"It's not nearly enough," Malik responded.

"Dude, you're a one-man shop. What more can you expect?"

"Ah… I don't want to talk about it today."

"Fine," she said. "Are you going with Ronnie?"

"Yes," Malik said.

"Well, tell him I say hello," Callie said.

"I think you should tell him yourself."

34

———

PUSHING PRODUCT

THE PARKING LOT AT THE DOCTOR'S OFFICE WAS EMPTY AS MALIK SAT IN his car, constantly checking the rearview mirror. The sun had set, and Malik could only make out the shadows of people walking on the sidewalk past the office. Finally, his car's interior was illuminated. He looked in the rearview mirror and saw headlights approaching. The car pulled up next to the driver's side, and the window rolled down.

"What's up, Malik?" Ronnie said.

"What's going on, Ronnie?" Malik said as he got out of his car and walked to his back seat. He grabbed his black backpack and threw several handfuls of atomizers in there. He tossed the bag under the driver's side seat, pulled the cooler out, and placed it in the backseat of Ronnie's car.

"How many do you have today?"

"A little over one hundred," Malik said. He held up the box his mom gave him. "Check this out."

"Dope," Ronnie said. "They'll be happy tonight."

Malik got into the car and pulled out five atomizers. "Here, before I forget."

"What are these for?" Ronnie asked.

"Give these to your gramps," Malik said.

Ronnie took one atomizer. "Ah bro, I appreciate it, but five is too many. One's enough for now."

Malik put two atomizers in the glove box of the car. "Just in case he runs low." Malik put on his seat belt. "Where are we heading tonight?"

"I figured we'd start in the Old Fourth Ward and head toward downtown, then work our way back here. Let's see where people are."

Ronnie put his car in reverse but then stopped. He put the gear shift back into the park position. "Found our first customer."

Malik watched as Ronnie snatched an atomizer from his hand, a mask out of the box, and jumped out of the driver's seat. Malik turned around to see Ronnie jog and hand the items to a person pushing a cart.

Ronnie ran back to the car. "One down. Let's see who else we can find." He put the car into reverse, and they were off.

A while later in their drive, Malik glanced at the clock in the car. "It's seven-thirty, and we haven't seen anyone out since that lady in the parking lot."

"Do you think it's too cold tonight?" Ronnie asked.

"It's sixty degrees." Malik pointed to the thermostat on the dashboard.

"This is a trip," Ronnie said. "My gramps was telling me that a lot of people have been turning up missing."

"My mom was telling me something about that too." Malik stared out of the window as they rode around in silence. Malik didn't want to think about what could be happening to those people, so he changed the subject. "I got a date."

"Wait," Ronnie gaped at him, "the nurse?"

"Yessir," Malik said.

"What!" Ronnie gave Malik's shoulder a nudge. "Check you out! What are you going to do?"

"I found this spot on the BeltLine. It has a heated patio and rooftop views."

"Nice," Ronnie said. "After that, you should bring her by the club. I'll be there with some friends. We'll make sure that you look cool."

"Shut up, fool," Malik said, but he really would appreciate any help he could get. He sat back imagining how great of a night it would be when a thought popped into his head for tonight's route. "Let's go to the library."

"You think people will still be there?" Ronnie asked.

"I can't imagine where else they'd be. I mean, no one is on the streets, and we've checked the soup kitchens, the shelters. The library closes at eight. That's the only place left that they'd be."

Ronnie drove them to the Toco Hill Library.

Malik got out of the car. "Where are you going?" Ronnie asked.

"George may be in there," Malik said.

"Crazy George Washington?" Ronnie asked.

"I told you not to call him that," Malik said.

"My bad. Do you want me to come in with you?"

"No, I'll be fast."

Ronnie held out an atomizer and a mask. "Just in case he's in there."

Malik reached for them but hesitated. He pulled his hand back. "I'll come back if I need them."

Malik saw several people sitting inside the library, with everything they own in a dirty, tattered bag next to them. Malik walked around the library, searching for George, but he didn't find him. He and Callie would spend hours in this library when they were growing up. This is where they met George Washington, who bears no resemblance to the first President of the United States. Their George Washington was tall, dark, and had a lot of wrinkles. *They have gray hair in common.* Malik laughed at the thought as he walked to George's corner.

George always sat in the corner by the windows that overlooked the second parking lot and the forest. Malik and Callie used to joke about that corner, but every time Malik would walk over there, he'd peek out to see if something was interesting to see. There never was. Not until tonight. Tonight, the dull concrete gray of the parking lot was replaced by metallic black, and a lot of it. Malik didn't realize what it was, but he knew it was bad news. He backed away from the window, unsure if he was being watched, then turned and quickly walked out. As soon as he was outside, he heard someone scream out what he had feared.

"Contact tracers!" someone yelled, just as the front parking lot was swarmed with black SUVs. Malik walked toward Ronnie. He and Ronnie locked eyes from a distance. Ronnie shook his head at Malik as Biotech tracers walked toward Ronnie's driver's-side window. Malik turned away to escape the parking lot, walking casually as to not attract any attention.

Malik made his way down the dark road until he heard, "Hey you, stop."

Malik didn't turn back. He just reacted, sprinting down the hill toward the DeKalb Tennis Center. He knew that he could lose anyone in those woods at night if he made it to the Mason Mill path. He heard the contact tracer chasing him while also trying to radio for backup.

Malik saw two people walking ahead of him, one with a cart, the other with just a backpack. *George!* Malik saw the two bodies vanish as they turned the corner. Malik followed George down the boardwalk path.

He startled George as he ran up behind him. "Malik, what are you doing?" George asked.

"Contact tracers are coming. You and your friend need to hide." Malik looked around and didn't see the other person with the cart.

"I'm not worried about any contact tracer," George said, but they both got quiet when they heard the static from a handheld radio.

"Still no sign of the individual on foot. Looking for one male, on foot, likely homeless," the contact tracer said.

"You've got to go," Malik whispered. "I'll lead them away."

"Don't be foolish, young man. If you've got a reason to run, then you better get out of here. I'll play ignorant. Now go." George grabbed his chest and panted. He sat on the bench as Malik walked down the path out of sight.

Malik heard George say, "Whew, all right, all right, all right. You got me. I'm too old to run. I don't know what I was thinking."

"Why'd you run?" the contact tracer demanded.

Malik watched from a distance as the contact tracer held up the portable test machine. He put the cotton swab in George's nose, collected a swab, then placed it in the small box.

"What's it say?" George asked. "I bet it says negative."

The contact tracer checked the result. "Negative."

"What'd I tell you? I'm virus-free, baby," George said, and he got up to walk away.

"Wait," the contact tracer said. He held up what looked like a smartphone. "Place your finger here."

George placed his finger on the phone's screen. "What is this? A second opinion or something?"

"It says negative as well," the Confidence Biotech tracer said as a couple of others approached. "This also says that you haven't tested positive in the past three years."

"Whew, it must be a miracle or something," George said. "Now, if you don't mind, I'll be on my way." He reached for his bag, but one man grabbed it.

"You're not going anywhere. We need to bring you in for a test."

The men grabbed George, and Malik ran in his direction. George discreetly motioned him away. Malik hid as they carried George away.

35

THE COUNCIL MEETING

Jessica and Vau were sitting in slightly elevated seats, staring at a large round table with thirteen empty chairs. Soon, several individuals entered the room and took their places at the table. Jessica recognized Evelyn, Ori, Jordan, Professor Raziel, Carlos, and Gabriel. She was surprised to see Silas there as well. Jessica didn't recognize the other five people seated around the table, but they were all chatting among themselves. Jessica could feel the air get tense as Aja walked into the room and took the final seat.

At that moment, Jessica felt a sharp pain in her forehead, followed by a steady throb. She closed her eyes and put her head in her hands, hoping to dull the pain. Jessica opened her eyes to a flashback of being in the woods late at night. It was chilly, and she was stumbling, trying to run.

"It's great to see everyone." Aja's voice brought her to the present. "I know it's been a while, but as we are getting close to the next major event, we thought now would be a good time to update everyone as to where we are and what we will need to do moving forward." Aja looked around the table. "Evelyn, do you want to get us started?"

"Sure," Evelyn said. "You should have received communication from me confirming that the next major reset will come in the form of a coronal mass ejection. As you all know, we can never be sure of the exact timing of the event, but we know that it doesn't occur long after being discovered." What appeared to be tablets rose out of the table in front of each person. Jessica leaned in to see if she could make out what was on the screen. Vau tapped her on the shoulder and pointed up to the ceiling. Suspended above their heads was a large screen for spectators to view.

"That projects whatever is on those screens," Vau whispered.

Evelyn continued speaking. "Here before you are the details of the universe at the forefront of the CME. This will be the existence within the multiverse that takes the first devastating blow."

Jessica saw a series of letters and numbers: 7.83HZ-25921-7.819.774.981.

"As you can see, this planet Earth resonates at seven point eight three hertz. It takes them twenty-five thousand nine-hundred twenty-one years to move through the Great Year, and their current population is," Evelyn quickly referenced her tablet, "let's just say over seven billion, eight hundred million."

Vau leaned over. "That just means that between Earth's crust and the ionosphere, which is the upper atmosphere, there's seven point eight three hertz of electrical power."

"What kind of electrical power?" Jessica asked.

"There are thousands of lightning strikes that occur each second, somewhere on Earth."

"What's the resonant frequency of the human mind here?" Aja asked.

"It's all over the place," Ori said. "But the majority operate on the beta wave, somewhere between fourteen and thirty hertz. About five percent of the population can shift their minds to function at alpha and theta waves."

"That's concerning," Aja said.

"Why is this the existence at the forefront?" Silas asked.

"It's the version of Earth with the largest population of people. These resets start there and then work their way down through every version of Earth in the multiverse."

"How prepared are they?" Aja asked.

Evelyn looked around the table. "Let's give a quick update on where the population is today."

"I'll begin," Carlos said. "This humanity is divided into roughly two camps. You have half of the people afraid of going missing, catching the virus, being homeless and hungry. Then you have the other half, who are not concerned with any of that. They are concerned about their freedoms being taken away. Some people are using chaos and uncertainty to seize power and wealth. This does not bode well."

"Silas?" Evelyn prompted.

"As you know, large-scale conflicts have calmed. The move away from using oil has given us hope that conflicts in the Middle East will decrease further. But," Silas nodded in Carlos's direction, "like he was saying, we still see divides and land grabs for power in both developing and developed nations."

"You've come a long way, Silas," Aja said.

"Thank you, ma'am." Silas gave a smile and a nod.

"Ori, what do you have?" Aja asked.

"If you add the health toll of the virus on top of the discord Carlos and Silas mentioned, I don't see how they'll be able to get the mental space to develop a solution to protect against the CME."

"Then so be it," Gabriel said. "Are we forgetting that they chose to be in the situation they are in by either their action or inaction? It's not our job to come in every time they get themselves in trouble and bail them out. If they can't survive the solar flares, then so be it."

"So what exactly is your recommendation then, Gabriel?" Aja asked.

"I say we let them figure this out on their own," he said. "They're already employing a solution."

"Which is?" Aja asked.

"They are using the plasma of the asymptomatic and immune to create an antidote to the virus. This is just until they can find a more sustainable vaccine, of course," Gabriel said.

"Have they successfully reduced the spread of the virus?" another council member asked.

"They've gone through waves of reduced physical and social

interaction up until now. They will need to continue with this, limiting direct interaction further and mainly communicating through various technology," Gabriel said.

"You're talking about allowing them to slip back to the second growth phase?" Aja asked.

Jessica felt a sharp pain in her forehead again. An image flashed in her mind of electrical currents being injected into a tree, causing the leaves to tremble while the branches remained still.

"It's the only way for them to get beyond the virus without our intervention," Gabriel said, bringing Jessica back.

"That will never work," Jordan said with passion. Ori and Evelyn both shot her a glare.

"Oh, it won't?" Gabriel replied indignantly. "Ori, what do you think?"

Ori was silent for a moment, his head down as if he was collecting his thoughts. He finally spoke, "This solution will help contain and control the virus until a cure is discovered. This is assuming that mankind, as a whole, can develop and maintain a level of discipline that it hasn't had to have for centuries."

"See," Gabriel said, "we need to let them dig themselves out of this mess."

"However," Ori continued, "what Gabriel fails to understand is that this approach of collecting plasma from the healthy to heal the sick is a very slippery and dangerous slope. This could escalate to an alarming situation quite quickly. It will be hard for the best and brightest people to imagine the technology that will save the planet from the solar flares if they are too busy trying to keep their freedom."

"That is unfortunate," Gabriel said. "But again, it's their world, not ours."

"You're right," Evelyn said. "However, there's something else you're forgetting."

"And what is that?" he asked.

"Mankind's ability to survive the solar flares is one thing, but Earth's survival is another. It won't be able to survive, not this time."

"What do you mean?" Gabriel leaned in as he looked at Aja.

"She's right," Aja said. "Humanity's deforestation efforts have been so devastating that the tree canopies aren't large enough to keep the planet cool, not on their own. We need mankind's creativity to come up with a solution."

"You mentioned that this is one of the universes, correct?" Silas asked.

"That's correct," Evelyn said.

"Well, what happens if this version of Earth gets destroyed? Will the others still exist?" Silas asked.

"What happens in a frontline existence will trickle and spread throughout the other existences. Each at different speeds, of course, but the spread will happen. It's just a matter of time," Ori said.

Evelyn continued, "And this version of Earth is leading all others in deforestation, desertification, animal extinction, homicide, genocide, and the list goes on. This is the version that we need to turn around."

"Ori," Carlos said, "you had a plan. How's it going?"

"We did have someone, Zach, who was slated to come up with a way to coexist with the virus. But he was incapacitated before he was able to share his knowledge broadly. He and Jessica were close." Ori pointed to the stands, and Jessica rocked back in her seat, surprised to have all the attention turned to her. "She lost some vital memories, so we have her here until she can regain them."

"How long has she been here?" one council member asked.

"She arrived a couple of days ago," Ori said.

"That's a long time. Is she aware of the risks?" the council member asked.

"She is," Ori said, "but she has decided the upside is worth it. Also, the virus has been mutating faster, and as discussed, if that isn't handled, there's no hope for confronting anything else."

"She can't stay past Match Day," Aja said. "If she does, the effects will be irreversible."

"Understood," Evelyn said.

"With Zach out of play," the council member asked, "now what?"

"We found a recruit," Ori said. "His name is Malik. His genius was the only one that accepted the task. He has been developing a solution."

"That's great news," Aja said.

"His solution alone doesn't have the necessary scale though. There's no way he can get to almost eight billion dosages in the needed timeline," Ori said. "Plus, we have been getting reports that there's an increase in interference around him."

"What do you need from me?" Aja asked.

"We need your support for a faster way to get the antidote to more people," Evelyn said.

"Also," Ori continued, "we will need to make sure that no one stops this young man's process. We need the approval to do whatever is necessary, without causing serious harm, of course."

"Allowing this crew to intervene in public will cause even more issues," Gabriel argued.

Aja stood up, walked toward the crowd, and lifted her gaze in Jessica's direction. "Professor Raziel, how important is this Malik?"

"He's the only one with the necessary background to pull this off," the professor said.

Aja was silent for a moment. "If my sources agree that the young man is worthy, then we'll figure out a way to get the antidote to more people." Aja turned and addressed Gabriel. "They'll do whatever is necessary to keep him out of harm's way." Aja then looked to Ori. "Please keep it discreet."

"Thank you," Ori said.

"Is there anything else?" Aja asked Evelyn. "If not, I need to get back to Match Day preparations."

"That's it," Evelyn said.

"This meeting is adjourned," Aja announced.

Gabriel stood up and stormed out. A couple of other council members followed. The crowd filed out, and the room quieted. Vau indicated that they should stay seated until the rest of the crew seemed ready.

Jessica saw that Carlos was lingering, and he caught Ori's attention. She could just hear their voices.

"Ori, you know you have my support, yes? Just let us know what you need," Carlos said.

Ori gave an appreciative smile and nodded. "Will do."

Carlos continued, "Few have done what you've done. You deserve it."

"How's she doing?" Ori asked.

"Jackeline is tough, she'll be all right. Her new identity is helping her through it."

"Nicolas was a tough one to recruit. She did all she could do," Ori said. "Her role is never the easiest, either. Seems like she's been making great progress."

"I have told her the same thing," Carlos said. "I think what is bothering her is that she didn't know you were involved."

"Please tell her that she wasn't meant to know. If she had, then that means I failed somewhere," Ori said. "Will she be ready for her next assignment?"

"She's incredibly motivated," Carlos said.

"That's very good to hear."

Vau then stood up, and Jessica followed his lead. They walked toward Ori, Jordan, and Evelyn, who met them halfway.

"Well," Vau started, "that could have been worse."

"I thought it went pretty well," Ori said.

"We got what we wanted," Evelyn said, "for the most part."

"What about Jessica?" Jordan asked, nodding in her direction. "Match Day is on Saturday. That's two days from now."

Jessica felt her heart beat faster. Jordan continued, "We all heard what Aja said."

"You worry too much," Ori replied. He made eye contact with Jessica. "Everything will work out. Your memories are coming back faster, aren't they?"

"I—I think so," was all Jessica could offer.

"See," Ori said. "Let's go grab some lunch."

As the team left the meeting room, Jessica asked, "What's Match Day?"

36

ZACH'S NORTH STAR

THE CREW MADE THEIR WAY BACK TO THE PROFESSOR'S HOUSE. JESSICA still couldn't get over how beautiful the forest was. There was something about the sound of the birds chirping and the cool breeze that made Jessica want to spend all day strolling down different, unknown paths.

"So Match Day," Jordan said, "is like a mix between a science fair and a career conference. Geniuses from all over come here and present their ideas for solutions that will help improve the world."

"It happens once every procession, typically during a period when two cycles overlap," Vau said.

"Wait." Jessica tried to wrap her mind around what they just said. "Match Day happens once every two thousand years?"

"Give or take a couple of hundred years," Vau said, "but yeah."

A large cloud of white fog filled the woods just off to the right. Jessica paused in place as she watched it move in. Everyone else continued walking as if nothing had happened. Within the cloud, something caught her attention. She saw flickers of small black particles that quickly got larger and larger until they came together to form a blurry outline of a person. As the image continued to sharpen, Jessica recognized Tony walking out of the fog. He fell in stride with Ori as if he'd been walking next to them the entire time.

Jessica jogged and caught up with the group.

"How was your trip?" she heard Ori ask Tony.

Tony shook his head. "Carlos's tip was right. They are snatching up anyone who's testing negative for the virus. How was the meeting?"

"We got permission to intervene," Ori said.

Tony replied, "That's going to be a lot of clean up."

"Don't worry." Ori had a big smile. He put his hand on Tony's shoulder. "Gabriel has to clean up anything that we miss."

Tony turned back to Jessica. "How are you doing? Anything coming back to you yet?"

"I—I don't…" Jessica tried to replay the image that popped into her mind during the council meeting. She focused her gaze on the ground, concerned that looking at the others would throw off her concentration. Something clicked into place in her brain. "Wait…"

Jessica looked up. Everyone's expression showed concern, except Ori's. He had a smile on his face. She continued, "I remember what Zach was building."

Back at the house, the team sat around the table, all focused on Jessica. Professor Raziel brought tea, and Jessica took a sip. "Is this peppermint?"

"It will help ease your headaches and help you concentrate," he said.

"Thank you," Jessica said with meaning. She then took a breath and started. "I remember that Zach didn't just oversee research and development for special projects. He was being groomed to take over the company after Leslie."

"That's right," Ori said in a soft, encouraging voice.

"His contact tracer technology," Jessica continued, "was based on the theory that we can communicate with plant life. He learned that trees send messages through the fungi network, exchanging nutrients and water. Zach found that if a tree was under threat by a parasite or something, then that tree would send a message or signal out asking for help. In response, the forest would send more nutrients to the tree in danger to help it heal faster. Even more interesting," Jessica stood up and started to pace, keeping the momentum, "was that the forest would also send out a chemical reaction in the air. These aerosols could call for help from other species. For instance, if beetles were harming some trees, the chemical reaction would attract woodpeckers, who eat the larvae. Zach saw this play out time after time. Then, he started trying to monitor trees while they were healing. Zach measured the number of nutrients the trees were consuming when they were trying to get healthy versus when they were healthy. Trees, like the human body, require more resources when they are growing or healing. One day, Zach noticed something peculiar. There were trees in the forest that were consuming more nutrients than usual. But to his surprise, they were perfectly healthy trees. Zach couldn't understand why, so he broadened his research and enlisted the world's top dendrologists. After extensive study, they found that trees consumed more nutrients when they were surrounded by large populations with respiratory illnesses. Trees not only capture carbon emissions and provide air, but they act as a type of filter."

Jessica realized that she had everyone's undivided attention. "Zach found that when we exhale CO_2, small DNA particles are exhaled as well, and trees capture all of that during the photosynthesis process. Zach found a way to tap into the mycorrhizal fungi network of large old-growth hub trees, to read the data that the trees were capturing."

"It's the most advanced bioengineering technology on the planet," Tony said.

Jessica kept following this trail of memory. "This was a pet project for him. Zach had a fascination with nature, and he just wanted to learn more. That's why he was willing to partner with... Ah." Jessica grabbed her head as the sharp pain returned. She shook her head, trying to refocus. She took a couple of sips of the tea and then said the last thing still in the front of her mind. "His main project was Alderamin7500. He didn't finish it."

"Well done, Jessica," Evelyn said. Jessica glanced around; everyone was smiling, and Tony was nodding his head with a big grin. Everyone looked pleased, except Ori.

"What's Alderamin7500?" Jessica asked.

"Alderamin7500 is an algorithm," Jordan said. "It's a program that will tap into government and university databases that the Singularity Group was able to get access to, aggregate the information, and create an easy-to-read output."

"We're talking some degree of cooperation from all the alphabet organizations, FBI, DOJ, EPA," Tony said. "It also would have combined data from the World Bank, the WHO, and it would have been able to cross-reference social media posts with official statistics."

"Why?" Jessica asked. "What was the objective?"

"It was meant to ensure that everyone on the planet had access to a fact-based, objective source of information," Tony said.

"How would it have been used?" Jessica asked.

"Anytime a person using a device with a Singularity Group screen would search for information, that algorithm would flag and deprioritize any resulting content not supported by credible, objective data," Tony said. "It would have made sure that everyone online had a shared version of the truth."

"A north star," Vau said.

Evelyn jumped in. "Society heavily relies on the internet to get their information. The world is fractured and is becoming more so. People with different views can live in micro-realities, their ideals being constantly reinforced as truth, even if they are not. This division alone is harmful, but it also opens people up to being controlled by whoever creates internet content."

"Zach was working on this algorithm under tight confidentiality," said Jordan.

"Why?" Jessica asked.

"Because if he were to launch it, then no one would be able to hide behind misinformation anymore," Vau said.

"Is that why he was attacked?" Jessica asked.

"No," Ori said, "that was unrelated. But only Zach can finish the Alderamin7500 algorithm."

"What makes you think that people will believe the truth anyway?" Jessica looked at Evelyn. "People are so divided that they only believe what's convenient for their own narrative."

"It's about longevity and consistency," Evelyn said. "Once launched, that tool will provide accurate, honest information year after year after year. At some point, people will realize that they've been lied to. When they see that this information has been accurate time and time again, we believe that people will start listening."

"This will not be a fast transition, but this tool needs to be out there," Ori said.

"You heard Gabriel," Jordan said. "If this virus doesn't get under control, then everyone will be living life behind a screen, experiencing reality through their internet connection. This puts everyone at risk of being manipulated by those who control the content and access."

This conversation was triggering more flashes of memory. Jessica felt little bits of information coming back. "Zach did talk about how close he was to finishing. He kept all of his secret work on an encrypted memory stick, never in the cloud. He was very cloak-and-dagger with this, which was so not Zach." Jessica gave a little laugh. "Part of why Zach and I connected was because he appreciated that I explained the Singularity Group's other technology to the world. He wanted more people to learn so that they could take the technology to the next level."

"Jessica." Ori's tone was steady, serious. "This is great progress, but I need you to try to remember where Zach got his ideas."

"I don't know," Jessica said quickly. She looked at Vau. He avoided eye contact. Jordan was staring at the ground, and Tony stood up and went inside.

"Do you mind, guys?" Ori asked. Jessica watched as Vau and Jordan followed Tony inside the house. Now Evelyn and Ori were left, staring at Jessica.

"Please," Evelyn said, "just try one more time to remember where Zach got his ideas."

Jessica felt a sense of panic in her chest. This was the first time she'd ever felt uncomfortable around them. "Okay, I'll try."

Jessica closed her eyes. She tried to replay the memories that had been coming back. Walking with Zach through the woods, walking past an exhibit at the museum. Then she saw a flash of Zach in Medlock Park. She saw him sitting on a bench like he was waiting for someone. It reminded Jessica of when she met with Ori the other day, and someone was sitting on the bench by the baseball field. *Zach was sitting on that same bench. It was early. Her skin felt the cold breeze of the morning; dew soaked through her shoes. She was walking toward Zach from the side of the baseball field. She looked down. Something was in her hands. It was a journal, with a beige cover and a green spine.* Then everything faded to black.

37

JESSICA'S BOARDROOM EXPERIENCE

Jessica tossed and turned in bed. Her mind was racing with thoughts she couldn't make sense of. She had flashes of Zach in a corporate boardroom, sitting at the head of a long rectangular table. There were at least ten people on each side of the table, all staring at a screen opposite of Zach. He was different. He was older. Zach's dreadlocks had grown down to the middle of his back and were gray.

Jessica was in the room, pacing back and forth on one side of the room by the floor-to-ceiling glass windows. Everyone was looking at the screen, engaged in a conversation, and seemingly unaware of her presence. She watched their lips move, but she couldn't make out anything that they were saying.

A flash of light from the window temporarily blinded her. She froze in place. As her eyes adjusted, she scanned the Atlanta skyline. Off in the distance, just over Kennesaw Mountain, she saw the flash again. It was like someone was using a mirror and reflecting the sun to signal to Jessica. *Impossible, that mountain is over twenty miles away.* The reflection caught her eye again. This time the glare lasted a little longer. Jessica leaned closer to the window, pressing her palms against the glass.

Suddenly, the mountain burst into flames. Jessica jumped back from the window. *Was this some sort of attack?* There were no planes in the sky. The blaze grew quickly, spreading toward Midtown Atlanta. Jessica turned and looked at Zach. He and the rest of the people in suits were still in discussion, staring at the screen. Jessica turned back to the window, watching the earth scorch on a path toward them. Jessica rushed over to Zach and shook his shoulders. He didn't respond. Jessica ran out of the room to the other side of the building. She saw flames coming from the other side of the city too, rapidly making their way inward. Jessica ran to the other sides of the building. Her fears were confirmed. There was a blaze coming for the heart of Atlanta, and they were in the center.

Jessica ran back to the boardroom, unsure of what she would say, but she knew she needed to do something. This time, only Zach was in there, sitting alone, still staring at the screen. Jessica approached him cautiously. She reached out to put her hand on his shoulder, but a familiar voice stopped her.

"Look now," Evelyn's voice said.

Jessica hadn't seen her in the room, but Evelyn was now standing by the glass wall, staring off at the mountain. As Jessica approached the glass, she saw that the fire had stopped progressing toward them. It was still burning, but something was preventing it from moving closer.

"Come down," Evelyn said as she turned and left the boardroom, the door closing behind her. Jessica tried to follow her. She opened the door and was back in her room.

Jessica sat up in bed and tried to shake off the dream. Once she collected herself, she headed downstairs. She saw Evelyn in the kitchen, standing next to the island, drinking from a steaming mug. "Would you like some tea?" she asked politely.

"You all are really into tea here," Jessica said. "No, thank you. How did you do that?"

"Magic," Evelyn laughed. "The complicated, real answer is that every thought you have emits a frequency, a wavelength. Ori can see each wave, like a trail of light or energy, from its origination to its destination. He can also see each ripple effect that your thoughts create. Ori figured that you would be restless, and he told us which frequency to monitor. It was my turn to watch you when you had the dream." Evelyn smiled and took another sip from her mug.

"Your turn to watch? How long have I been asleep?"

"A little over a day."

Jessica's heartbeat quickened. "When is Match Day?"

"Tomorrow."

"Can you read my thoughts too?"

"Like Ori?" Evelyn shook her head. "No."

"Good, so you can't tell how much I'm freaking out."

"Ha." Evelyn seemed amused. "I don't need to read your mind to pick up on that. But, based on your dream and Ori's vision, you shouldn't have anything to worry about." Evelyn placed her mug on the counter. "Let's take a walk."

The sky was clear, and Jessica could see every star. *It's always a clear night sky here.* She stared up at the sky, expecting to see one of the thousands of satellites fly past, but there was nothing. An image of her and Zach camping on the South Rim of the Grand Canyon appeared in her mind. *"See, there's another one," Zach said, pointing at the orbiting satellite. "One day, we are going to have to find a way that doesn't rely on those things polluting space."*

Jessica shook the thought out of her head. "What's happening to me? I keep having these flashes of Zach. Some seem real, but others seem like dreams. I'm not sure what to think."

"Your rational mind is having a hard time letting go. It's trying to make sense of things that logic can't explain." Jessica walked in silence while Evelyn continued. "When you're born, your brain starts to collect all kinds of data to program itself. It takes cues from your guardians, family, friends, television, news, everything. That creates the foundation for how your brain works. The things you are learning and experiencing here go against everything you've been programmed to believe. That's an incredibly difficult thing to comprehend, but your brain is doing a great job of it."

"Those journals," Jessica said. "I gave Zach those ideas?"

"Sort of," Evelyn said. "To you, it seems like you pulled a book off the shelf with all the secrets to the universe. To Zach, you inspired him in different ways. Maybe on a trip in the woods, you made a passing comment about how the woodpecker knows which trees have food and which don't. Remember, we never give answers. We just point people in the right direction."

"Why are things so muddled in my mind?" Jessica asked. "In my dream, Zach was older, much older than the last time I saw him. How is that possible?"

"You saw the version of reality that we need to have occurred," Evelyn said. "A future in which Zach—"

Jessica finished her thought, "Becomes the CEO of the Singularity Group."

"That's right."

"And the fire…" Jessica continued, staring at the dirt path as they walked into the forest. "The solar flares. Zach has the company focus all of its efforts on identifying a solution to save the world from the solar flares." Jessica looked over at Evelyn. "That's why the fire stopped in my dream."

"That's correct," Evelyn said, nodding along.

"But how does the Alderamin algorithm come into play?"

"We need diversity of thought to help build the technology that will save the world. The world is still incredibly divided. Once we get people operating off the same objective data points, more people will move from the extreme edges toward the middle. We need more people working together, people from all different backgrounds. You never know who carries the final piece of the puzzle that will save humanity, so no voice must be discounted."

Jessica felt a sharp pain in her head as an image flashed of her stumbling through the woods. She stopped and put her hands on her knees.

"Headache again?" Evelyn asked.

Jessica nodded.

Evelyn put an arm around her waist for support and urged her forward. "Come with me."

Jessica heard water, and the pain in her head subsided. They were back at the pond. Jessica thought back to the image of Ori standing there, his flesh replaced by the darkness of space, his features replaced by the stars and galaxies. "If Ori can read my mind and can see the future, why doesn't he just tell me what happened and what I need to know?"

"It doesn't work that way. We only operate in your subconscious. That way, you are more likely to take ownership of your thoughts, words, and actions. The answers never leave your subconscious. That's where all of your shadow beliefs are held."

"Shadow beliefs?" Jessica questioned.

"These are the beliefs that are buried deep inside, that were programmed in you at a very early age. Most people aren't even aware that they exist." Evelyn kneeled and put her hand in the water as the sizable koi fish approached. When Evelyn's skin touched the water, her forearm turned the black of deep space, and Jessica could see small glowing stars, just like she had with Ori. "When you are all alone, daydreaming about your perfect life, you might picture everything that you ever want to happen. Once you get a clear picture of what that looks like, how happy you would feel, you ask yourself, 'Do I deserve it?'" Evelyn looked up at Jessica. "Your shadow beliefs about yourself will be answered. Too many people don't believe they are worthy." Evelyn pulled her hand out of the water. It returned to its flesh and blood hue. She stood up. "Your shadow beliefs feed your subconscious, which drives your conscious thoughts and behavior. There's nothing wrong with your shadow beliefs. You wouldn't be here if there was."

"Then why can't I remember everything?" Jessica asked.

"Zach's the problem," Evelyn said. "Your two minds have formed a powerful bond and have become entangled. You have a shared vision, so powerful that what's happening to his conscious mind is impacting yours."

"What else do I need to do to fix it?" Jessica asked.

"You've got to remember what it is that has created such a strong bond between you."

Jessica said, "He mentioned a godson. I've spent a lot of time with him, though, and I—I can't remember anything about a godson."

"Well, we know Zach's thoughts are scrambled," Evelyn said.

"Because of interference?"

"Zach has information that he's keeping, and someone is trying hard to get it. They are driven, and they are determined. But what's in your mind is equally important, and it's the only way we can save him."

"What if I can't remember?" Jessica asked.

"Don't think like that," Evelyn said. "You've already remembered. Now you just need to let the rest come to you."

38

———————

MATCH DAY ARRIVAL

Jessica was surprised by what was hanging in her room when she awoke. On the door hung a sleek black gown, with golden waves painted across it and diamond detailing. It was the most regal thing she had ever seen. She walked downstairs to check in, and in the main room was a beauty salon set up with a hairstylist, a manicurist, and a massage therapist. When Jessica hesitated on the stairs, Tony peered around the corner and said, "Hurry up, you're next."

Before Jessica knew what hit her, she stood in front of a full-length mirror, not recognizing herself. Her hair was intricately braided and put up, with a single large ruby as the centerpiece, perfectly embedded.

Jessica walked out to the patio area to see Ori, Evelyn, Jordan, Tony, and Vau sitting. When she stepped out, everyone stood to greet her. They were all elegantly dressed in tailored attire, clearly designed to highlight each of their beautifully unique physiques. Jessica noticed shimmers of sapphire and emerald shining from little adornments. The effect was magical.

In unison, they all gave a single nod of approval. "You look majestic," Professor Raziel said, joining them outside.

"I feel like we're about to go to the Met Gala, not a science fair." Jessica laughed.

"Tradition." Evelyn smiled. "Dreamy outfits and sensible shoes." She motioned down to her flats with a little wink.

"It's incredible," Jessica said appreciatively. "Thank you all, by the way. I know I still have more to remember, but having you all show me behind the scenes, it's been unforgettable. Well, let's hope."

Ori smiled in return. "Just remember that no matter what, the universe is always on your side."

Jordan interrupted the silence. "This is a beautiful moment, but it's time to go."

Something felt a little like high school as they walked together, all dressed up, down the path and into the forest. Surrounded by thick old-growth trees, they stopped. Jessica watched as they all lifted their wrists, fingers on the outer rings of their timepieces.

"Alright, who's coordinating?" Jordan asked.

"Let me get this one," Tony said as he walked over to Jessica. He got right next to her, so she had a good view of his skeleton watch. Tony pointed to a dial he was adjusting to 7.83. "This shows where you're anchored. Your version of Planet Earth, on average, resonates at 7.83 hertz. Sometimes it's different, but then that's when there's overlap with other realities or there's multidimensional interference, blah blah blah. For now, let's keep it simple. So if I'm your escort, we'd set this at 7.83."

Tony placed his thumb and index finger on the largest ring around the face of the watch. "This bezel, the big one, you tune this to where you want to go." He twisted it and said, "Where is it again?"

"President John C. Lewis High School," Vau said.

"No," Tony said, "I mean…"

"It's at six one nine," Ori said.

"All right," Tony whispered, focusing as he adjusted the large dial on his watch until the second sub-dial lit up and flashed "6.19 hz." "Okay," Tony continued. "Now you have to clear—"

"Wait," Vau interjected. "I just remembered it's my turn. Why does Tony get to do it?"

"Because I designed it," Tony said.

"Fine, but I'm going to show her around Match Day," Vau said.

Jessica saw Evelyn shake her head, while Jordan rolled her eyes, and Ori laughed.

"Just hear me out," Vau said. "This will be the first time she'll see Match Day. She's like a recruit, and I'm up."

Tony looked at Evelyn, who said, "Well, he's not wrong."

Tony scoffed and stepped back. Vau strutted up triumphantly. He held his wrist up to Jessica so she could see his clouded watch face and dials. "Now, grab my arm." Vau pressed the circular 6.19 hz on his watch, and Jessica felt a burst of air all around her. "Take a deep breath, imagine Match Day, and we'll travel through time and across the multiverse. Relax and enjoy the ride." Vau patted Jessica's arm reassuringly. He closed his eyes, inhaled deeply, and Jessica was surrounded by white clouds. She couldn't see anything else, even her hand when she tried to put it in front of her face. Jessica felt like she was floating in the ocean and parachuting through the air simultaneously. Aside from the gust of wind, the only thing she could feel was the steadiness of Vau's arm.

A few moments later, they were strolling through a park, walking as if they'd never missed a step. She could see Vau now, and he said, "Once you find your watch, you'll be able to see everything." *My watch?* Jessica's thought stopped short as she stared ahead. What she saw had to be an illusion. Their destination looked like a city enclosed in a glass dome, elevated in the sky. "Is that a city-sized snow globe?" Jessica asked, half-jokingly.

"Something like that," Vau said.

The city appeared to hover over a thick rainforest. As they got closer, Jessica saw that a golden pyramid was rising out of the treetops, making contact with the bottom of the dome. The city appeared to be balanced on the pyramid's point. Jessica followed Vau and the team as they stepped into a glass box. It was like an all-glass gondola lift, but it wasn't connected to any cables. Once they were all in, the unmanned container elevated off the ground and flew directly toward the elevated city. If Jessica didn't see the ground passing below them, she wouldn't have thought they were moving.

39

—————

MATCH DAY EXHIBITS

Jessica was surprised at the number of different transport carriages arriving at the docking station and the passengers disembarking. Some people were dressed in formal wear similar to hers, and others in little more than animal coverings. Everyone pleasantly greeted one another as the massive influx of travelers walked toward what Jessica figured was the city's center. There were no concrete streets or sidewalks anywhere, only grass pathways. The city was in the shape of rings, with the outermost ring holding the shorter buildings. Each ring inward from there had progressively taller buildings. The very center of the city featured what could have been the inspiration for the Burj Khalifa in Dubai.

"Don't get too distracted," Ori said, talking to Vau. "Make sure you take care of what needs to happen first."

"I know, I know," Vau said.

"All right," Evelyn said as they got closer to the city center, "we'll meet up with you after the builders' finale." Evelyn and Ori broke away from the group.

"Oh, I almost forgot," Tony said, as he pulled two small cone-shaped items out of his pocket and handed them to Jessica. "Put these in your ears. This is the best workaround we have until you get your watch back."

All around them there was music, dancing, and delicious-smelling food.

"This isn't quite what I expected," Jessica said, thinking about the description of Match Day as a mix between a science fair and a job convention.

"This," Tony said, as he waved his hands toward the festivities like a circus ringmaster presenting his next great performers, "is the birthplace of genius. At the end of every Great Year, all the geniuses come together and present what they believe are the tools needed for the next twenty-six thousand years. We have a representation of people from almost every major version of the multiverse."

"Those who come from places sanctioned to attend," Jordan said.

"Are they, umm, celestial beings too?" Jessica asked.

"They are part of the team," Jordan said, "but they're more like you. They started as recruits and have elevated."

"All right," Vau said, "time to split up?

"Cool." To Jessica, Tony said, "Hey, enjoy this."

"See you at the finale," Jordan said, and they both walked off.

"So the first exhibit is…" Vau looked around, "over here."

"What's our role here?" Jessica asked.

"We're shopping," Vau said. "C'mon, they're about to start. First up, the aquatic exhibits." A small crowd had formed around the first booth, which was crewed by two young women. One had long black braids that went past her lower back. The other had lively curly hair the color of a bright red hibiscus. As Jessica and Vau approached, the crowd made way for them, and Jessica could swear she heard at least one person whisper, "It's the scribe."

Jessica surveyed the booth to see several transparent balls lying on the table.

"What do we have here?" Vau asked.

The young women had been staring at Jessica. At the sound of Vau's voice, the one with the long black braids cleared her throat. "This allows someone to breathe underwater."

The young lady with the red hair picked up one of the rubber-looking balls and handed it to Jessica.

It felt cold and soft, like gelatin.

"How does it work?" Jessica asked.

The young women looked at each other.

Vau encouraged them. "Do you mind showing an example?"

The two women spoke simultaneously and then traded off words as if they had done this countless times. "This technology is made of chemical components that, at an atomic level, feed oxygen directly into the human being," said the one with red hair.

"All they have to do," the other chimed in, "is place the device over their nose and mouth." The young woman pressed the ball against her nose and mouth, which then morphed into a transparent mask. The girl took several deep breaths and spoke. Jessica could hear her words, although her voice was a little muffled.

The one with the red hair bent down behind the booth and pulled out a transparent block that was the size of a Rubik's cube. "Please stand back," she said as she placed it on the ground and squeezed the sides. The cube then expanded into a glass tank that was taller than Vau.

The girl with the transparent mask stepped inside, closed the door, and pressed her hand against the inner wall. The tank then filled with water, submerging the girl, who exhibited her ability to keep breathing with no issues, thanks to the mask.

"Remarkable," Jessica whispered.

"Where is this viable?" Vau asked.

"It ranges from five hertz up to eleven hertz," the woman said.

"Are there limitations on duration and depth?" Vau asked.

"This allows for three circadian rhythm cycles of breath, regardless of depth."

Vau explained, "So this will allow you to breathe underwater for at least seventy hours before you have to come up for air. Right?" Vau glanced back at the presenter.

"Correct," she said.

"This is excellent. Thank you." Vau gave a slight bow.

"Thank you," Jessica said.

"It's an honor," the presenter said.

"Let's see," Vau said, taking in the surrounding booths. "Next up?

Ah, soil. We have some time before the next presentation, so let's explore."

Jessica and Vau slowly made their way through the different exhibitions. Vau pointed toward a group of people. "This is the transportation section. You'll find all sorts of technology tied to time and interdimensional travel."

Jessica saw demonstrations of people teleporting fruit from one location to another. There were several versions of flying vehicles. She saw a demonstration where an elderly man stepped into a large stone or quartz box. The demonstrators sealed him in, and after a few minutes, he stepped out, looking several decades younger.

Everywhere that Jessica and Vau walked, Jessica noticed that people would stop midconversation and stare at her.

"Why do I feel like people here know me?" Jessica asked.

"Because of your role as a scribe," Vau said. "What you see here will not exist in your world unless it is written or displayed somewhere, in some capacity, so that it plants a seed in the imagination of someone who will be brave enough to try and bring it to life. Over there," Vau pointed across the convention area, "is the agriculture area. The next thing you need to see is about to start."

At the next exhibit, Jessica saw an empty tank on the ground. The tank was only a few feet long, but it was as tall as Jessica. Next to the tank was a table with a row of test tubes filled with a golden liquid.

One exhibitioner, a young man, walked around to the front of the glass tank, knelt, and with one hand, lifted the tank off the grass-covered ground.

"Please note," the young man said, "that there is no bottom to this tank."

The other presenter dumped a jar of sand on top of the table, creating a small mound. "This is sand from the driest desert on the planet. It has not grown life in thousands of years."

The young man by the tank now stood on a ladder and poured buckets of sand in the tank, filling it to the top.

"What we have here," the presenter behind the table held up a vial of the amber liquid, "is a special formula. When this interacts with barren earth, it triggers the dirt on an atomic level and sends a message for help to the nearest living organisms."

The young man on the ladder held up a beaker full of the golden liquid in an exaggerated demonstration. The crowd cheered him on. He poured the liquid, and the area of sand where the liquid touched it clumped. Nothing happened, and Jessica turned away to look at another exhibit when Vau grabbed the top of her head and turned her face back to the tank. That clump of sand sank to the bottom of the tank. Once it reached the bottom and interacted with the grass, the surrounding sand changed from a light tan to a dark brown to black. This transformation moved upward in the tank until the sand had become black dirt. Jessica hadn't noticed that she was moving closer to the tank until she was a foot away. From there, she saw that there were tiny white threads, like white veins, weaving in and out of the now dark, fertile soil.

The presenter continued, "As long as there's still some life somewhere down in the earth," he held up the vial again, "this sends out a distress signal to all the living organisms. Once they consume this, they can multiply quickly to convert the soil to a healthy state."

The presenter then held up a tiny seed for the crowd before he walked over to the tank and handed it to the young man on the ladder. The demonstrator gently buried the seed in the newly created fertile soil, and quickly got down from the ladder, moving a few feet away from the tank.

"We recommend waiting for at least one circadian cycle before planting anything, but for presentation purposes, we wanted to show the effects when you plant seeds in the soil while the bacteria are at their peak state of stimulation and reproduction."

The seed sprouted within seconds. Jessica saw the roots reach down toward the bottom of the tank. A green shoot glided out of the soil like a snake carelessly moving through a field. The leaves quickly multiplied as the plant grew tall, stretching toward the sun. The young man climbed back up the ladder, wrapped his fingers around the plant's stem, getting a firm grip near the roots. He effortlessly pulled the plant out of the earth and held it up high. The crowd erupted with applause.

"That's wasabi," Vau said.

"Why wasabi?" Jessica asked, staring at the plant with the corners of her mouth upturned in delight.

"Wasabi is incredibly difficult to grow."

After a moment, Vau said, "There's one more thing you should see."

40

THE BUILDERS

Jessica and Vau left the main convention grounds.

"Where are we going?" Jessica asked.

"They're setting up for the finale," Vau said. "I want to make sure we get there early."

"The finale?" Jessica said. "But it's still light out." She expected some grand display with fireworks.

"If you wait until dark, you won't be able to see," Vau said. "Each year, the best builders and architects come together to put on a show to celebrate early innovations. They recreate old structures in the old way. I love it." Vau turned and looked at Jessica. His smile reminded her of a kid walking into a theme park. He continued, "It reminds me of the good old days." Vau led Jessica to the outermost ring of the city, toward a transport trolly. Just as they were getting close, Jordan and Tony ran up to them.

"You guys finished already?" Vau asked.

"We figured you were going to the finale early," Tony said before Jordan interrupted.

"We couldn't let you be the only one to see the expression on her face."

"What is so special about this show?" Jessica asked.

"Just wait for it," Tony said as they boarded the glass vessel and gently sailed down to the ground.

The group got out and walked through the thick rainforest on a well-worn path.

"So, what'd you think of Match Day?" Tony asked.

Jessica opened her mouth to respond but was interrupted by a loud boom. The ground trembled beneath her feet, and she stopped and looked around. It reminded Jessica of her family's time near a base that often tested artillery in the mountains.

Tony continued talking as if nothing happened, "Did you get a chance to check out the section with the latest for black hole travel?"

"Uh—no," Jessica said, very distracted. "Did you feel that?"

"Yes, I did. It's nothing." Tony continued, "What about the aquatic section?"

"I did see something there," Jessica said as several consecutive booms, followed by mini earthquakes, took her attention.

"It's hard to concentrate when they're warming up," Vau said.

Jordan chimed in, "From the sounds of it, they may be training some new builders."

The path expanded to the size of a one-lane road, and the dirt converted into a hard floor. "Is that marble?"

"Granite," Tony said.

The walkway was easily wide enough to fit two large trucks on it. Jessica knelt to see that each granite brick was cut precisely, with sharp corners and not a crack or chip to be seen.

Jessica walked quickly to catch up with the rest of her group. As she got closer to them, she heard an array of instruments getting tuned, followed by another loud boom.

"The band is still warming up," Jordan said. "The show will not be anything like this."

"Are they using explosives or something?" Jessica asked.

"Explosives?" Jordan said, "Oh no, they use—"

Vau interrupted, "Patience, Jessica."

Tony looked at Jordan. "Don't ruin the surprise." He then turned to Jessica. "Just wait, we're almost there. You'll get a kick out of it."

The walkway ended at the entrance of an outdoor amphitheater, surrounded by dense green on all sides. There was a full orchestra with strings, horns, and a percussion section facing the stage. Instead of a traditional stage, the orchestra faced what Jessica could only describe as a climbing wall. It was several stories high and resembled something that could have been inside a sporting goods store. The only thing it was missing was the colorful hand and foot grips.

The group walked by the orchestra on their way to claiming seats in the front row. Up close, the instruments appeared different. The string instruments looked like they had speakers embedded in them. The brass instruments had some sort of cone on the bells of the horn.

"What are those?" Jessica asked, still staring at the instruments.

Vau gently grabbed her arm and guided her so she wouldn't trip as she got to her seat. "Those help the instruments hit a larger range of octaves."

On cue, the horn section played a loud note, and Jessica saw a stone the size of a truck elevate in the air. The louder the group played, the higher the stone raised until they gently lowered it back to the ground.

"That's it!" Jessica heard the conductor shout. "Just like that."

"That is impossible," Jessica said to herself, not even thinking about the probability of the things she'd seen since she had arrived at the Point.

Vau and Jordan were laughing when Tony trotted down to speak with some of the crew working with the orchestra. "There's nothing impossible about it," Vau said. "Music moves the entire universe."

"Don't you know that everything, and I mean everything, moves to music?" Jordan asked. "Just like the right music makes you want to dance, the right sound can make anything in the universe move."

Tony sat down in the row behind her, holding a small cloth sack. "Even black holes enjoy music. The one by the Perseus cluster sings at a B-flat. Take out those earpieces I gave you earlier." Jessica did as instructed while Tony turned to the conductor and signaled one more time. The horn section then lifted their instruments and played. She heard the same note. This time, however, it also sounded like her eardrums were flooded with water. Her hearing was muffled. Tony took the earpieces from her hand and placed them back into her ears.

The muffled sound went away. "That B-flat note is fifty-seven octaves below anything a human being can hear. The trick is to find a way to play music at both an octave that resonates with the natural world and a level that's audible. And this," Tony held up the sack in front of Jessica's eyes, "this is the other part of the secret. Let me see your hand."

Tony cupped Jessica's hand and poured some of the contents of the bag into it, which could have been black and silver grains of sand. "Sand?" Jessica asked.

"It looks like it, but there are tiny computers that can convert the music we hear to the appropriate octaves that resonate with the granite. These tiny computers bond incredibly well with the atomic structure of the granite," Tony said, as he pointed at the stone wall. Jessica observed the crew members, who were each carrying similar cloth sacks and applying the nanotechnology to the granite slab with what looked like a paintbrush. When they were done, there were ten rectangular outlines, each as big as a truck.

"You'd be surprised at how close you are to creating these," Vau said. "There's already a computer that's one millimeter by one millimeter."

"You're closer than you think," Tony confirmed.

41

THE FINALE

THE ORCHESTRA HAD LEFT, AND JESSICA SAT BACK AND LISTENED AS Jordan, Vau, and Tony exchanged stories of past adventures. Jessica couldn't follow most of the discussion, but she enjoyed seeing their banter and hearing their inside jokes. Watching them play around made it easy for Jessica to forget these were beings that some cultures would consider divine. While she knew the severity of her situation, that if she didn't regain her memory, she would lose it forever, she also finally felt a little more at ease.

Jessica stood up and walked to the highest seats in the theater, which overlooked the rainforest. The view allowed Jessica to see the traffic gliding in and around the domed metropolis, balanced so delicately on the tip of the pyramid.

Jessica watched the dark outline of birds flying against a backdrop streaked with orange, pink, and blue sky. *Is any of this real? How would I know what's real and what's not? Who would I tell? Who could validate it? Would Mikiko believe me?* Then she became angry with herself for even raising those questions. *How can it not be real? Why do I need anyone's validation?*

The sound of voices filling the theater brought Jessica's attention back to the present. She turned to see a crowd of people flowing in from the conference. The orchestra of perhaps a hundred members made their way back. Like the conference-goers, the musicians represented a range of cultures or universes. Some wore gowns and tuxedos, while others wore clothes made of animal hides, decorated with intricate, colorful beads. The jewelry brought Jessica back to her childhood, reminding her of the time in second grade when her dad took her to see a powwow held on Fort Huachuca to celebrate Native American heritage. The singing and dancing were majestic, of course, but the clothing with the colored beads captured her imagination. She marveled at the discipline and dedication it must have taken to create something like that.

The orchestra was now tuning their instruments, which Jessica found odd because they had done so earlier. She heard the crowd gasp and applaud as they stared at the granite wall. Jessica settled into her seat between Vau and Jordan. She searched for the cause of the crowd's reaction and saw white dust floating near the wall. "What's that?" Jessica asked.

"It's from the granite wall," Vau said. He had a big grin on his face as he stared at Jessica. Unhappy with her lack of enthusiasm, he said, "Look closely at the outline."

Jessica looked again. There were gaps in the wall where the stage crew had applied the nanocomputer chips, as if someone had taken a wet saw and cut along the lines. Jessica leaned forward, marveling at how quickly and precisely the technique worked.

The conductor tapped her baton, and the orchestra went silent. A man walked on the stage and said, "To celebrate the end of the Great Year and the beginning of a new one, the builders have decided to pay tribute to the Pyramid of Khufu, or as some call it, the Great Pyramid of Giza. After the concert ends, please join the rest of the citizens at the celebration in the city center." The man bowed to the crowd then nodded at the conductor. "Maestro, they are all yours."

The crowd applauded as the man walked off stage. Then the amphitheater was silent again.

Da-Da-Da-DUUUUUUUUUUUUUUUUUM.

Jessica knew the start of Beethoven's Fifth Symphony anywhere. It was the first and only classical song she knew growing up. The orchestra held the fourth note much longer than Jessica remembered.

As the orchestra played the fourth note, Jessica watched as the gigantic stones slid out of the granite wall like someone pulling open a dresser drawer. The orchestra held that fourth note until all ten stones were out of the wall and gently lowered onto the stage.

Da-Da-Da-DUUUUUUUUUUUUUUUUUUM.

As the musicians played the next three notes, the colossal stones raised in the air. They were elevated over the crowd by the time the orchestra played the eighth note. The rocks floated over the crowd as the performers held the note again for an extended period. Jessica observed as the stones divided into hundreds of smaller cubes. Once the parts of the granite stones separated from the whole, the orchestra played on at an upbeat allegro tempo. Moving in sync as if a specific instrument controlled each stone, each cube danced to the notes. The sun had almost set when the stones converted from their pinkish hue and took on an assortment of vibrant neon greens, blues, and yellows. It was like a fireworks exhibit with all of the excitement and none of the disappointment from the vanishing act.

Jessica pinched herself.

"This is real," Vau said. "I can assure you of that."

Jessica felt the vibrations of the music through her seat. Her heart was racing. She felt goose bumps rise on her arms, and her eyes watered. Jessica wasn't sure how long the show lasted, but she wanted it to continue forever. She closed her eyes and allowed her body to sway with the notes of the music. The sharp pain on the side of her head returned, forcing her to shut her eyes harder. She squeezed her eyelids so hard that she felt the corners of her eyes tremble. White flashes of light replaced the pain in her head. Each burst brought back a different image. First was a picture of Zach, standing in front of an exhibit in the MoMa, smiling. The next image was of her, lying in bed in the house where she lost her memory, under the sheets, laughing with Zach. Another scene flashed into her memory, one of the little girl in the meadow. Jessica heard the child say again, *"I know who you are, silly."* "Nia," Jessica whispered to herself. The next image was different; it didn't seem like something from a dream or the past. Now Jessica was seeing a reflection of herself in the bathroom mirror. She was old, her face and hands were wrinkled, and she had dark skin tags under her eyes. This scene felt like the present—like it just happened or like it was currently happening. *"Wait for me, grandma,"* a little voice called from somewhere behind her. Jessica's heart felt like it was about to explode. She opened her eyes, stood up, and looked around frantically. Vau, Tony, and Jordan stood up with her.

"Malik," Jessica said.

Jordan smiled. "Ori's at the block party. Let's go find him."

42

———

THE BLOCK PARTY

As they approached the center of the city, the group first bumped into Carlos.

"It's nice to see you again, Jessica," Carlos said as he extended his hand.

Jessica shook it and tried to smile politely as Jordan spoke. "Have you seen Ori? She's getting her memory back."

"He's around here somewhere," Carlos said. "Oh, here they come now."

Jessica followed his gaze. Ori, Evelyn, and another familiar face walked toward her. Jessica's heart thumped when she recognized the doctor with the decaying eyes from her visit to Zach's nursing home.

Carlos continued as the three approached, "I believe you've met my colleague, Dr. Serrano. Yes?"

"Don't worry, Jessica," Ori said. "He won't harm you. Dr. Serrano's specialty is understanding and manipulating the physical network of the brain. You can think of him as a type of neurologist."

"The rest of my memory is coming back," Jessica blurted out.

"What have you remembered now?" Ori said.

Jessica focused on the grass, making sure nothing distracted her. "I remember how I met Zach. Leslie brought me in to meet him. Zach wanted me to write a piece on their technology. He figured that if more people knew how it worked, then there would be a leap in technological discoveries."

She looked up and studied Ori's face.

"Go on," he said.

"I was skeptical."

"Why?"

"Because I knew exactly how it worked, how everything worked." Jessica rubbed her temple instinctively. She had flashes of herself writing in the journals with the green spines. She saw herself at the Point walking around the gardens, sitting in her room, or even sitting at the round table in the command center.

"I remember tagging along with you." She glanced at Jordan, Vau, Tony, and the rest. "With all of you. You've taken me around before, explained everything to me."

"Why were you skeptical?" Ori asked again.

"Truly understanding how the dark energy technology worked was a complex thing. I wasn't sure that a piece by me would enable broad understanding and use of the technology. But Zach not only understood it well; he could clearly and simply explain it all." Jessica smiled, and she felt her eyes water. "His brain was so fascinating that I just kept finding excuses to meet with him. From then on, it was like everything I learned here, Zach had dreamed about as well, without me telling him."

"Your minds became entangled," Dr. Serrano said. "No one can explain how these things happen, and it's rare, but it does occur."

"What happened on the night you lost consciousness?" Ori asked.

"I was in town for the forum on the virus, and I visited Zach's place. He had something important that he wanted to share with me."

"Do you know what it was?"

"He didn't trust the people from Confidence Biotech. He found out that they were using the Global Breadth system to identify and capture healthy people. Then they used them to create an antibody. He'd feared something like that happening, so he'd given them a beta version of the system. He also downloaded the entire system on a memory drive and gave it to me. He made me put it in my car then and there. I'm so thankful I did. I had to check some emails, and when I went back into the house, Zach was unconscious. Some men were in the middle of dragging him out. They approached me and sprayed some liquid in my face. I collapsed and couldn't move or speak, but my mind was still working. After a minute, I don't know how, but I managed to get up and get to my rental car. I vaguely remember driving and crashing somewhere. The next thing I knew, I was at the Point by the pond." Jessica grabbed her wrist to find nothing there. She gasped, "I lost my watch."

"Jessica," Ori said, "why did you go visit Zach?"

"He said that he had something to tell me."

"And what did you have to tell him?" Ori asked.

Jessica gently placed her hands on her stomach. Tears rolled down her cheeks. "Oh my God."

"Your baby is fine." Evelyn grabbed her hands. "She's healthy, strong, and determined. Just like her mother."

Evelyn released Jessica's hands. Dr. Serrano then stood in front of Jessica and placed his hands on her shoulders. Jessica jumped back, but Ori assured her, "Dr. Serrano is one of us. When they sprayed you with that chemical, your connection to us was severed. Carlos sent the doc to assess the damage. You saw him clearly at Zach's care center, which was a good sign. But then when you didn't recognize him at the park, I knew things weren't right."

"We had to get you here to jump-start your memory," Evelyn said.

She relaxed as Dr. Serrano adjusted his grip on her shoulders. "Take a deep breath and relax." Jessica stared into his eyes. His irises were light brown, but they turned a bright white before they eroded. Just like she had seen before, the doctor's eyes, eyelids, and sockets cracked and flaked like ash on a burned log. Just as quickly, they returned to normal. "Her full memory should return." Dr. Serrano looked back at Ori and Evelyn. "She should be good."

Evelyn stepped closer to Jessica again. "We need your help. Malik is in danger, and only you can provide the missing piece. We need to get back to the command center immediately."

Jessica watched as everyone, including Carlos and Dr. Serrano, were adjusting their watches. Jessica nodded, and the group made their way to the gondolas out of the city and back to the edge of the rainforest. With precise timing, as soon as the group stepped off the glass transport, the thick white fog was waiting for them. Jessica hooked her arm with Evelyn's as the chilly mist and air took her away.

43

THE RUSH TO SAVE MALIK

ONCE AGAIN, JESSICA HAD LITTLE VISIBILITY AND JUST HELD ONTO Evelyn's arm firmly. Jessica felt the strong winds blowing against them on both sides. Instead of emerging in the forest, this time the fog cleared as they entered a dark cave-like hallway. Vau, Jordan, and the others waited for Ori, who was bringing up the rear, before proceeding. The group then waited for a glass door to open, and once they walked through, Jessica saw they were back in the control center. This time, they must have entered from the same door that Tony exited the other day.

Most of the group headed straight for the briefing room. Jessica hung back a little, watching Evelyn as she walked farther down the hallway to a separate doorway. Aja appeared to wait there for her. The two had a quick exchange before Evelyn walked back to Jessica and held out a skeleton watch. "Aja took your watch when she found you by the pond. It's very dangerous to have it if you can't control your thoughts."

"How could one spray of that chemical do so much damage?" Jessica asked.

"Well, you also probably took some impact either from your collapse or your crash or both. Plus, this didn't just happen to you; it happened to Zach too, and your minds are entangled. Your memory was and is impacted by recurring medicinal treatments that are happening to Zach," Evelyn said.

Ori came over to join in. "Now that you've regained your memories, there's a chance that Zach can recover his. But, we've got to act fast."

Jessica nodded in understanding as she took the watch and secured it on her wrist. She followed Ori and Evelyn into the briefing room. Jessica felt her stomach turn, and a sense of panic overcame her. "Malik is in danger?"

"He is," Vau said.

Jordan added, "We just needed to make sure that you were good before we took action."

"I'm fine. Please save him," Jessica couldn't help but say, even though she knew that's what they were all there for.

"We got him," Ori said. "Go ahead, Carlos, what were you saying?"

"Outside of the morning hours between three and five, for there to be such severe interference with Zach, not to mention a recruit," Carlos looked at Jessica, "a scribe no less, the person must be incredibly driven and blinded by ambition. We know that these requests have to be coming from Roy Mengele."

"Who's that?" Jessica asked.

"He's the president and CEO of Confidence Biotech," Jordan said.

"Since when?" Jessica asked. *How much time has passed?*

"Jessica," Ori said quietly, "you understand that Malik's world is quite different from the one you remember?"

"I suppose," Jessica replied.

"What do you remember about Confidence Biotech?" Ori asked.

"They were a questionable company, but I was never able to substantiate anything definitively criminal. We believed they were taking advantage of senior citizens, claiming to have a solution for dementia, but their clinical trial data was fishy. Complaints would pop up, but then seemed to be quickly quieted."

"That's exactly how they are or would've been if Zach's path hadn't been interrupted. In the reality you lived in, the one that should be the truth, you're exactly right. But when Zach was attacked, it threw everything off," Evelyn said.

Jordan spoke up. "What's happened with the absence of Zach and you is that Confidence Biotech has become one of the most powerful companies in the world. They've used their tactics to convince the world's powers that they've created a solution for the virus. Their answer is inhumane, yet they are still pursuing that strategy to the bitter end."

"That bitter end is with Malik," Tony said. "He's the last link to a sustainable, effective, humane resolution for the virus."

"Unfortunately," Carlos said, "Roy is circling." Carlos shook his head. "If Roy and his Biotech contact tracers get ahold of Malik, it's game over. Roy is so far down this path that he will do anything to be viewed as the savior."

"We'll stop him," Ori said simply.

"How?" Dr. Serrano asked. "There's such limited time."

"We'll intervene directly," Evelyn said.

"And you believe Gabriel will comply?" Dr. Serrano asked with some surprise.

"His job is to watch over humanity until they either destroy or embrace one another. Since the virus is an act of nature, it's technically Aja's jurisdiction," Ori said. "But by now Gabriel has to realize that if Earth is at risk, there can be no humanity. And if we can put back in motion a path that allows Earth to survive, we have to think about the type of society that will exist. Because humans are a part of Earth's ecosystem, some will survive the reset. But even those people will bring to the future what they thought worked well in the past. Suppose people believed that sacrificing some for the benefit of others is the way to develop a society. In that case, the next version of mankind will be no different from this one."

"And Gabriel knows," Evelyn interjected, "that any one society with that type of belief system is prone to endless war and oppression. Gabriel would have to continue to watch this loop of human existence, on repeat."

"But," Ori said, trading off with Evelyn like this speech was rehearsed, "with a universal reset, like the great deluge or solar flares, humanity is much more likely to come together and embrace one another for mutual survival. That only happens if they get through this test as one."

Dr. Serrano considered this and asked, "So is there a way back for them from this barbaric path they've gone down?"

"Aja has agreed that we should be more assertive since it's for the survival of the entire planet, not just humanity," Evelyn responded.

Ori added to her reply, "Gabriel needed proof that there was another solution to the virus that was being overlooked. He and I made a deal. If Malik finds that solution, Jessica gets her time back. Now that Jessica has her memory back," Evelyn placed a hand on Jessica's shoulder as Ori continued, "we can help Malik tap into what's at his fingertips."

The room was quiet for a moment. Carlos made eye contact with Dr. Serrano and then turned to Ori and asked, "All right, what do you need from us?"

Ori smiled but said no more and just looked at Jessica.

"Jessica," Tony said, "it's your moment."

"What can I do?" Jessica asked.

"Zach gave you a small hard drive that was encrypted," Tony said. "We need you to remember the password."

"And in the meantime," Ori said, "we'll go help Malik."

44

MALIK'S LAST PATIENT

The Fridays when Dr. Patel was on call were Malik's favorite days in the office. The entire staff spent the first half of the day getting caught up on work while everyone got a chance to play their music of choice for an hour each. Then, they went out to lunch together before most of the staff headed home for the rest of the day. Malik and Christine would typically hang around to take any calls, though the phones were usually quiet. Christine would head out early to pick up her kids from school, and then Malik had the office to himself for a couple of hours. Living at home with his family, Malik rarely had time all to himself. He liked to spend the time jamming to music or lost in a book, but he couldn't focus today. This Friday was different.

Malik checked his watch and then wiped his sweaty palms on his pant legs. *Ten minutes until five,* he thought just as he smelled a light fragrance in the room, the sweet yet subtle Chanel Coco Mademoiselle. Malik had selected Magaly's name for last year's holiday party. He knew that she only wore one type of perfume. Everyone made fun of him for not sticking to the twenty-five-dollar max. He turned around and lost his breath when he saw Magaly in her black blouse, form-fitting jeans, and heels. He wasn't used to seeing her in anything other than scrubs. Her black hair was pulled back and tied with a red scarf, but her curls still cascaded down from her ponytail to just past her shoulders. Her golden hoop earrings were a final touch.

"I wish you had let me pick you up," Malik said.

"I live too far out of the way. It wouldn't have made sense."

"I should at least change out of my work clothes," he said.

"I like your slacks and dress shirt," Magaly smiled.

"I think it's okay that we close a few minutes early today." Malik stood up and walked to the front door. He twisted the deadbolt until it clicked into place and turned off the virus detection machine.

As soon as Malik walked back to the patient area, he and Magaly both jumped when they heard a loud pounding on the entrance door. They waited for a minute, thinking the pounding would go away, but it didn't.

"Open up!" a stern voice said from the other side of the door.

"Who in the world—?" Magaly started.

"I don't know. All of our patients know that Dr. Patel is working at the hospital today."

Malik walked to the entrance and peeked out of the window to see two large bodies dressed in black tactical gear, with helmets that blocked their faces. They were pushing a gurney with a person covered in a sheet on it. "They're CB tracers. It looks like they have a patient."

"We're not open," Malik shouted. "The doctor's at the hospital."

"Open up. It's an emergency," one guard shouted back.

"We are closed, and Dr. Patel isn't here," Malik shouted again.

"We know," the guard said impatiently. "He's at the hospital. He told us to come here. Open up."

Malik looked back at Magaly. "You should grab a mask. There are some behind the desk."

Malik waited until Magaly securely put on her mask and then opened the door. "What's going on?"

The men eyed Magaly, and then Malik. "Are we the only ones here?"

"Yeah, we aren't seeing patients today," Malik said.

"Why?" Magaly asked from behind the desk.

"Good." The man ignored Magaly as he and his partner pushed the gurney inside. "We don't want to put anyone at risk."

Malik noticed that the other person on the gurney was also wearing tactical gear. "What's going on?" Malik asked again. "What happened to him?"

"We were out on patrol when our colleague here," the man patted the side of the gurney, "collapsed. We tested him, and he came up positive for the virus."

"Then you should be at the hospital right now, not here," Magaly said.

"We were on our way to the hospital but were instructed to come here instead."

"Why here?" Malik asked.

The man talking patted the man on the gurney. *Why does he keep touching him?*

"He had no symptoms at all this morning; then a couple of hours ago, he just collapsed into an unconscious state. We believe that he may have contracted a new strain of the virus. Dr. Patel told us we could use his office since no one would be here today. Is there a room we can put him in?"

"S—sure," Malik said as he locked the door behind the men and turned to lead them through to the patient area.

The man said to Magaly, "Can you please go to the hospital and tell Dr. Patel that we are here?"

"I can just page him," Magaly said.

"No, we need to ensure that he gets here quickly. And you don't need to be in here. If this is a new strain, we need to minimize who comes into contact with it."

"I'll go too," Malik said.

"No!" the man said, too loudly. "You stay here. We need someone here who knows where everything is." He looked back at Magaly. "Now go, and hurry."

Malik nodded at Magaly, then she turned to leave. Malik pointed the men toward a patient room when there was more loud knocking on the front door. Malik sighed. "I'll be right back." He went back through to the waiting room.

"Where are you going?" The lead man tried to follow him, but the door auto-locked.

Malik said, "I'll be right back. Go ahead to the patient room. Just a minute."

The men reluctantly pushed the gurney down the hall.

Malik looked out of the window to see three more figures wearing all-black tactical gear. Malik opened the door, and the first person said, "Are they in the back?"

"Yeah," Malik said, "I'll show you where." Something about this trio was different. Maybe it was their demeanor. They seemed calmer than the first group. It could also have been their headgear. These had dark-tinted visors that obscured even more of their faces, leaving only their mouths visible. After Malik let them in, he went to lock the door again.

"There's no need for that," the man in charge said. "We'll be out of here quickly. You can go to the hospital and get Dr. Patel."

"But— Your friend just said that I needed to stay here until Dr. Patel comes."

"It's okay; we can cover them. You should get out of here too until the doctor comes back."

Malik left and went to the hospital.

45

THE FIGHT SCENE

Once Malik was gone, Ori, Jordan, and Tony walked to the patient room where the Confidence Biotech tracers were. When Ori opened the door, the gurney was empty, and all three men were standing. One of them was behind the door.

"Who are you?" one man asked, standing up taller.

Ori, Jordan, and Tony took their helmets off and closed the door. Jordan winked at one man.

"Who the f—" he started to say.

Jordan swung her helmet. It landed directly on the man's jaw, and he flopped back onto the gurney. Another Biotech tracer lunged toward her, and Ori struck him on the ear with the palm of his hand. The man wobbled and bent over. Ori kneed the man, splitting his headgear. The blow was so forceful that the man's entire body elevated and was briefly horizontal in the air before thumping on the ground. Tony kicked the third man above his knee, dropping him to the ground. Tony slammed the man's head against the counter, knocking his helmet off and breaking the cabinet door into several large pieces that were struggling to hold on to the hinge.

"Why did you do that?" Jordan asked, exasperated.

"It was there," Tony said. "What was I supposed to use?"

"I don't—" Jordan shook her head, "maybe the gurney or your knee."

"It's fine," Ori said. He flicked his fingers, and the busted cabinet door was back on the hinges, and there was no sign of any damage.

Tony smiled. "See, no issues. It's like it never happened."

"Now's not the time to joke around," Ori scolded lightly. He pointed his fist at the brick wall and window that faced the vacant parking lot. He opened his hand wide. As Ori extended his palm and fingers, the bricks of the walls stacked onto themselves like a set of children's magnetic tiles, creating an opening to the parking lot. Vau was waiting with an official black Confidence Biotech vehicle. Jordan and Tony carried two of the men to the back of the truck. They placed the unconscious Biotech tracers inside, next to the unconscious driver, before returning to the examination room. Ori closed his hand, forming a fist again, sealing the opening in the brick wall. Ori glanced back at the remaining man on the gurney. "Don't forget about him."

All three of them put their helmets back on. Tony put the helmet back on the unconscious man and covered him up to his neck with the sheet. Just then, they heard the door open.

46

DR. PATEL AND MALIK ARE BACK

Malik was speed-walking next to Dr. Patel and Magaly, trying to articulate his thoughts. "I don't know who they were. They claimed to be Confidence Biotech tracers, but something seemed off. They told me that you sent them to the office."

"It's okay, Malik," Dr. Patel said. "We will get to the bottom of this."

Malik opened the door to the examination room and saw one of the contact tracers adjusting the sheet on his sick colleague.

"What in the world is going on here?" Dr. Patel demanded. "I didn't authorize anyone to be brought to my office. This is ridiculous. Who is your superior? I'll be calling him now."

Malik had never seen Dr. Patel angry with anyone.

"There's no need for that," the man said. "There was a misunderstanding, and it's been all straightened out."

"What about the positive test result?" Magaly asked. "Didn't you say he has some new strain? How would you know that?"

"That was a false positive," the man said.

"And the symptoms?" Malik pressed.

"We think it could be the flu."

"This is all very strange. You stay right here." Dr. Patel pulled out his phone, and Malik saw him dialing 911. "What's your name? Show your face."

The man reached into his pocket and pulled out an identification card to show Dr. Patel. Malik couldn't get a look at it.

Dr. Patel inspected the information, put his phone away, and let out a big sigh. "Ah, thank you for the information. I appreciate it." As Dr. Patel tried to hand the card back to the man, Malik caught a glimpse. It just had a bunch of zeros and ones on it.

"No," the man said, "you can keep it. We apologize for the inconvenience. We got here as fast as we could."

Two of the tracers pushed the gurney out of the room, down the hall toward the reception area. The third walked next to Dr. Patel. The two were chatting like old buddies, laughing and joking.

"I wish I would've known." Dr. Patel smiled wide, as he unlocked doors for their exit. "Why didn't you tell me it was—never mind. Do you need any help?"

What? Malik said, "Wait a minute, Doc—"

"It's okay, Malik," Dr. Patel patted the contact tracer on his back. "We have a connection."

"There is something else I'd like to run past you," the man said. "I'll swing back after we sort this out if that's all right."

"That would be great," Dr. Patel said. "But you have to stay for dinner."

"I couldn't turn that down."

"Wait," Malik said. "There were six of you. Where did the other two go?"

"You must've missed them on your way back," the man said as he walked out of the office.

"We're gonna get out of your way. Thanks again for letting us use this space," one of the other tracers said as they pushed the gurney out of the last door.

Dr. Patel closed the door behind them and twisted the deadbolt into place.

"What in the world was that?" Malik asked.

"I don't know exactly, but it's all good now," Dr. Patel said. "Now, don't you two have someplace to be? A date?" He smiled with raised eyebrows.

"Bye, Dr. Patel," Magaly said, laughing as she pulled on Malik's arm.

"You two have fun."

47

MALIK AND MAGALY'S DATE

THE REST OF THE EVENING FLEW BY AS MALIK AND MAGALY LAUGHED until their stomachs hurt. Malik couldn't remember the last time he'd had such a great conversation. Malik looked around and realized that he and Magaly were the last people in the restaurant.

The waiter stopped by. "Let me know if there's anything else I can get you guys."

Malik asked, "Are you closing up?"

"Just about," he said, "but don't worry about it. There's one more table in the back. Stay as long as you want. I don't want to mess up your groove. He winked and smiled before walking away.

"That's embarrassing," Malik said, low enough for only Magaly to hear him.

"What? You don't think we are in a good groove?" she said.

"No, I—I do. It's just…" Malik shifted in his seat.

Magaly grinned. "I'm just messing with you."

They both laughed and continued talking the time away. Not much could take Malik's eyes away from hers until there was some unexpected movement in the periphery. He looked over to see several people in suits walking directly toward them. Oddly enough, it was Chance and Roy from Confidence Biotech, along with two other people.

"What a coincidence, seeing you twice in one week," Roy said.

"It is, isn't it," Malik said. He couldn't help feeling like this wasn't a coincidence at all. "I thought that you'd be back in New York by now."

"Our meetings down here required more time than we anticipated," Roy explained.

Malik stood up, and his napkin fell from his lap. "I'm sorry," he said, looking at Magaly. "Magaly, this is Roy Mengele, the CEO of Confidence Biotech."

"Hello," Magaly said.

"It's nice to meet you, Magaly. It looks like I'm interrupting a special night, so I'll make this brief." Roy turned to Malik. "Please, sit down. It's quite fortunate that we ran into you. After our meeting the other day, I had Chance here," he tilted his head toward Chance, who was standing behind him, "do a little research. I wanted to figure out what it would take for us to negotiate a deal for that antique you have."

Roy squinted his eyes and rubbed his temples as if he had a headache. "I'm sorry, it's been a long week."

He refocused on Malik. "I'm just curious, why does an intern go through what you went through, finally get a full-time job offer, only to turn it down and go work at a doctor's office?"

"What's wrong with Dr. Patel's office?" Magaly interjected. "Dr. Patel is the best in his field."

Roy put his hands up and backed up a step. "Why yes, he is. It's just, with a mind like Malik's, he could be at Confidence Biotech creating cures that will heal millions of people. Instead, you're, what," Roy looked at Malik, "seeing thirty patients a day?"

Malik rubbed the back of his neck. "Yeah, I know. My family needed me closer to home though, so I decided to move back. I'm still learning a lot at Dr. Patel's."

"Well, you know, Malik, many of our employees work remotely now. With someone like you, it wouldn't be a problem at all to get you set up working right out of your home."

Malik smiled politely, sitting up straight in his seat. "I appreciate it, but I'm great where I am."

Roy's mouth smiled back, but his eyes communicated something different, something uneasy. "I'm happy to hear that, though it's a shame for us. You're a once-in-a-generation talent, Malik. If you ever change your mind," Chance stepped forward and placed a business card on the table before Roy continued, "you can reach out to Chance. We'll find a home for you."

"That's very kind of you," Malik said.

Malik stood back up and exchanged handshakes with the two men. They each nodded at Magaly before leading their group toward the front door.

After a few steps, Chance turned around abruptly and said, "Your previous internship sponsor spoke the world of you. He mentioned that you have some ideas that could be very beneficial to our company. If you come back, I'd love to give you everything you need to make that dream come true."

Malik grew stern. "Thank you for the generous offer, but I believe my previous sponsor gave you outdated information. My ideas weren't so special."

Chance shrugged with a skeptical look in his eye and continued on his way.

Malik watched Magaly, who was glaring at the CEO. Once the door closed behind the group, Magaly turned to Malik. "Man, they want you there, huh?"

"I guess so," Malik said.

"I bet that if you were to go work for them, they'd pay you whatever you wanted."

"Probably," Malik said.

"Why would you say no to that?"

"I don't have the best memories of that place. Plus, I'm much happier where I am now." Malik looked down, thinking the groove was officially ruined. "Do you mind if we talk about something else?"

"Sure." Magaly paused, and then said, "Hey, do you want to get out of here? We should get a change of scenery."

"What do you want to do?" Malik asked.

"I don't know," she said. "Surprise me."

"There's a club with good music just off the BeltLine. How do you feel about dancing?"

48

MALIK AT THE CLUB

MALIK HAD NEVER BEEN TO THIS CLUB BEFORE, BUT HE TRIED HIS BEST TO make it seem like he had. Ronnie had told him that the main entrance was around the side of the building, and it looked like a large garage door. Malik led Magaly around the corner and saw the open garage door with a couple of bouncers posted near the entrance. *Just like Ronnie said.* Malik and Magaly approached and handed their identification cards to one bouncer, while the other bouncer reached for a couple of nose swabs. The pair pulled down their masks while the bouncer took samples from each of their nostrils. The bouncer put the swabs into the portable viral test kit and, after a few seconds, said, "They're good."

The first bouncer handed their ID cards back to them, and Malik held up his phone to pay the entry cover. The entrance was a long, gradually declining concrete driveway that led them to an underground level. The space was dark, but the walls and bar were illuminated by neon paint and black lights. There were two dance floors, each playing a different style of music. Malik's ears were still adjusting, but Magaly caught his attention. She motioned around at the other patrons, pulled out her phone, and put it within inches of her eyes. Malik glanced around and saw what she meant. Everyone who wasn't dancing had a blue light reflecting on their faces from the light of their cell phones.

Malik and Magaly shared a look and each smiled. Then he leaned over and shouted, "Would you like a drink?"

Magaly nodded her head, pulling down on his arm to bring him closer to her height, and said, "Vodka cranberry, please."

Malik almost missed her order. The scent of her perfume was distracting, and her lips were so close to his ear he thought she might have kissed him. "Oh, okay," he said, trying to pull it together.

The couple were migrating toward the bar when somebody jumped in front of them.

"Hey, you two! I'm so happy that you got this guy out," Ronnie said as he threw an arm around Malik's shoulder. "I usually have no luck convincing him to come out, but when you agreed to go on a date with him, he was so panicked that he didn't know where to take you." Ronnie gave Malik a wink and said, "I told him we'd make him look cool."

Malik elbowed his friend. "Magaly, this is Ronnie."

Before Magaly could answer, Ronnie stuck out his hand and said, "You must be the nurse I've heard so much about."

Magaly laughed and shook his outstretched hand. "Oh, he's been talking about me, huh?" she said.

"Well—" Malik stammered.

"Malik, weren't you going to go get us some drinks?" she said, letting him off the hook with a playful smile.

"Yeah, Malik, why don't you go get some drinks," Ronnie said. "You can put them on my tab."

"I'm buying top shelf," Malik said in vain as the two walked off. Malik could see Ronnie running his mouth and Magaly's head falling back in laughter. *Lord only knows what that dude is telling her.*

Malik waved his hand casually to get the bartender's attention. She came over, and just over her shoulder, something caught Malik's eye. There was a man in a blazer and button-down shirt across the bar staring at him. The stranger wasn't trying to get the bartender's attention, and he didn't have a drink. He just stood there, staring at Malik.

Malik then realized that the bartender was talking to him. "What can I get you?"

"Oh, uh, one vodka cranberry and one gin and tonic, please."

"What type of vodka?"

"Whatever you recommend," Malik said as he glanced back toward the mysterious man, who was now gone. Malik got the drinks and reviewed the bill on the screen. He nodded in agreement as he leaned closer to the screen and spoke the command, "Approve the transaction."

Malik brought the drink to Magaly, who was standing at a high table with Ronnie, both of whom were laughing hard.

"I had no idea," he heard Magaly say. "He never said a word."

"I'm telling you," Ronnie said, "this dude has had a crush on you for such a long time."

Malik handed Magaly her drink. "What are you guys talking about?"

"Oh, nothing." Magaly smiled and took a sip of her drink.

She doesn't seem scared off. Malik couldn't help but smile back.

"So, as I was saying, Magaly," Ronnie cleared his throat, "thank you for convincing Malik to grace us with his presence. He never comes and hangs out anymore."

"That's not true," Malik said.

"Oh yeah," Ronnie responded, "when was the last time you and I hung out?"

Malik was about to speak when Ronnie interrupted. "Riding around the city doesn't count."

"Well, I've been working a lot," Malik said.

Ronnie looked at Magaly. "We used to hang out all the time, but then after Callie…"

"I know," Malik said, cutting him off.

"Well, you're still coming to volunteer tomorrow, right?"

Malik sucked his teeth and averted his eyes.

"You said you would be there," Ronnie reminded him.

"Volunteer, to do what?" Magaly asked.

Ronnie responded, "Callie always wanted to clean up the woods around Mason Mill and Medlock Parks. Her dad started an annual event in her honor. Tomorrow we're going to clean up that scrapped car that she was so obsessed with."

"Those woods were always your thing," Ronnie added, with intentional eye contact, as if Malik needed reminding.

"I'll go with you, Malik," Magaly offered.

"Really?" he said.

"Of cour—" Magaly started to say before Ronnie interrupted.

"Great! We'll be out there at nine o'clock." Ronnie then suddenly looked past them. "Okay, I've got to go. There's someone I've been waiting to see." He caught Malik's eye one last time. "You'll be there, then?"

"I will," Malik said.

"Good." Ronnie gave Magaly a conspiratorial look. "Malik always keeps his word."

49

THE MOB

MALIK'S SHIRT WAS SWEATY, AND HIS LEGS WERE BURNING, BUT HE WASN'T leaving that dance floor if Magaly was out there. Every time Magaly danced close enough to brush up against him, he thought, *This is the most fantastic night of my life.* They had switched to soda water a long time ago in anticipation of needing to drive at the end of the night. Malik hadn't expected to feel this comfortable with her. It was as if they had their own rhythm. The night couldn't have been going any better when the music stopped abruptly, and the DJ spoke.

"Attention, everyone, we apologize for the inconvenience, but please put your masks on and move toward the emergency exit."

"Wonder what's going on?" Magaly said. The bright lights came on, and Malik knew that something serious had happened. He scanned the bar with the light now exposing all the dinginess the darkness had been hiding.

Ronnie was out of breath when he got to them. "You've got to go, bro." He held up his phone. "There's a photo of you posted on the contact tracer site. It's saying that you may have some mutated strain of the virus."

"What?" Malik was stunned. *This can't be right.* "Magaly, does your app say the same thing?"

"I don't have the app," she said.

Malik stared at Ronnie's phone, trying to process what he was seeing. "How—" he started to say until he felt Magaly tugging on his shirt.

He looked up to see several people looking from their phones to him and whispering to each other with panicked expressions. Malik noticed someone move toward him and stop at a distance. It was the man in the blazer from the bar, who was now standing between Malik and the exit. Malik's instincts kicked in, evaluating exit options. Malik scoped the main entrance and saw Biotech tracers marching down the ramp. His heart was pounding as he contemplated what to do. In a room of commotion, a very still person caught his attention.

There was a woman behind the bar with curly, light brown hair and green eyes who was looking directly at Malik. He recognized her from somewhere, but he didn't have time to think from where. The woman turned, while holding Malik's gaze, and disappeared behind a wall on the other side of the bar. Malik grabbed Magaly's hand. "C'mon, I think there's another way."

Malik ran behind the bar in pursuit of the curly-haired woman. Once behind the bar, they went down a hallway filled with liquor cases. They passed by an office, a kitchen, and a walk-in freezer. Malik paused. "What next?" he whispered. Then he heard what sounded like the hinge of a door. They followed the sound, and Malik was about to push the door open when Magaly stopped him. She stepped in front of him and opened the door, just enough to stick half of her body out. *She's protecting me.* Malik felt his chest tighten. After looking around, she said, "Okay, we can go now."

They hurried across the parking lot where Malik's car was parked, both looking back toward the club. Malik looked forward just in time to avoid colliding with a homeless woman pushing a shopping cart. "I'm so sorry," Malik said quickly as he danced around the woman. That was when he caught sight of his car, which was surrounded by a Confidence Biotech vehicle and two tracers.

"What do we do now?" Magaly whispered.

"I—I'm not sure."

"Stop right there," one of the men shouted and walked in their direction, and Malik's body locked up. "What are you doing back there? Come here, and let me scan your ID."

It was too dark, and the Biotech tracer was too far away to recognize Malik's face. As the Biotech tracer approached him, Malik saw the other one walking closer as well.

Magaly stepped forward, got out her phone, and pulled up her ID code. The man scanned it, never taking his eyes off Malik. "You're all clear. Now yours." The Biotech tracer continued slowly toward him. Malik could see the green scan bar on the screen of the Biotech tracer's mobile scanner.

Malik's hands shook as he tried to pull his phone out of his pocket. His lucky pen wasn't living up to its name, as his phone kept getting caught on it. Malik pulled the pen out of his pocket, making room to grab his phone. As Malik went to put the pen back in his pocket, the Biotech tracer lunged forward, reaching for Malik's hand that held the pen, and shouted, "I've got it!"

Everything happened quickly, but the next thing Malik knew, he was face down on the ground. The Biotech tracer had his knee in Malik's back, one hand holding Malik's arm out, while he used the other to try to pry the pen out of Malik's hand.

"Get off him!" Magaly screamed.

Malik didn't know why, but he knew he couldn't let the pen go. He clenched his fist harder.

As the contact tracer tried to wrestle the pen away, he said, "Just give it up, kid, and this will all go away." His partner was on the radio saying, "Target acquired."

Malik clenched his eyes tightly, hoping this was all just a bad dream. All he wanted was to open his eyes, wake up in his bed, and go spend time under his trees.

"Get off him!" Magaly screamed again. "You have no right!"

Magaly's screams brought Malik back to the moment, which, sadly, was no nightmare. The man's knee was heavy on his back. Malik tried hard not to inhale the fumes from the tar and oil that covered the asphalt parking lot.

Out of nowhere, a dark shadow entered his view. He watched as it ran down the street. The speed and stature reminded Malik of an Olympic sprinter or a gazelle trapped in a sprinter's body. At the same time, the tracer's radio static got incredibly loud, forcing him to adjust it, which took a little pressure off Malik's back.

Malik heard a voice on the radio say, "I repeat, we lost the target. He got away. He's heading toward Freedom Parkway."

"What the—" the contact tracers started to say, and then Malik felt an intense burst of wind. The weight lifted off of his back, and Magaly was by his side in an instant, helping him stand up. They looked around to find both tracers lying on the ground several yards away.

Now on his feet, Malik asked Magaly, "What happened?"

"I don't know," she said as she stared at the men. "He just flew off you."

A woman's voice came from behind them. "Our distraction won't last long." It was the curly-haired woman from Malik's dreams. She knelt, picked something up from the ground, and handed it to Malik. It was his pen.

"You're," Malik hesitated before saying, "Evelyn."

Evelyn nodded, but kept her serious tone. "You've got to go." She looked past them, and Malik followed her gaze to the two men getting up. "I'll take care of them." Evelyn nodded her head in a single quick motion up to the sky. As she did, two large chunks of asphalt rose out of the parking lot. Then with a wave of her hand, they crashed against the helmets of the contact tracers, knocking them both back to the ground.

"Now go!" she shouted.

Malik and Magaly did as she said. After getting enough distance from the scene, they transitioned from a run to an up-tempo walk.

"Who was that?" Magaly asked.

"I don't know," Malik said.

"How do you know her name then?"

"She's been in my dreams."

Magaly shook her head. "I don't understand, but I guess now's not the time. We need to figure out where we are going."

"We're in the Highlands, right? Dr. Patel lives in Morningside. His house is a couple of miles away; we can go there until we can figure out what to do next."

50

THE WALK TO DR. PATEL'S HOUSE

MALIK ALWAYS APPRECIATED THE VIRGINIA-HIGHLAND AREA, WITH THE older homes and tree-lined streets. It was an active area, with a few strips of shops and restaurants. When he was younger, his dad used to bring him here for festivals with live music and artists. It was odd to be this deep in the neighborhood so late at night. He wasn't used to seeing it so quiet.

"So..." Magaly's voice interrupted his thoughts. "How do you know Ronnie?"

"He and Callie used to kind of date," Malik said.

Magaly laughed. "How can two people kind of date?"

Malik was silent, thinking about how to respond. "Can I ask you something?"

"Answering a question with a question?"

"No, I'll answer, but I just want to know something first."

"Ooookaaaay," Magaly said, eyeing him.

"Why didn't you leave back there? I mean, those guys were after me, not you," Malik said. "You could be home by now, out of this mess."

"Oh," Magaly's expression lightened, "because I like you. And I don't trust those Biotech tracers. I never have. Call me paranoid, but I probably got it from my dad. Once ConBullish..."

"ConBullish?" Malik said.

"Oh, sorry, I know you worked for them and everything, but that's what my dad called them."

"Why did he call them that?"

"My dad swore up and down that they were just a bunch of con artists."

"Is that so?"

"Yeah. Did I ever tell you that my aunt was an architect?" Magaly asked.

"I didn't know that," he replied.

"She had this incredible imagination. She saw things in a different way than everyone else."

"Did she design anything here?"

"More so overseas. She designed all sorts of things. She and my uncle had a business together and were inseparable. But there was an accident, a long time ago now, and my uncle went into a deep coma. My aunt didn't handle it well. Most people thought she lost her mind, but my dad knew that she just needed to find a way to get her mind back by focusing on creating. My aunt ended up seeking professional help at a Confidence Biotech psychiatric center, but instead of getting better, she rapidly declined. She lost her ability to communicate with people. Before long, she was just sitting there in a chair all day in front of a screen. Dad always believed that they did something to her, but he could never prove it.

"Once Confidence Biotech took over the contact tracing business, staffed a bunch of questionable ex-cops, and went from simply tracking people to aggressively quarantining them, Dad felt vindicated. That's another reason I stuck around; I don't trust them. I figured you might need a witness. But, it was mainly because I like you."

"Cool," Malik said. "Thank you." Malik stared down at the street, trying to hide his smile.

"Cool, thank you." Magaly used a deep voice, mocking Malik. "A girl tells you that she likes you, and that's all you can say."

"I—I like you too."

"That's better," Magaly said.

"This is kind of my first real date," Malik said.

"I know." Magaly smiled. "Why is that, though? I figured all the girls were after you in school."

"Me?" Malik said, surprised. "Why?"

"You were always smart, kind, and not too hard on the eyes either."

"I could say the same about you."

"Well, this isn't my first date though." Magaly gently nudged him with her shoulder as they walked in stride. "I haven't forgotten. What's up with you and Ronnie?"

"I have only had two good friends my entire life," Malik said, "not including my parents: Callie and Ronnie. Ronnie came around because he really liked Callie, and Callie and I were always together, so he got two for the price of one."

"That seems like a pretty small circle. Why is that?" Magaly asked.

"I don't have an online presence, which means I grew up pretty sheltered, I guess."

"That's right," Magaly said. "I was going to ask you about that. I tried to look you up, but I could never find a profile or anything."

"Callie didn't either. It was great having Ronnie around because we caught a glimpse of everything through him," Malik said.

"Did your parents have the same opinions of social media as my dad?" Magaly asked. "He tried to convince me to get rid of my accounts. Although he never succeeded, I did limit my presence on social media."

"Sort of," Malik said as he rubbed the back of his neck. "Can I tell you a secret?"

Magaly stopped and searched his face, which made Malik's heart beat faster. "Malik, anything you tell me will always remain between us."

Malik nodded. "Here goes," he whispered. "I've never been sick before. Like ever."

"Never?" Magaly said.

"Nope." The two began walking again.

"You mean, you've never caught a serious illness."

"I've never even had a stuffy nose," Malik said.

"Wow, lucky you," Magaly said.

"Lucky-ish," Malik said. "I'm an ASIM."

"Are you asymptomatic, or do you have immunity?"

"The latter," Malik said.

"I have so many questions," Magaly said. "Umm… How did you find out that you could never get sick?"

"It started when I was in daycare, so maybe around two or three years old. Every kid in the daycare caught the virus, but I always tested negative. My pediatricians couldn't explain what happened. They said that I was lucky. My parents were worried that the government would come and take me away for tests or something. They decided to pull me out of daycare until I was old enough for kindergarten. That's when I met Callie. We hit it off because we both loved exploring nature and learning about creatures. We became best friends. Although we shared a passion for nature, we were opposites in health. She would get sick all the time; like her nose never stopped running." Malik laughed, thinking back to his friend's ever-present tissues. "When I never caught any of her colds, especially after spending so much time together, that's when my parents became suspicious."

"What made them worried about the government finding out?" Magaly asked.

"Probably similar to your dad, the aggressive quarantining that was happening. And there were the rumors that the government was considering allowing trials around antibodies in the blood plasma of kids."

"I remember that," Magaly said. "That was freaky."

"Yeah, and my dad took it to an extreme. Our entire family deleted all of our social media accounts. Say goodbye to the connected world. Although to be fair, I was young, so I didn't care. It only mattered later when I got to middle school."

"What was Callie's reason?" Magaly asked.

Malik swallowed. "When we were maybe nine or ten, she found out that she caught a mutated version of the virus. Dr. Patel had never seen it before. No one had. She had to go into an intense quarantine. It was wild," Malik said. "I remember when she got home, her room was like a literal bubble. Completely enclosed in plastic, and it was airtight. She had to wear these special masks to ensure that it didn't spread. Fortunately, I couldn't get sick, so it was perfect. Her parents moved their family next to us, and we spent our childhood exploring the woods near our house."

"Wow, did it stay that way for her?"

"As we got older, she still had to be more cautious than most, and of course, wear her mask. But she didn't require the full quarantine or sterile environment. It was her long-haul symptoms that were the biggest problem," Malik replied. "Seeing Callie like that got me interested in working at Confidence Biotech. They were supposed to be on the cutting edge of virology. I had been working on this idea that I believed could help cure the virus. Well, if not cure it, at least it would ease some of the severe symptoms."

"What was the idea?" Magaly said. "Is this what you've been researching at Dr. Patel's office too?"

"You're going to think I'm crazy," he said.

Magaly stepped in front of him and put her hand on his shoulder, stopping him in the middle of the sidewalk. "That word gets thrown around way too much." She put her hand down. "Now, try me."

Malik nodded slightly. "I think that the secret is in the trees."

"Go on," Magaly said, strolling again as she listened.

"As I said, Callie and I spent most of our time exploring nature. Almost all we did was roam around the woods, looking for trees that we could climb and spend all day in. Since we were the only ones around, Callie didn't have to wear a mask, and she felt great. By middle school we were reading books about trees, how they communicate with each other and support one another. They are stronger in clusters, so if one tree sends out a distress signal through the root system, other trees will send it nutrients. We also read that trees can emit aerosols that other creatures pick up on. If there's an invasive species, for instance, a tree can project a mist that attracts a predator of that species."

"That's incredible," Magaly said.

"Right? Well, we got even more invested when one of our favorite climbing trees had a terrible beetle infestation. We thought that it was going to need to be cut down. Our parents paid for the best arborists, but all of them said that there were too many and that the tree would inevitably die. The trees' natural defenses were too weakened.

"So sad."

"We were devastated. But then one day I had to clear out the attic at my grandma's house, and I found some old journals. There were notes about various plants and trees. I remember seeing her talk to the trees when I was a kid. I always thought that it was part of her medical condition. But according to her notes, she believed that they heard and responded to her in their way. Callie and I started researching that theory and found out that trees do respond to sounds and vibrations. If a tree hears the sounds of a threatening caterpillar that eats its leaves, it will release oil that the bug doesn't like to deter it. From what the arborists said, we figured that the tree was now too overwhelmed to do this by itself. So then we thought, what if we could find a way to trigger this tree and surrounding trees to emit an aerosol to attract the right predator? Maybe we just needed to find the right sound. I developed a computer code to play and record sounds at an infinite number of frequencies. We would spend every free moment by that tree, just playing different sounds, and waiting to see if something would happen. Then one day, sure enough, woodpeckers came and ate the larvae."

"Are you serious?" Magaly said.

"We were so excited." Malik felt his cheeks hurting from smiling. He hadn't talked about his history and details of this work with anyone since Callie. "It gets better. That journal I found was just the beginning. My grandma had all sorts of notebooks that my mom was going to donate to Georgia Tech. We weren't sure where they came from, and much of them I didn't understand, but they had a lot of interesting theories and thoughts in there related to nature. You want to hear something cool?" Malik paused, looking at Magaly's face.

"What's cooler than what you've just told me?" she asked.

"Did you know that the willow tree releases a natural painkiller into some water supplies?"

"Yes actually, the bark has a substance that converts into salicylic acid," Magaly said.

"Right, a natural remedy for pain relief and inflammation," Malik said. "We knew that we could get the medicine from the bark, but we wanted to see if there was another way to receive the dosage. I can't tell you how much time we spent under a willow tree, just playing different sounds."

"Did it work?" Magaly asked.

"Yes, to an extent," Malik said. "Certain sounds produced different aerosols that we were able to capture. We had Callie's aunt test them in her lab, and they did contain traces of salicylic acid. But we got small amounts at a time, with a ton of trial and error. That's why I wanted to do well at Confidence Biotech. I just knew that if I had their resources, we might discover something big."

"Why didn't you take Roy up on his offer to return then?"

"Because—" Malik stopped and looked around. "Wait, we passed the doctor's house. It's back there."

51

AT DR. PATEL'S HOUSE

MALIK'S FINGER WAS INCHES AWAY FROM THE DOORBELL WHEN THE FRONT door swung open. Dr. Patel was standing there in pajamas and a robe. "Hurry inside, you two." He closed the door quickly behind them.

"So you know that the Biotech tracers are after me?" Malik asked.

"An alert was sent out statewide saying that you were a potential carrier of a new strain of the virus," Dr. Patel said. "Knowing your medical history and your daily test results, I knew that wasn't true."

"Why is this happening?" Malik asked, almost rhetorically.

"It's not because of your alleged new strain of the virus," Magaly said.

"What do you mean?" Dr. Patel asked.

"They didn't seem to want Malik," she said. "They lunged after him as soon as he pulled out that pen. The same pen that guy tried to buy."

Malik had assumed that the Biotech tracers reached for his pen in error. Maybe they thought it was a knife or something. *Could it have been for the pen itself?*

"May I see the pen again?" Dr. Patel asked.

Malik handed it to him. Dr. Patel examined it and then nodded as if confirming a suspicion. "Yes, the Singularity Group only made a handful of these. They were testing the mycelium to see what could be made from it."

"So, is it something about the mycelium?" Magaly asked.

"Well, this pen is different," Dr. Patel said. "You notice how half of the pen is black, and the other half is white. The black part is holding ink, and it's stored externally in these grooves. It's a trade secret why the pen doesn't leak ink."

"Which is why I think it's cool," Malik said, "but why would they care?"

"Look at how thick this pen is. But why?" Dr. Patel continued, not awaiting their guesses. "Other pens need the space inside to keep things like the spring and the ink chamber. But for this pen, everything needed is on the outside. So haven't you ever wondered what's inside?"

"Not really," Malik admitted.

"Where did you get this pen?" Dr. Patel asked.

"It was my grandma's. She used to take it with her everywhere she went. Back when she was talking and had lucid moments, she gave me the job of making sure that I never let her lose this pen. She said that it was her lucky pen. When she stopped using it, it became my lucky pen."

Dr. Patel nodded and looked more closely at the pen in his hands. Then he squeezed each end simultaneously, and the middle popped ajar. He pulled the pen apart to expose a USB drive. "Malik, I need to show you something."

Dr. Patel walked them back to his home office. On his desk was the box from the storage unit that the delivery person dropped off earlier that week. Dr. Patel searched around inside and pulled out a magazine. He sifted through several pages until he landed on one. It was a man with dreadlocks sitting on a desk with his arms crossed. "Do you know who this is?" Dr. Patel asked as he pointed to the picture.

Both Malik and Magaly shook their heads.

"That is Zach Carver," Dr. Patel said, nodding as if the name should be familiar to them. "You know, the person who designed the system that the Biotech contact tracers use to identify who's infected."

"ZC," Malik whispered to himself. He didn't know why, but something made him take note of those initials. Malik knew the name, but he'd never seen a picture of him anywhere.

"These were items left behind by my previous partner, Dr. Wen Shen. She knew the virus better than anyone, and she didn't believe that Confidence Biotech found a cure. She believed that they were kidnapping people who were immune or were asymptomatic and using their DNA to create an antidote. She was constantly looking for proof."

"She's a legend." Magaly nodded.

"There's more." Dr. Patel pointed to a name on the page. "Look at who wrote this article."

Malik saw the name "Jessica Ifill." "Grandma?"

"It gets better." Dr. Patel lifted the magazine and shifted his finger onto a different spot on the page. "Look closely."

Malik and Magaly both leaned in. "What?" Malik wasn't sure what he should be looking at.

"No way," Magaly said. "Look at what's plugged into the computer."

Malik finally realized that the item plugged into the computer looked a lot like his lucky pen. Putting the pieces together, Malik said, "Zach built the program that is fundamental to Confidence Biotech's contact tracing capabilities."

"That's right," Dr. Patel encouraged. "Do you know what happened to Zach?"

"They say that he was a mad genius, and shortly after the system went live, he had a mental breakdown and was institutionalized."

"That is what they say, isn't it?" Dr. Patel seemed doubtful. "His technology was brilliant. I remember when it was first launched, you could identify anyone around the world based on what they exhaled." Dr. Patel's eyes grew wide. "It worked with such precision and accuracy. Then the rumors started spreading in the medical field that the system became less accurate over time. A few even questioned if the system worked at all. But by that time, the Global Breadth system was so ingrained in the fight to control this virus that anyone who questioned it was silenced." Dr. Patel looked at Malik.

"Rumor had it that Zach never fully trusted Confidence Biotech and that he built a flaw in the system, just in case his mistrust was founded." Dr. Patel put the pen back together and handed it to Malik. "If this is your grandmother's pen, then there could be something vital on it. It could even be the key to the Global Breadth network."

"Which would explain why those guys wanted it so badly," Magaly said.

THUD THUD THUD. The loud pounding on the front door made Malik and Magaly jump.

Magaly looked at Malik wide-eyed. "Do you think they followed us here?"

"If they are after that pen, then they are probably searching everywhere to find you two. It would only make sense to check here since I live so close." Dr. Patel replied, walking behind his desk, then grabbing a leather crossbody bag. He quickly threw the contents from the box into the bag. "Follow me." Dr. Patel led them downstairs to his garage and gave them a set of car keys.

"Your Jag?" Malik asked.

"They won't be looking for you two in a Jaguar, at least not for a while." Magaly sat in the passenger seat, and Dr. Patel handed her the bag. They heard the pounding on the door again. "I'll talk to them." He pointed to the small windows at the top of the garage door. "I'll turn those lights on when I answer the door. Once I turn them off, that means they're gone, and you are safe to go. You two need to go someplace where no one would think to look."

52

WHAT REALLY HAPPENED AT CONFIDENCE BIOTECH

Malik and Magaly sat in the car, staring at the light shining into the garage.

"I'm sorry that you've gotten involved." Malik sighed.

"None of this is your fault," she said.

"I don't know. I could have postponed after that weird contact tracer incident at the office earlier."

"Why would you have done that?"

"I wasn't completely honest with you about why I decided to decline that job offer."

Magaly was silent while Malik went on. "All I wanted was to work for Confidence Biotech, thinking it was my best chance at discovering a cure for the virus. It was my final year of college and my fourth year interning with them. My boss was awesome. I told him about my theory on the trees, and he took me under his wing. He helped me think of different ways to test my theory, but he insisted that we never do anything in the office. He lived in Westchester, New York, and every weekend, I'd meet him out there and we would spend the weekend running different simulations. He and I made huge strides on my project. He cautioned me that any work being done at corporate would be considered corporate property, even though we never used any of their resources, and he didn't trust that the company would do right by me. That should have been enough of a red flag about the company. At the end of every year, he made sure that I mailed the latest prototype and all my notes back home. Well, he insisted that I send everything to Callie's address."

"Why?" Magaly asked.

"I just always thought he was paranoid. But it turned out the company monitored the mail that employees, even interns, sent and received. Corporate espionage was a big deal."

"Were you able to confirm that your idea worked?" Magaly asked.

"We got close," Malik said, "but it was still quite laborious. I can get an antidote, aerosolize it, and put it into atomizers. But I can only do this in relatively small quantities, about one hundred to one hundred and fifty per week. And that's if I'm pushing it. I need to find a way to scale up. To reach more people."

"It sounds like you were on to something, though," she said. "Why didn't you and your boss branch out on your own?"

Malik's eyes watered as he shook his head. "My boss went missing."

"What? Do you think the company had something to do with it?"

"I know they did. You see, one day in the office, we were running some trials on people who were infected. My hazmat suit got snagged, and I was exposed to the virus. My mentor freaked out, but I told him that there was nothing to worry about because I was an ASIM. I went into his office afterward to complete an incident report. Everyone who was exposed to the virus had to fill one out. When I went into his office, he said he didn't have access to the incident report system. The next day he acted as if nothing ever happened.

"At his house that weekend, he told me that I shouldn't let anyone know that I'm ASIM, especially anyone at the company. And that was that, for a while.

"When there were just a few weeks left in my internship, my mentor and I decided I should send home the latest prototype, and then we'd have a celebratory dinner at his house. I went to the post office in the city and hung out around there for the afternoon. I caught a later train out, and when I got to his house, a couple of black vehicles were out front. I went ahead anyway and walked in through the basement door, thinking I'd do a little cleanup and make sure I wasn't leaving our workstation in a mess before dinner. Then I heard a conversation upstairs and started up just to let my mentor know I was there. He saw me and motioned me to head back downstairs. From what I could hear, there was an emergency in the lab, and they needed him and his wife there right away. They had received data that the next wave was coming, and it was more mutated than before. To keep everyone safe and ensure that the best minds were on it, they needed to isolate them somewhere else. My boss said that he needed to grab his notebook from downstairs. When he came down, he was worried and insisted that no matter what happened, I needed to go to work and finish my internship as if nothing happened. No one must know that I was at their house that night or ever. He said that he feared that the company found out that he and his wife were ASIMs. He went back upstairs, and I never saw him again."

"What do you think happened?" Magaly asked.

"There were rumors about the cure to the virus being in the plasma of people who are ASIMs and that Confidence Biotech was trying to identify the gene. Have you noticed how rare it is to find people who are ASIMs now?"

"I haven't thought about it," Magaly said. "But that sounds like something ConBullish would do." Magaly froze, then whispered, "Look!" She pointed at the window. "The light's out. We need to go."

The two drove around I-285 for a while. The roads were practically abandoned, which allowed Malik some time to think.

"Where should we go?" Magaly asked.

"We need to find a place where we can see what's on this pen," he whispered.

"We could head to my house," Magaly said.

"No, I've gotten you involved enough. I don't want them to have a reason to involve your family."

Malik focused on the road, trying to think. Magaly turned on the flashlight from her phone and looked through the contents of the bag.

"What else is in there?" Malik asked.

"There's an old notebook, a photo of the old office staff, and this. This is interesting—" Magaly's voice trailed off.

"What?"

"Didn't Ronnie say that you guys were going to clean up some old, wrecked car in the park tomorrow?"

"Yeah, why?"

"Is it blue?" she asked.

"Yes." Malik turned to Magaly. "How did you know that?"

"Because there's an old article in here about a crashed car in the Mason Mill trail area. The police were still looking for the car thief who stole a blue rental car and crashed it. They believed it was a couple of kids on a joy ride."

"Wonder why that's in there?"

"I'm not sure. Wait," Magaly said, "it says here that the rental company said that the car was registered to a journalist. There's a sticky note with 'J. Ifill question mark' circled. Do you think this could be your grandmother?"

"I'm not sure," Malik said.

"She was a journalist?"

"When she was young, but not since I've been alive. She still journaled a lot, but I thought that it was a way for her to deal with her dementia. She was diagnosed well before I was even born. There were a lot of references to ZC in her journals. Now I'm wondering if that stood for Zach Carver."

"This is creepy," Magaly said.

"I keep thinking about what Dr. Patel said about the Global Breadth system, that the algorithm perhaps wasn't complete, or had an intended flaw. I have an idea. We need to go to Callie's house."

Magaly pointed to the dashboard, and Malik followed her fingers to the green glow coming from the clock. 12:43 AM.

"It's way too late to go there, right?" Magaly said.

"No, we should be good." *That's the only place I know I can go this late.* "Callie had the same computer as I do with a port like this."

Malik parked the car on a darkened street with a wooded area on one side and houses facing the woods on the other.

"Where are we?" Magaly asked.

Malik pointed down the street. "We are at Callie's house."

"Which one?" Magaly asked.

"It's down the street and around the corner."

"Just trying not to draw attention?"

"Yeah, and if we parked on the other side, we would have passed by my house, and I'm not sure if the Biotech tracers are watching it. Ready?" Malik opened the car door, took the bag off Magaly's lap, and got out.

There were no clouds in the sky, and the full moon was bright, providing all the light they needed. Callie's house sat atop a slight hill. As the two approached the hill, Malik spotted the dim blue glow from the living room windows. He paused, and he felt Magaly stop moving too. "Callie's mom always falls asleep in front of the TV," he said. "There." Malik pointed as if Magaly could see his hand. In the distance, he saw some movement in the kitchen. "That's Aunt Lily. She's a night owl and is always on the phone with someone." They watched as she opened the refrigerator door, took something out, and closed it again.

"Okay, let's go," Malik said before he moved again. Rather than heading directly for the house, he led them around the side. They walked to a side door and waited.

"Now what?" Magaly whispered.

There was a flowerpot next to the door. Malik bent down and reached his hand inside the clay pot. He pulled out a whistle and blew it.

The sound that came out wasn't what Magaly expected. "What is that?"

"It's a duck call," Malik said before he blew into the whistle two more times. He then stopped and waited.

"Are you sure we should be here?" Magaly asked.

"That car," he replied, "the blue one from the article, they are volunteering to clean up that car because Callie was obsessed with it. Every time we would walk by it, she'd rattle off some new theory about how it got there. Near the end, she became determined to learn the truth. Callie would go on these rants about VINs being missing and gaps in the police report." Malik laughed. "How she got access to those, I don't know." He paused as he thought about his lack of involvement in his friend's last adventure. "I barely listened. I—I was just so focused on trying to find a way to make the project viable."

He felt Magaly's hand touch his back. "It's okay."

He cleared his throat. "Callie was convinced that the car wasn't there from some botched robbery."

"Why did she think that?"

"Because it was a low-end battery electric vehicle in an area where there were way more valuable cars. So why go to the trouble? She told me that she found proof, but she was put on a ventilator before she had a chance to show me." Malik squeezed his eyelids tight, trying to prevent his tear ducts from doing their job. He shook the memories out of his head and inhaled deeply. "I haven't been to her house since."

53

***

CALLIE'S HOUSE

MALIK BLEW THE DUCK CALL ONE MORE TIME AND STOPPED WHEN HE heard a tap on the door.

"Wha—" Magaly started to say.

"Shhh," he said, holding his finger to his lips.

There was a tap on the door a second time. Malik tapped back, and then he heard the deadbolt turn.

"Malik! Come in, come in," Aunt Lily said. "What are you doing out there? And why didn't you text me? Nia has been worried sick about you. You're not answering your phone."

Malik pulled his phone out of his pocket. There were eighty-seven missed calls from *Mom*. "I forgot that I put my phone on silent. I didn't want to—" Malik started to explain as he walked into the house.

"Oh, you are lovely. I love those curls," Lily said to Magaly as she unconsciously touched the back of her own hair. "You must be Magaly, Malik's date."

"Hi, thank you, nice to meet you," Magaly said.

"Can you tell my mom that I'm fine?" Malik asked, squeezing Aunt Lily's arm.

"You better call her yourself. Biotech tracers are looking for you."

"We know," he replied. "They tried to grab me while we were out. I think I know what they want. I just need a little time."

Aunt Lily locked the door behind them. "What is going on?"

"I'm not entirely sure, but I think it has something to do with my grandma," Malik said. "Some Confidence Biotech guys tried to buy grandma's lucky pen, and I said no."

"Then the Biotech tracers tried to take it from him tonight," Magaly chimed in.

"I need to use Callie's computer to see what's on it."

Aunt Lily looked at her phone, "Nia's calling me again. I'll talk to your mom. Several of Callie's dad's guys are sick, so he is pulling a late shift tonight to cover. Her mom is pretty tired and won't hear much, so you should be good for a while. Do you guys need anything?"

"I need to use the bathroom, and water would be great," Magaly said.

"Of course," Aunt Lily said. "There's a bathroom down the hall on your right. And we keep packs of water down here, so feel free to grab as many as you'd like."

Magaly nodded and walked toward the bathroom.

"Caaaalllliiiiiieee," Malik heard a weary voice moan as he and Lily walked up the first flight of stairs.

"How's she doing?" Malik asked while looking at Aunt Lily.

Lily sighed and shrugged. "It's been rough. Negotiating the mounting medical bills is just," Lily rubbed her temples with her fingers, "painful, and it's forcing her to relive things that she'd rather not. It's taking its toll, but we'll get her through."

Malik walked toward the living room, and Aunt Lily stopped him. "She wouldn't want you to see her like this."

Malik nodded. He understood.

"Why don't you go ahead to Callie's room?" Aunt Lily said.

Malik tiptoed through the dark house and up the stairs to Callie's room. It had been a while since he was last there, but it looked the same. Malik took a minute to look at the collage of photos on her bulletin board. Malik's favorite picture was of him and Callie when they were maybe four or five years old. It was Halloween. Malik was dressed as a koala bear, and Callie was dressed as a bumblebee.

"Dude." Callie's voice made Malik jump.

"Where have you been?" Malik said.

"I can't believe you are hanging out with *Magaaaaly.*" Malik could just see Callie's smile in the dark room as she mocked him.

"So what?" Malik tried his hardest to pretend it wasn't that big of a deal.

"Oh, BS," Callie said. "Don't try to pretend like you haven't had a crush on her for forever."

"Now's not the time, okay," Malik said. "Something serious is happening."

"Well, then now is a perfect time. There's all this danger and tension." Callie hugged herself and laughed. "Yaaaay!"

"Shhh…" Malik said, trying not to laugh, and checking behind him. "Be quiet. You don't want to wake your mom."

"She's out for the count," Callie said. "I know what you're looking for. It's in the drawer."

Malik walked to the desk next to Callie's bed and sat in the chair. He opened Callie's computer while he searched the desk drawer. There was the old notebook with a green spine. "I'm going to need it for a while."

"I'm not going to need it," Callie said. "It's all yours now."

Malik pressed the power button, but the computer didn't come on. He decluttered the top of the desk to find the laptop's power source and plugged it in. Once it booted up, he inserted the USB drive but was disappointed to find it was empty. Deflated, he sat back in the chair, not sure what to do next.

"Malik," Callie said more softly, "there was more you were looking for, wasn't there?" She nodded her head toward a flip notepad next to the laptop. He opened it to find all her notes on the abandoned car in the Mason Mill park area. He flipped through it.

"I told you I had discovered something big," she continued. "I think that car was wrecked there for a reason—to be found by us."

"Why?" Malik asked.

"ZC," she said. "Zach Carver. His initials appear throughout your grandma's notebook. He also happened to live in the area where that car wrecked. I found his old address and walked from the house to the wreckage site. That small compact car was the perfect size to navigate that narrow trail. I spent hours looking around that wreckage site. I felt like an archaeologist. And believe it or not, I happened to find some proof." Callie nodded her head back toward the desk drawer.

Malik looked inside. "What? It's empty."

"Look harder," she said.

Malik pulled out the entire drawer, and a pen, much like his grandma's lucky pen, fell to the floor. This pen had similar grooves but was entirely off-white.

"I almost missed it," Callie said. "It blended into the ground like it was just an overgrown mushroom. If I didn't know what your grandma's pen looked like, I never would've found it. I get it now."

"Get what?"

"I get *it*. I understand my role now, and it's okay."

"But—" Malik started to say, but Callie cut him off.

"Shhh—" she said urgently. "Do you hear that?"

"Hear what?" Malik said.

"I think someone just pulled into the driveway." Callie rushed to the bedroom window. "Someone is walking up the driveway. You guys have got to go. Grab the laptop."

Malik did as instructed and started toward the door. He paused, turned back, and Callie was gone. He grabbed the laptop's charger, some headphones, and a long speaker. Malik placed them in the bag strapped around his chest and quickly walked down the steps. He found Aunt Lily back down in the basement just as he heard the doorbell ring.

"Who else would be coming here at this time of night?" Aunt Lily said.

Ding dong. They heard the doorbell again.

Magaly peeked into the hallway, looking to see what they would do.

"Caaalliiie." The three heard Callie's mom again. *Poor woman.*

"You've got to get up there," Malik told Lily. "It might be Biotech tracers."

"How would they know to come here?" Aunt Lily asked.

"Maybe your call with my mom?"

Lily winced.

"It's okay, we've just got to get out of here. I'm sorry that we came here and got you involved."

"Hey, Malik," Aunt Lily touched his shoulder, "it's okay. Callie loved you like a brother, and I love you like a nephew. Take this," Aunt Lily gave Malik her phone. "I'll go distract them. You guys wait here and stay quiet."

Malik and Magaly were quietly waiting in the dark. Malik attempted to monitor his breathing but found it hard to stay calm.

"I'm sorry to have gotten you involved," Malik whispered to Magaly. "You're going to be okay, I promise."

Magaly nodded and gave an understanding smile.

Malik and Magaly looked toward the door when they heard Aunt Lily shout, "Okay, let me just get my phone. I'll text him. He always answers."

Aunt Lily came back. "I need my phone back, and you guys have got to go. Two guys, dressed in suits, are outside the door, and they are looking for you."

Malik handed the phone to Lily, and she quickly returned upstairs. Malik and Magaly escaped out the same basement door they had entered and ran down the street to Dr. Patel's car.

They jumped in the car, and Malik pressed the button to start the engine. Then, suddenly, the block seemed to light up. SUVs were not only out in front of Callie's house, with their headlights on bright, but more were showing up at each corner.

"They're blocking all the streets," Malik said as he looked back and forth between the rearview mirror and the windshield.

"What are we going to do?" Magaly asked.

"I have an idea." Malik kept their lights off and turned into the woods.

"What are you doing?"

"There's an access road down here for people who maintain the nature preserve. It goes all the way through and comes out near Highway 78," Malik tried to say as he and Magaly bounced around in their seats. *Dr. Patel will be so mad.*

"Look," Magaly said, pointing to distant people walking with flashlights in the nature preserve.

"That's okay," Malik said and kept driving. "See," he said as they got on the access road, "they won't be able to see past the bamboo growth. Plus, if they are on foot, it should take them some time to catch up."

They drove for several minutes before Malik turned on the headlights. "They shouldn't be able to see us here. We are almost to the highway. There." He pointed to a steep hill up ahead.

"I don't know if this car can make it," she said.

"It has to," Malik replied as he stepped on the gas pedal as hard as he could. *We're going to make it,* he thought as they lurched up the hill. Suddenly, Malik heard metal scraping metal. *That's not good.* They jerked forward, and the airbags deployed, protecting them from cracking their heads against the dashboard. Once they had settled from the impact, Malik tried the gas pedal again, but they weren't going anywhere. The cab of the car had filled with smoke.

They stepped out of the car, and Malik saw that the tires were caught on a wire fence. "Hmm, I never noticed that fence there before."

"Well, you've never had to drive up this hill before," Magaly said.

"Yeah, maybe."

"Do you think anyone heard that?"

"I'm not sure." *I hope not.*

"Now what are we going to do?"

"We're close to a major road. Maybe we could get someone to call a tow truck or something," Malik said.

54

WAITING FOR A TOW

Malik stayed just out of sight while Magaly stood on the side of the highway, waiting for a car to flag down. There was no one on the road in either direction.

I can't remember the last time I was out this late at night. "This must be the worst first date you've ever been on, huh?"

Magaly laughed. "It's unforgettable, that's for sure. So, do your parents know about your research and how far you've gotten?"

"Yeah, they're supportive," Malik said. "If I think about it, all of this probably started with them. My parents are super into nature and instilled an appreciation in me at an early age. We've always done a lot of hiking and camping together."

"That sounds like a nice childhood."

"The best." Malik smiled. "My dad always insisted that was what kept him healthy, despite the prevalence of the virus. He had an interesting theory."

"Which was?"

"It was around the origin of the virus." Malik paused, waiting for her reaction. "Everyone knows that the virus originated from bats that lived deep inland in China. Of course, animals in the wild carry numerous viruses that, if exposed to mankind, would be devastating. This virus was one of them. Dad's theory was that the virus was nature's defense mechanism. When human beings moved too far into areas that supported Earth's ecosystem, the virus was released to push them back. Think of this virus as a type of antibody for the planet trying to neutralize another virus that's spreading too much."

"And we are the virus," Magaly said.

"Humanity on Earth is a pretty invasive species if you think about the massive deforestation, pollution, and other destruction of nature," Malik said.

"Fair." Magaly nodded. "What about your mom?"

"This is a shared interest for them. My mom grew up spending her time in the forests, but old-growth forests. She is on another level about how magical the trees are." Malik rolled his eyes. "That's why my parents bought a house in this neighborhood, close to the nature preserve. My parents loved that most homes in the area came with huge old trees. Our house has two white oaks that are at least three hundred years old."

"Sounds perfect for you guys."

"Absolutely. I can even do some of my work in our backyard with our trees, which is nice."

"So did Callie stay involved in the work, or did it become your pet project?"

"She stayed involved as long as she could," Malik replied. "We tested aerosols on her. The more we experimented, the less she coughed. She even got to where she could go on runs—that's how much her lungs strengthened."

"Wow! I have not seen patients who can do that."

"We were also fairly active and spent a ton of time in fresh, clean air. But, that's what inspired us to try to fully build out the technology." Malik stared off in the distance. "I went to school to study business and understand how to market and sell the technology. Callie studied Forestry at Northern Arizona University. She planned on getting a PhD."

"What happened?" Magaly said.

"No one knows. Callie was back home, applying for PhD programs, when she had trouble breathing. Her health faded pretty quickly. Most people say she was lucky to have lived as long as she did. After that, I felt I owed it to her to finish what had been our life's work."

Headlights flashed the area, and they both turned to see a truck slowly heading their way.

The truck looked old, like it was from before all the carbon emission and vehicle electrification laws were established. But, it looked like it was made to drive through a brick wall and keep on moving.

The truck pulled over and came to a stop a few feet in front of Magaly. Malik stepped out in front of Magaly and stood between her and the truck. The headlights were bright, and Malik couldn't make out who was in the driver's seat. He saw a large shadow as the driver's side door opened and someone stepped out.

"You guys need some help?" Malik heard the deep voice say. It sounded like the voice of a man who is never in any particular hurry.

"Yes, please," Malik said. "I accidentally drove my frie—" Malik caught himself. "We got stuck on the fence."

Malik saw the man's shadow pause, likely looking over at their car. "Well, I've seen worse."

The man continued to walk forward and was illuminated by the headlights. He was tall and thick, like he could have been a former bodybuilder or defensive end. He was wearing a short-sleeved shirt, jeans, boots, and a mesh baseball cap. His arms were covered in tattoos.

"I may be able to help. This old thing here is stronger than she looks." The man extended his hand to Malik. "I'm Vau. Nice to meet you."

"I'm Malik," he said, "and this is Magaly."

Magaly nodded, and Vau shook her hand as well.

"You guys want to hop in, and we can see about rescuing your car?" Vau said.

55

LESSONS FROM DREAMS

Vau maneuvered the truck into the best position he could and then hopped out to connect a cable to their car. Malik and Magaly waited in the cab of the truck. It smelled of oil and had the gear shift on the floor, requiring Magaly to lean her legs against Malik's. He wasn't going to complain. Malik stared at the roof of the truck, trying to focus and think about what to do next. Should he call an attorney? Would the police help? Everyone knew that if you went to a Confidence Biotech quarantine center, you likely wouldn't return for months, maybe longer. Those who came back were never the same, Malik had heard.

"There's something that I just can't get out of my head," Magaly said, breaking the silence.

"What's that?"

"You said that the lady from outside of the bar was from your dreams."

"It's strange, I know. I've always had pretty wild dreams. But lately, they've been much more vivid, and that Evelyn lady has been in them."

"What were the dreams about?"

Malik thought back. "In one, there's this wealthy lady from olden times, British aristocracy or something. I saw her as she developed a crazy rash or infection on her skin with massive red bumps." Malik got the chills, and the hair on his forearms stood up. "It looked painful. Then later she was at a mosque, and it appeared as if they were inoculating babies for the same rash."

"That sounds like the story of smallpox, or one of them. I've read about it in school. Lady Mary Wortley Montagu," Magaly said.

"I think Evelyn called her Lady Mary."

"Some say that she was the first Westerner to discover how Muslims in the Ottoman Empire performed smallpox inoculations."

Malik paused, and then shared, "There was another dream too."

"Oh yeah?" Magaly looked curious.

"It was about a cowboy who was selling cocktails at a rodeo. That one felt way different, but part of it stuck with me."

"What part?"

"He said that if they aren't going to help me, then I should do it myself."

"It has been said that dreams are your subconscious trying to tell you something. What do you think your subconscious is trying to tell you?"

Malik thought about it in silence, remembering the third dream. *Do you have what it takes to go all the way? Do you trust and believe in yourself?*

56

OUT OF THE DITCH

"ALL RIGHT," VAU SAID, CLIMBING INTO THE CAB, "I WAS ABLE TO PULL the car out of the ditch. You're pretty lucky. I'm not seeing any damage to the frame, which means that it's most likely not totaled. I want to bring it back to my shop to take a closer look. Does that work?"

"Yeah," Malik said, "that works."

"Is it your car?" Vau asked, raising an eyebrow at Malik.

Malik paused. He thought about lying but decided there wasn't much of a point. "No," Malik admitted, "it's not. A friend of mine loaned it to me. He has my car."

"And this friend? Who is he?" Vau asked, patiently awaiting Malik's response.

"He's my boss."

"You must have a pretty cool boss to let you borrow a car like this, huh?"

"Yeah, he is."

"That boss wouldn't happen to be Dr. Patel, would it?"

Malik was surprised and stayed quiet a moment.

"It's okay. He's a customer of mine." Vau looked out the front windshield and turned the keys. "Doc and I go way back." The engine was louder than expected and made it hard to hear any conversation in the cab of the truck. This was a welcome silence; Malik needed to think about what to do next. He wanted to check the pen Callie found but needed to find a moment of privacy.

After a few minutes, Magaly put her head on his shoulder and seemed to fall asleep. Malik couldn't help but smile, and he tried to stay as still as he could.

"Man," Vau shouted over the sound of the engine, "sorry your night had to end this way. I'm sure you had some other ideas in mind." Malik could see the wide grin on Vau's face.

"Oh, this evening got derailed a while ago," Malik replied, hoping not to wake Magaly.

"You two make a cute couple."

"This is our first date," Malik said.

"You could've fooled me," Vau said. "I mean, she stayed out with you this long. Plus, your car broke down, and she stuck around until someone came to help. It says a lot, right?"

I guess it does. "So, how bad was the damage?"

"I'm not sure yet. We need to get it to the shop and take a better look. What were you doing in those woods in the first place? I can't imagine that's what Doc had in mind when he let you borrow his Jag."

I'm a fugitive being chased by Confidence Biotech tracers for some unknown reason. And if they catch me, I'll likely never be seen again. Malik mustered up, "I got lost." After another moment's thought, he added, "Hey—um, maybe it would be a good idea if you just pulled over and let us out here. You can take the car back to the shop and call Dr. Patel to pick it up."

"What are you talking about?" Vau asked.

"Hey, man, you seem like a nice guy, and we don't want you to get into any trouble."

Vau's eyes were focused on the road. Malik wasn't sure what type of response to expect. "So is it fair to assume," Vau finally said, "that Doc gave you his car to help you get out of some sort of trouble?"

"That's right," Magaly spoke, her eyes still closed and her head on Malik's shoulder.

Had she been awake the whole time?

She said, "He gave us the keys and just told us to drive."

"Listen, you two, Doc is my guy," Vau said. "If he trusts you and thought it was important to help you, the least I can do is let you hide out at my garage until you figure out your next move."

"Are you sure about that?" Malik asked. "We are being chased by Biotech tracers."

"You can tell me more about it at my shop," Vau said. "Maybe there's some way that I could help."

"You'd do that for us?" Magaly asked.

"That's what I do." Vau nodded. "I help people."

57

BACK AT THE GARAGE

Vau's garage reminded Malik of what you'd see in the movies. The outside looked like a no-frills storage facility and scrapyard combined. The truck rolled to a stop in front of a sizable chain-link fence at least ten feet high that seemed to surround the entire compound. Just beyond the barrier stood a large metal building with several white garage doors. All entrances were closed but one. Vau stopped at the call box and said, "Open up." The gate slid open, and Vau pulled into the gravel lot toward the open garage door and parked the truck. "We do a night shift on Fridays for the late-night weekend accidents," Vau explained to Magaly and Malik. The three got out of the pickup to see someone walking toward them.

"What do we have here?" the man asked. He was slightly taller than Malik with brown curly hair and dressed in coveralls and boots.

"Tony," Vau said, "meet Malik and Magaly. They're friends of Dr. Patel's."

Tony seemed to assess Malik and Magaly and nodded. "What's up."

Malik nodded back, and Magaly said, "Hi."

"I found them on the side of the road," Vau explained. "Doc loaned Malik his car. They got into a little trouble and needed some help."

"The Jag," Tony said, seemingly impressed. He walked around the car, inspecting it. "It doesn't look like there's any major structural damage, but we will have to get it on the lift to check it out."

"How long will that take?" Malik asked. He felt his voice rise a little and cleared his throat.

"Why?" Tony asked. "Do you guys have somewhere you need to be?"

"Well," Malik said, "I— I—"

Vau cut him off. "They are in trouble with those clowns from Confidence Biotech. That's why Doc loaned them his car. I'm sensing a bit of panic in the kid," Vau said, looking at Malik. "I get it. You have no idea who we are, and we are about to put your only way out of here on a lift, stranding you here for the foreseeable future."

Malik didn't say anything. Vau was spot on.

"How about this," Vau continued. "Is there anyone you can trust to pick you up and take you someplace safe? Someone who isn't connected to any of this?"

Malik had been thinking about this all evening, and the same name kept popping into his head. He should've called him a while ago, even before tonight. The last time they spoke, it was a difficult conversation. It was Malik's fault, and he knew that. "I know one person I can call," Malik said.

"Who?" Magaly asked.

"Coach O," Malik said.

Magaly opened her mouth to ask more about him, but Malik rushed on, "I'll explain everything later, I promise." Malik turned to Vau. "Do you have a phone I can use?"

"Tony, do you mind getting that on the lift?" Vau asked, pointing to the tow truck. "You two follow me."

The inside of the garage was like a museum exhibit. There were rows of antique cars from various decades, all in mint condition, buffed chrome all around.

"I've never seen this many shades of green before," Magaly said.

"Neither have I."

"They don't make them like this anymore," Vau said. "Malik," he pointed to a glass window carved in a brick wall, "there's a landline phone in the office."

58

MALIK AND HIS MENTOR

After making the call, Malik walked back to the group. "He'll be here in about thirty minutes."

"Cool," Tony said. "Do you guys want a coffee or something?"

Magaly shook her head, and Malik said, "I'm okay too."

While Vau was examining the car, Magaly was sitting in a large chair, watching the news. She turned the TV off and looked at Malik. "Do you think your Coach O will be able to get us out of this mess?"

"I'm not sure, but he's the first person that came to mind when everything started to go down," Malik said.

"Why didn't you call him earlier?" Magaly asked.

"We haven't spoken in a while," Malik said.

"Why not?"

Malik sighed. "Well, I kind of let him down."

"How so?"

"He was a mentor of mine when I was transitioning from high school to college. He helped me figure out what I wanted to study, where I wanted to go, and what internship opportunities I wanted to pursue."

"Okay. So what happened?" Magaly asked.

"I was focused on Confidence Biotech, and he tried to get me to look at other emerging biotech companies. Around the time I got my first internship offer from Confidence Biotech, he had set up some coffee chats for me elsewhere. I didn't take them very seriously, and it probably didn't reflect well on him."

"Yeah, I can see why that would make him upset," Magaly said.

"He tried to talk me out of Confidence Biotech, but I didn't listen," Malik continued. "After that I was too wrapped up in other things to maintain the relationship well. Then once I realized that he had been right, I was too embarrassed to reach back out."

"I'm sure he understands you had to make your own choices and find your path," Magaly assured him.

"Yeah, he was easy on me just now. No questions asked, like he was expecting my call," Malik said.

"So, kid, what did you study?" Tony asked.

"Business mostly, but my favorite side study was cymatics," replied Malik.

"What's that?" asked Magaly.

"Learning new ways to better tie sound with results in the physical and natural world," Malik said, then looked around. *We have a little time to kill. Maybe I can show her.* Malik motioned to two flat metal plates and a long pipe. "Can I use these?"

"Sure," Tony said.

Malik grabbed one of the plates and the pipe and used them to create a makeshift music stand. Then he picked up a bag of kitty litter, checked with Tony, who gave him a nod, and sprinkled some of it on the second plate.

"Why do you have kitty litter in a garage?" Magaly asked.

"It's to help clean up spilled oil," Tony said.

Malik moved around searching for things. "Do you have any fishing line?" he asked.

"We do," Tony said as he disappeared down a hall.

Malik found a piece of wood about an inch or two thick and a couple of feet long. When Tony returned with the fishing line, Malik took it and quickly went to work connecting the fishing line to the piece of wood.

"Violà," Malik said.

"What is it?" Magaly asked.

"It's my beautiful violin bow."

Magaly looked skeptical.

Malik sat down next to his makeshift music stand. "Everything in the universe is moved by sound, vibrations, and frequencies that most human beings aren't even aware of. I believe that's why most people have a love for some form of music. I also believe that music can help do more than we know." Malik placed the string of the bow against the metal plate and made one quick movement, creating a sound like a violin.

"Did you see?" Malik asked. "The kitty litter on that plate moved to the sound." He played more notes, experimenting with these homemade instruments.

Magaly was watching as the kitty litter vibrated and shifted around the plate.

Malik focused hard and finally hit the note he was looking for and held it just long enough. To his delight, Magaly's eyes lit up as she saw the kitty litter form a vertical line in the middle of the plate.

"And different frequencies and vibrations can create different patterns," Malik said. "So this is one of my passions. If we crack this code, we will be one huge step closer to understanding how the universe works."

"This plays into your work with trees, right?" Magaly asked.

"Yep, and I've been putting it into use. Trying to make an impact."

"You've been putting the study into use or your actual treatment?" Magaly arched her eyebrows questioningly.

Man, she's sharp.

"The aerosols that help with the virus and its symptoms, and the atomizers I told you about—every other week or so, Ronnie and I ride around and hand out inhalers to the homeless around the city—that and masks. Ronnie's granddad uses the atomizers too. They're helping."

Magaly remained quiet but smiled at him.

Malik realized he hadn't done the one thing he needed to do. He grabbed the bag, pulled out the laptop, pen, and charger. "Is there someplace I can plug this in?"

Tony responded, "We can go into the office. If you need WiFi, the password is Archerspoint-seven-eight-three-exclamation point, capital A, and no spaces."

"It's also written on a Post-it note on the desk," Vau shouted. "Don't make things so difficult," he said, looking at Tony.

Malik took a seat and plugged the laptop in to charge. Magaly scooted a chair up next to him. Tony sat on the shorter filing cabinet against the wall. "So, Biotech tracers are after you, huh?"

"Unfortunately," Magaly said.

"What do they want?"

Malik and Magaly exchanged looks.

"Listen, you two, if I wanted to, I could've taken your stuff and called up those Biotech fools already. We don't like them any more than you do."

Malik sighed. "I think they want what's on this." He held up the white grooved pen.

Tony nodded. "A mycelium pen. It's been a while since I've seen one of those."

"You know what this is?" Malik asked.

"Of course I do. I know who invented them."

"You do?" Malik was surprised.

"You think I don't know who Zach Carver was?" Tony smiled. "Close your mouth, son; don't be so surprised. I know I'm a mechanic, but I know things about things. Do you know what's on it?"

"Not yet," Malik said.

"Then I guess you better see what it's all about."

59

MALIK ACCESSES THE SYSTEM

MALIK TURNED ON THE COMPUTER AND ENTERED CALLIE'S PASSWORD. Once the computer was ready, Malik plugged the pen into the USB port.

"It looks like there's just one large file on here," Malik said as he double-clicked the icon. The laptop's monitor briefly flickered black. Then a small pop-up window appeared.

Run the Global Breadth Program? Confirm or Cancel.

"This can't be," Malik said as his pulse quickened. He raised his finger and gently pressed the *Confirm* button on the screen.

Running System Diagnostics... Installing Program... Installation in Progress... Installation Complete.

Initiating Two-Factor Authentication.

The screen turned black again, and five small ovals in an arc pattern appeared on the screen.

"What do you think that is?" Magaly asked.

"I think it's for your fingerprints," Malik said. "The question is, whose fingerprints?"

"This was given to your grandmother, right?" Magaly said.

"Mm-hmm," Malik said.

"Try your hand," she said.

"My fingerprints are not a match."

"Maybe it's not just asking for fingerprints." Tony picked up the laptop and examined the bottom. "Is this screen one of those vision screens by the Singularity Group?"

"Yeah, it is," Malik replied, remembering when he and Callie upgraded and felt so fancy at the time.

"I read that some of the security programs for those screens can also tap into trace amounts of DNA from the skin on your fingers."

"Do you think this could have been set for my grandma's DNA?"

"Why not?" Magaly said.

Malik carefully placed his fingers and thumb in the ovals on the screen.

Scanning in Progress…

Scanning Complete… Approved.

The black screen vanished and was replaced with a map. There were various numbers and symbols at the bottom of the screen.

Malik felt a nudge on his shoulder. "What'd I tell ya, huh?" Tony said.

"Don't get too excited," Malik said, trying to figure out what he was looking at.

"Is that the entire globe?" Magaly leaned in to get a better view. "What do those numbers mean?"

The map of the globe took up the top three-quarters of the screen. The bottom quartile had multiple columns of numbers. The numbers ranged from zero to one hundred.

"I have no clue," Malik said, as a rectangular window popped up. *Enter Password.*

Malik was so excited that something was happening he forgot about the second part of the two-factor authentication. Malik's palms were sweaty. He was so close to having access to one of the biggest technological mysteries of all time. The only thing that stood between him and it was a password.

"Can you guess?" Tony asked.

"Ha, I wish." Malik sat there, deflated.

"What about your grandma? Where is she?" Tony said.

"She's at home, but she has severe dementia and hasn't even spoken in a long time." Malik rubbed the back of his neck, trying to think of his options. "Maybe if I just try, I could find a way to communicate with her. God, we're so close."

60

A NEW ARRIVAL

BANG! BANG! BANG!

Malik jumped in his chair when he heard the loud thumping on the garage door. *Maybe it's Coach O?* Malik, Magaly, and Tony made their way out of the office toward the garage door entrance, where Vau was already standing.

BANG! BANG! BANG!

"What if it isn't Coach O?" asked Malik.

"What time is it?" Vau said, looking at Tony.

"Not the time we want it to be," Tony said. "It's a quarter till three."

The pounding on the door sounded again. *BANG! BANG! BANG!* This time it was more forceful. Vau and Tony looked at each other.

Malik felt his panic returning. *What if it's tracers again?*

Vau looked at him and said, "Just sit tight and be quiet."

The banging stopped, and the group waited patiently to see if it would return.

Tap... tap... tap. Everyone but Tony made a one-hundred-and-eighty-degree turn back toward the office.

"Where is that coming from?" Magaly asked.

"It's coming from the back door," Tony said.

Malik stared down the hallway, and just as he was ready to turn away, he saw a dark figure. He took a step back until he recognized his former mentor. He sighed with relief. "Coach O!" Malik walked over to the man and shook his hand happily.

"Are you okay?" Ori asked.

"Yeah, I'm good." Malik looked back at Magaly. "Coach Ori, I'd like to introduce you to Magaly. We work together at the doctor's office."

"Nice to meet you," Magaly said with a smile.

"It's a pleasure," Ori said with genuine warmth. "I believe I'm acquainted with your aunt and uncle. It's good of you to still visit your aunt."

Malik watched Magaly, who appeared as stunned as he was.

"Malik, I'm glad you called."

Malik shook it off, focusing on the matter at hand. "Coach, I need your help."

"I've heard," Ori said.

"You're early," Vau said, looking at Ori.

"I know," Ori said. "That was not my intention."

Now Malik was confused again. *Do they know each other too?*

"What are you doing here now, then?" Tony asked.

Ori gave Tony a side glance and then shook his head.

BANG! BANG! BANG! It started again.

Malik looked around. *So was that not Coach O?*

Ori smiled at Tony and Vau and said, "Two for the price of one?"

"Technically, we do have two," Tony said as he tilted his head at Magaly and Malik.

"All right," Vau said, "ready?"

"Yeah," Ori said. "Open it up."

Tony checked his watch. "Five till," he said, looking at Vau. "Ori, I don't think—" Tony started to say, but Ori interrupted.

"It'll be all right," Ori said. Ori nodded his head at the door. "Go ahead; open it."

The sliding garage door at the front opened, and Vau quickly walked toward the office and vanished in the back of the building. Malik's eyes followed the bottom of the garage door as it rolled up, looking for a clue as to what stood on the other side. He expected to see several pairs of black boots, followed by tactical gear. To his surprise, it was a small woman, dressed in dirty, ragged clothes. She was quiet and still, hands resting on a shopping cart in front of her.

"Please, come in," Malik heard Ori say.

The lady smiled, and Malik recognized her. She was the homeless woman from the club parking lot earlier in the evening. He felt like he'd seen her before then as well. She pushed her cart into the garage.

"Do you know her?" Malik asked, looking at Ori.

Ori didn't answer him.

"I figured that you were in town," the woman said.

"How did you figure that?" Ori said.

She eyed Malik. "This young man's ideas and designs were…" the woman paused, "of another world." She reached inside a plastic bag from her grocery cart and pulled out one of his atomizers.

"Inspiration comes from everywhere," Ori said.

"This is true," the woman said. "There's been a lot of commotion lately about what he possesses, so I had to see it for myself." The woman observed Malik's face. He kept looking back and forth between her and the door that was still slightly ajar.

"Don't worry," she said, giving him a devious look, "everyone scatters when Wen Shen comes around. Everyone except Ori."

Wen Shen? Malik said, "Dr. Wen Shen? Did you work with Dr. Patel?"

The woman smiled. "Something like that."

"Would you like some tea?" Ori asked.

"I would love a cup of tea," Wen Shen responded.

Ori looked at Tony. "Do you mind?"

"I've got you," Tony said. "Standby."

Malik blinked and couldn't believe his eyes. The woman's appearance had transformed. Dr. Wen Shen was now attired in a beautiful red silk robe with golden lace detailing. Her black hair was now as elegant as her dress, pulled back at the base of her neck with a jade comb. A table was between them, set with a porcelain teapot with two matching cups.

Ori motioned his hand to the two empty chairs, and Wen Shen

nodded. Malik wanted to say something, but he just stood there, frozen in place, as the two took their seats.

"So, Ori," Wen Shen sat down and placed the atomizer on the table, "how do you know this young man?"

Ori leaned back. "How do you think I know him?"

"I think that he has a gift that you want to be realized on Earth," Wen Shen said.

Ori didn't reply.

"Is this true?" Wen Shen asked.

"Now, you know the work we do," Ori said.

"Hmmm," Wen Shen said, "but why would direct interference be permitted?"

"Let me ask you something. Why did you show yourself to Malik?" Ori said. "He saw you at the office and in the parking lot."

"He interests me," Wen Shen said.

"Why's that?" Ori asked.

Wen Shen got quiet and looked at Tony. Vau walked back into the room and leaned against the far wall. Wen Shen smiled and returned her attention to Ori. "You're not here for the boy, are you?"

Ori smiled in return. "Why would you think that?"

Wen Shen sighed. "You're here for me. What do you want?"

"We need you to lay off a bit," Ori said.

"Now you know this is a necessary part of the balance," Wen Shen said.

"We understand, trust me, we do," Ori said. "But, you must admit that the viruses and diseases that you command are getting out of balance."

"What makes you say that?" Wen Shen asked.

"They are claiming too many lives," Ori said.

"Humanity needed to be reined in," Wen Shen said. "The virus knows it can't survive without hosts though. It will prioritize survival."

"That's true, but we're coming up on the reset," Ori said. "I've been sent to represent the whole."

Wen Shen leaned back. "Aja?"

"That's right." Ori nodded.

"But she's been silent for a very long time."

"Oh, I know, which is why I'm here."

"You have my attention." She leaned back in.

"The system is at risk," Ori said. "Earth is shifting, and the humans aren't ready. All must move, or none will move. They must move forward with a common goal."

"I'm fully aware of this. They always come together in times like these though."

"They typically have, but right now, they are more divided than ever, and it's getting worse. People are fracturing into smaller groups in an attempt to preserve what little they have."

"That's their choice."

"True. The issue is that they think that's their only choice. Malik has been matched with a gift that could allow the human body a chance to coexist with the virus."

"I'm aware," Wen Shen said as she held the atomizer up, inspecting it. "But this is impossible. He won't be able to reach the number of people needed in time."

"I know, that's why I'm here. That's why we need your help."

"If they find a way to coexist, then who's to say that they'll miraculously come together and do what's needed?"

"Don't worry about that. For now, we just need to slow this virus down, if you'll allow it."

"You said that you have Aja's support?"

"That's right."

"Then why are you asking me?"

"We need to work together on this. Aja wants your support."

"I can't show them the source. Not this time. We're not talking about rats and fleas like the plague. This is different. This virus is quite keen on surviving."

"I know. We just need the mutation to slow down. Aja has agreed on an expedited delivery of an antidote."

"So you just need me to slow the mutation. That I can manage."

"Well, we also need you to help him see."

61

THE DRIVERS

Wen Shen addressed Malik. "Young man, please come here."

Malik blinked, and there was another chair at the table, steam curling into the air from a hot cup of tea positioned in front of it.

Malik slowly walked to the chair and sat down. He looked into Wen Shen's eyes and took a deep breath.

"Malik," Wen Shen said. "You've been hesitant to accelerate this invention, and I'm not sure why. I need you to be honest with me. What drives your fear?"

"What do you mean?" Malik replied. "I've been honing the technology for years, trying to do all the right things. What fear?"

"Let me start with an easier question," Wen Shen said. "Do you believe your solution works?"

"Absolutely," Malik said without hesitation.

"Then, what's driving your fear?"

"I just haven't found the right sponsor to help scale it. That's all."

Wen Shen gave him a skeptical stare, and asked, "What's stopping you?"

"Nothing. I'm working on it."

"I've been watching you, Malik. I see the fear in you, deep down. You fear being wrong, and even worse, you fear being right."

"You're wrong."

"Oh, am I?" Wen Shen's eyebrows rose, prepared to challenge his statement. "You're telling me that you aren't afraid that you'll get to the end of this road and nothing will happen? No widespread cure? That you'll be ridiculed?"

Malik stared at the cup of tea, no longer able to hold her eye contact.

"And you also have a thought in the back of your mind that if you are successful with the cure, that if you would've pushed a little harder, a little faster, then maybe, just maybe, you could've saved your friend?"

Malik felt his stomach clench. "You don't know me."

"I know you much better than you think." Wen Shen paused, letting Malik think for a moment before continuing. "Between your and Callie's families, you could have found a way to file for a patent based on what you currently have. You had come far enough to post your findings online and let others help take it further, but you chose not to. You've hidden under the excuse that you want it to be perfect, to ensure that it works before you tell others. So now you tinker with this gift all alone in the woods."

Malik steeled himself and looked back up at her. "What do you want from me?"

"Your friend Callie lived far longer and far better than anyone else who contracted that strain of the virus. You had a brilliant scientist take an interest in and help you develop your work. When you pursue something that you are passionate about, Malik, something from the heart, I promise you, you'll never be alone."

Malik cleared his throat. "I know it works, but I'm worried I won't be taken seriously on a broader scale without a PhD. I don't have the time to do that; that was Callie's job." He continued, "It took us so long to sequence each tree species to produce for the strain of the virus that Callie contracted. I always figured that there would be a magic frequency to get to, and once there, everything would unlock. But what if there isn't? I'm afraid that I don't have what it takes to keep going that long. Even more, I'm afraid of what will happen if I stop."

Wen Shen nodded. "There's a lot to understand about our

ecosystem. Since the very beginning, humans have acted as gardeners for the planet. In exchange for tending to and caring for the trees, they in turn provided humanity with what was needed to live a long and healthy life. Since the trees absorb carbon dioxide from all the air humans exhale, they are the best at identifying respiratory issues. They know what clean air should be. Your grandmother knew this and made sure that your mother Nia had early exposure so that it would be ingrained in both her and your DNA. Why do you think you developed immunity?"

Malik pondered this for a moment. He had always thought it was genetic but hadn't thought about it much further.

"But trees adapt and react more slowly than you do. And if you move tree-by-tree, species-by-species, it's hard to get the speed and scale you need. But above all, if they are under strain, it's hard for them to care for humanity as well, and they have been increasingly under strain with each passing generation." Wen Shen sighed, then took a sip of her tea. "Zach Carver, he was brilliant, and on the cusp of a critical moment for humanity."

"His Global Breadth system?" Malik assumed. "I can't tell how it fully works yet."

"He figured out that one must find the hub trees and then tap into the mycelia there. Then you are connected to what connects all trees. It's like a back door. His technology could propel human civilization to an entirely new level and lead to a new wave of thinkers and thinking. It could be used as a template for how to think differently about a problem."

"If only I can figure out the password," Malik said.

Wen Shen took another sip of her tea. "Remember, you're never alone, Malik, not when you are pursuing great things."

"You can't see it all yet, but we can," said Ori. "Now's the time to be brave."

Malik glanced at Magaly, who had been quietly watching, then looked back to Wen Shen and Ori and nodded.

Wen Shen got a twinkle in her eye and asked, "Was your plan to just continue to create these bootleg atomizers?"

"As many as I could," Malik said with a smile.

Wen Shen laughed. "We can't allow that, can we? Not if you're ready." She closed her eyes and rubbed her temples in small circles. "All right, all mutations are temporarily paused. If you can find a way to get the antidote you've created into distribution in the next forty-eight hours, I'll maintain the pause long enough for appropriate balance."

"Excellent," Ori said.

"What?" Malik said. "That's imposs—"

"Have faith," Ori said. "I have a plan."

Wen Shen looked at the clock. "It's after three in the morning," she said.

"That it is," Ori said.

"What are you leaving behind?" she asked.

"I'm not sure yet," Ori said. "I'm open to recommendations."

"You should include—" Wen Shen started to say, but Ori interrupted.

"Hold that thought, I'm expecting one more."

"Two in one?" Wen Shen said. "That's pretty aggressive."

"It's out of necessity."

Malik opened his mouth to speak, but no words came out.

62

ANOTHER CHAIR APPEARED

Malik noticed there were now four chairs at the table.

BANG! BANG! BANG! BANG!

Here we go again! Who this time?

This time, the noise got louder and was no longer isolated to the garage door. It reverberated through the entire building and did not stop. Malik felt the vibration in his stomach and braced himself in his chair. He watched as neither Ori nor Wen Shen reacted. They continued drinking their tea as if they were on a pleasant picnic. The banging grew louder and louder. Malik couldn't hear himself think. He tried to focus his gaze and his mind on the teapot in front of him. Just as everything blurred, Malik isolated other sounds, which allowed him to focus. He heard Wen Shen's teacup being placed on its saucer. He heard Vau's and Tony's voices in a side conversation. He heard Ori scoot his chair back ever so slightly. Malik's vision cleared up completely. The thumping on the walls was still loud, but it faded to the background. Malik heard Tony more clearly say, "Ori, check him out."

Ori was looking at Malik and smiled. "See, I told you he could handle it."

"Enough!" Wen Shen said. The loud thumping stopped.

The garage door rolled up quickly, and Malik saw a man in a black suit with a white shirt and a black tie. As he entered the garage, Malik recognized him. "Chance?" he said.

"Hello," Ori said politely. "We haven't met before."

Chance stared at Ori, silent. Then he turned his gaze to Wen Shen and asked, "What are you doing here?"

Wen Shen continued to sip her tea, not looking up at him. In a soft and steady tone, she replied, "I think the better question is, what are you doing here?"

Ori interjected. He spoke in a calm voice. "I, we, have been called in."

Chance looked from Ori to Vau and Tony and back again. "Ori?"

"Ding, ding, ding," Wen Shen said, still peacefully drinking her tea. "You didn't know you were in his web, did you?"

The man glared at Wen Shen. "Just because Ori decides to grace us with his presence doesn't mean anything."

Ori looked down at the table like he was thinking about what to say. Malik wanted to say something, but every time he opened his mouth, no words came out. He tried hard to speak, but his bottom lip just trembled. All the hairs on his arms stood up.

Ori, still looking down, calmly said, "I was called all the way in."

Chance took a deep inhale. "So what are you going to do?"

Wen Shen set her tea down on the table, then lifted a doughnut to her lips.

Is that chocolate? Malik's stomach rumbled.

"Stay with us, Malik," Wen Shen said.

Ori sighed. "I need to ensure the right events are set off in the right order."

"Too late for that, isn't it?" Chance asked. "Besides, I've just been fulfilling my purpose. Gabriel is aware of everything."

"I know, and I understand," Ori said. "But Roy has utilized you too much for the wrong purposes. Too much greed has taken him, his company, and society in a dangerous direction and thrown off humanity's course."

Chance focused on Ori's face. "How can you be sure of the right course and the right order of events?"

"I've examined them all," Ori said simply.

"You're telling me that you consciously traveled all the way through?" he said.

Ori nodded.

"You've seen it all?" Chance sounded incredulous.

Ori nodded.

"Not unscathed," Vau said from a distance.

"I'm so sorry," Chance said somberly. Malik thought his expression was one of shame.

"You did exactly what you were wired to do. Your job was to bring to life whatever was envisioned by the bold. Not all bold visions are kind. Unfortunately, this went way too far."

Chance's face hardened. "So, the reset is near? Enough will survive this next cycle. They've done it before."

"Not without Earth as well," Ori said.

"Is that possible?" Chance asked.

"Yes, unless we take direct action quickly."

"You've spoken to Gabriel?"

"Yes, and Aja," Ori confirmed. "Otherwise, I would not be here with the two of you."

Chance nodded toward Malik. "What's his importance to you?"

Wen Shen slid the atomizer across the table. "Haven't you been curious about these?"

Chance picked it up and inspected it. "It was you, Malik, who created this?"

Malik tried to talk but could say nothing still.

"Clever, very clever. You know, I saw the genius in you. Roy just… had other visions."

"Greed and power will do that to you," Wen Shen said.

"And then you must have known why Malik's pen was so important to Roy?" added Ori.

Chance gave a small nod, then held up the atomizer. "This alone isn't going to be enough."

"Wen Shen has agreed to temporarily pause mutations. And in the meantime, Aja is willing to help."

"Really?" Chance looked from Ori to Wen Shen. "Then, what do you need from me?"

"Two things," Ori said. "First, you need to get the Biotech tracers away from Malik's house. He needs access."

Chance closed his eyes and was silent for a few seconds. He opened them quickly. "Done. And the second thing?"

"Malik needs the password," Ori said.

"From Jessica?" Chance said.

"Yes."

"She was your recruit, wasn't she?"

"She is," Ori said.

"I knew there was something different about her. None of that felt right." Chance nodded toward Malik. "Are they?"

"They're prospects. They have lots of potential."

"What do you think of them?" Wen Shen asked Chance, tilting her head to Malik and Magaly.

"From what I can tell, they've got grit." Chance leaned in, looking Malik in the eye. "Listen, kid. Here's something that they don't tell you. Yes, you'll have all the access to amazing universal knowledge. But, you're not the one in control, and you won't be happy or proud of everything you help manifest. And that's something you have to live with."

Malik suddenly felt sorry for Chance.

"Okay, let him talk to his grandma," Chance said, looking at Ori.

63

FINAL CHAPTER

MALIK JUMPED AWAKE TO FIND HIMSELF SITTING ON THE LOVE SEAT ON the lower level of Callie's house. His movement woke Magaly, who had been resting her head on Malik's shoulder. She wiped the drool from her mouth, and Malik pretended like he didn't see.

Malik heard footsteps on the stairs and turned to find Aunt Lily quickly coming down. "The coast is clear. The Biotech tracers left. Your dad, Callie's dad, and a couple of neighbors are walking around the neighborhood. They'll send out a signal if the contact tracers return."

Malik's eyes were burning. He looked out the basement door window. It was still dark outside. He checked his watch. It was just before four in the morning. He rubbed his face, trying to collect his thoughts.

"I just had the wildest dream," Magaly said. "We were driving and wrecked in some woods nearby."

"Did we go to a garage with a giant man with tattoos?" Malik asked, not expecting her reply.

"Vau?"

Both of their jaws dropped.

"You gonna try to get to your house while you can?" Aunt Lily asked.

Malik and Magaly both looked down at the satchel. Malik frantically opened it but couldn't find what he was looking for. "Was that real?" he whispered as he looked up toward the stairwell.

It was like Magaly was reading his mind. "The pen in Callie's room?"

Malik darted up the two flights of stairs to Callie's room. The laptop was on the desk, unplugged, and the desk drawer was slightly ajar. He waited, half expecting Callie to appear again. Nothing. He ran toward the desk drawer, pulled it fully open, and stuck his hand inside. Malik felt around until his fingertips touched something with the grooved sides he knew so well. He slowly pulled his hand out to see the all-white mycelium pen. "How is this possible?" he whispered to himself.

"Find what you needed?" a voice came from behind him. He turned, expecting to see Callie standing in the doorway, but instead, it was Aunt Lily. "You should go."

Malik grabbed Magaly and his things, and they ran out of Callie's basement and up the street to Malik's home. They burst into the door to find Malik's mom waiting, strain and fatigue on her face. She squeezed her son tight. "I was worried sick about you. Are you okay?"

"Yeah, we are," Malik said. "Mom, this is Magaly." He turned to his date. "Magaly, this is my mom, Nia."

"Hi, dear," said his mom, pulling her in for a hug too.

Malik snapped back into the urgency of the moment. "I need my laptop."

"Why?" Nia asked.

He held up the white pen. "I think we found the missing link to the Global Breadth system. I think this could help find a cure for the virus." Malik started toward his room; Magaly and Nia followed. In his bedroom, he powered up his laptop and inserted the USB drive. As they waited for the USB files to open, Malik looked to his mom and said, "Did you know that grandma knew Zach Carver from the Singularity Group?"

"Your grandma knew all sorts of people, Malik. She was a famous journalist," Nia said, "and more."

The system popped up just like it did in his dream. *Run the Global Breadth Program? Confirm or Cancel.*

The heart thumped in his chest. He raised his finger and gently pressed the *Confirm* button on the screen.

Running System Diagnostics… Installing Program… Installation in Progress… Installation Complete.

Initiating Two-Factor Authentication.

The five small ovals appeared on the screen, just like in his dream.

"This is the best date I've ever been on," Magaly whispered over his shoulder. Malik looked up to see her face brimming with excitement.

Malik turned back and placed his fingertips on the screen.

Scanning in Progress…

Scanning Complete… Approved. The rectangular window popped up. *Enter Password.*

"We never got the password," Magaly said.

"Grandma has it," Malik said with confidence. He grabbed the laptop, and they ran downstairs to her bedroom. Her wheelchair was there, facing the window, but it was empty.

"Where is she?" Nia asked. "Mom!" she shouted while darting out of the room, Magaly in tow. Malik was right behind them but stopped as he got to the bedroom door. He hadn't spent that much time in his grandma's room, not lately anyway. Her room had a beautiful view of the old white oak tree in the backyard. Malik could see its entire canopy. He walked to the window and saw a small, frail figure with silver hair standing in front of the tree. She seemed to be talking to someone, but Malik couldn't see who.

He walked downstairs through the basement and outside to the tree. Although Malik couldn't make out what she was saying yet, his grandma was still having a full-on conversation.

Hoot! Hoot! The loud hoots of the owl startled his grandma, and she slowly turned around. She smiled at Malik with a look of recognition. She turned back and continued talking to a figure up in the tree's branches.

"I'm very proud of this boy," Malik heard his grandma say as he got closer. "I'm proud of you too. You had a tough part to play, and I know your father is going to be proud." Malik saw a little movement but could only clearly see the night sky through the branches.

"Come here," his grandma said, motioning him closer. "It's a rare opportunity that you have."

"Well done, Malik." The voice was familiar to him. It was one that he'd known since he was a little kid.

"Callie?" Malik said.

"Yep, it's me." From the starry sky, he saw an outline emerge. It was her. "We don't usually show ourselves like this. And I can't stay, but I wanted to say thank you for going after this and goodbye."

"But wait," Malik said, "you can't leave this fast." He noticed fog drifting over from the neighboring trees.

"It's my time," Callie said. She tilted her chin to indicate the space behind him. "You've got everything you need back there," Malik turned around to see Magaly holding his mom's shoulders as she cried, "and in there." Malik saw the dark finger point at his heart, then at his forehead. "I'll always be around. We always are." As the fog moved past the tree, he could no longer see her.

Malik stepped forward when he felt his grandma's hand on his forearm.

"It's time. You'll see your friend again. Don't worry." His grandma looked down, and Malik followed her eyes to the laptop he held in his hands.

Malik held it up on his forearm. "I need your help. Zach Carver put a password on it, and we think that only you know what it is."

Jessica turned to see Nia, who was slowly approaching them. She cupped her mouth with both her hands and cried. "Try 'Nia Carver.'"

Malik's mind reeled, realizing that perhaps it was odd that he never knew who his grandad was. His mom never talked about it, and so he never pressed the issue. Malik looked back at the screen. *Enter Password.* He typed N-i-a-C-a-r-v-e-r.

Initiating System Scan… The screen went black, and there was only a network of trees on the screen. There was a pulse of light, almost like sonar radar. As it pulsed, some new trees showed up on the screen, and others were no longer visible.

Hub Trees Identified….

Detecting Virus Strains….

Magaly was now next to Malik. "What's happening?"

"It showed hub trees. Now I don't know."

Malik felt his grandma's gentle tug on his arm again. He looked over at her, and she was inhaling deeply. "Do you smell that? It smells like mint or…"

Malik followed suit, lifting his head higher and inhaling.

"I smell honey," Magaly said.

"It smells like lemon to me," Nia said.

Malik saw that the screen was now being populated with an array of numbers.

Virus Detection Complete.

Negative.

Initiate Global Network Scan? Confirm or Cancel.

Malik tried to confirm.

Scan Incomplete…

"It's not working," Malik said, racking his brain for what the issue could be. "Maybe the network or satellite connection is no longer in place?"

What now? This was supposed to be the solution. Malik thought back to his dream, sifting through the conversations. Then he saw Coach O walking toward them from the mist around the cluster of trees in the back of the yard.

"Glad to see you guys made it," Ori said, looking from Magaly to Malik.

"Ori?" Malik's mom said, sounding surprised and happy.

"Are you still chasing butterflies in the field?" Ori asked her.

"Not nearly as often as I used to," she admitted.

"Having some trouble?" Ori addressed Malik again.

"It seems to be getting tripped up at the global scan," Malik explained.

"Confidence Biotech hasn't been properly maintaining the network. The Singularity Group will be able to help." Ori took the laptop and handed it to Magaly. "In the meantime, you're part of Aja's accelerated solution as well."

"I am?" Malik asked.

"You and your mother. We need to get the antidote that you carry in your DNA to as many people as possible."

Malik then heard a sound growing louder, breaking the quiet of the dawn. It was a buzzing, like insects' wings. He watched as a thick cloud moved toward them.

"Female mosquitos," Ori explained. "They will take your blood back to their eggs, and billions of mosquitos will then carry a form of the antidote."

Ori walked closer to the trees. Jessica grabbed Malik's and Nia's hands and led them the same way.

They stood under the tree as the sound grew even louder. The cloud of mosquitos surrounded them and lightly landed on his exposed skin. He glanced over at his mom to see the same thing happening to her.

"Don't worry, just take deep breaths," Ori said. "What does that smell like?"

Malik inhaled through his nose. "Lemons."

"Keep breathing that in. It's an aerosol that will protect your bodies from any damage."

It ended quickly, and Malik saw the insects disperse into the darkness like smoke dissipating in the air. He stared at his hands and forearms, then at his mother's face. There wasn't a single telltale sign of a mosquito bite.

"What happens now?" Malik asked. "Will this cure the virus?"

"No," Ori said. "The virus has a right to survive, just like you. But what you've just done has given a lot of people more time."

Malik and his mom made their way back over to Magaly. Ori and Jessica were still in earshot, and Malik heard Ori say, "He did well."

"Yes, he did," his grandma said, looking at Malik and smiling.

"He came through, and without you in play, so you get your time back," Ori said.

Malik's grandma looked happy and weepy simultaneously. Malik watched as she made her way to Nia and hugged her. "I love you more than you can ever know, and I'll see you soon." She then put her hand on Malik's shoulder and gently pulled him down so she could kiss his forehead. "I can't wait to meet you again, and this time, I'll be present for every single second of it."

Malik searched her eyes. "Wait… What—"

DING… Ding… Ding…

Jessica opened her eyes. The plane's overhead lights illuminated the dark cavern as Jessica heard the flight attendant's announcement.

We are now beginning our descent into Hartsfield-Jackson Atlanta International Airport. Please ensure your tray tables are stowed and your seats are in the upright position. We want to apologize again for the delay, and we hope you enjoy your time here in Atlanta, Georgia.

Jessica looked down at her watch. It was just after 3 AM. She gently rubbed her finger across the face of the watch. The minute, second, and hour hands vanished, and she saw all the gears clicking together in sync.

CHARACTER LIST

In Alphabetical Order

1. *Aja:* Resident of the Point and council member responsible for Earth.
2. *Callie:* Malik's childhood friend.
3. *Carlos:* Council member and friend to Ori. First appeared in *The Recruiter* and was widely believed to be the head of La Tiniebla Cartel.
4. *Chance Domagk:* Chief of Staff to the CEO of Confidence Biotech.
5. *Christina:* Receptionist at the doctor's office.
6. *Evelyn (Blackwood):* Ori's team lead. First appeared in *The Recruiter* as an FBI agent as well as friend and colleague to Mikiko Shikibu.
7. *Gabriel:* Council member responsible for human affairs.
8. *Jessica Ifill:* Investigative journalist for Str8 Truth Media. First appeared in *The Recruiter* when she was assigned a story on Ori Clayborn. She was also chosen by Ori's team to be the Scribe.

9. *Jordan:* Member of Ori and Evelyn's team, responsible for field operations. First appeared in *The Recruiter* as a personal assistant for Ori at the Singularity Group.
10. *Magaly:* Nurse and romantic interest of Malik.
11. *Malik:* Inventive young man who is developing a treatment for the virus.
12. *Mikiko (Shikibu):* Deputy Directory of the FBI. First appeared in *The Recruiter* as a colleague and friend of Evelyn Blackwood.
13. *Nia:* A little girl that Jessica encounters at the Point.
14. *Ori (Clayborn):* Member of Evelyn's team and the recruiter himself. First appeared in *The Recruiter* as the CEO of the Singularity Group and the target of an attack.
15. *Dr. Patel:* Doctor of internal medicine and Malik's boss.
16. *Professor Raziel:* Resident of the Point. First appeared in *The Recruiter* as a mentor to Ori.
17. *Dr. Serrano:* Member of Carlos's team who is sent to check on Zach's state of mind. First appeared in *The Recruiter* as an enforcer for Carlos.
18. *Ronnie:* Malik's friend and Callie's ex-boyfriend.
19. *Roy Mengele:* CEO of Confidence Biotech.
20. *Silas (Stillman):* Council member. First appeared in *The Recruiter* as an elite soldier with a decorated military career. Jessica interviewed him for her article on Ori Clayborn and the attack at the Singularity Group.
21. *Tony:* Member of Ori and Evelyn's team, responsible for overall programming and cleanup. First appeared in *The Recruiter* as a private investigator for the Singularity Group.
22. *Dr. Wen Shen:* Former partner of Dr. Patel and co-founder of the practice where Malik works.
23. *Vau:* Anthropologist and member of Ori and Evelyn's team. First appeared in *The Recruiter* as a medic.
24. *Zach Carver:* Head of Research and Development at the Singularity Group, known for creating new, innovative technology. He is also Jessica's source.

DISCUSSION QUESTIONS

1. If you were Jessica, would you travel to the Point? Is there anything else you would've asked of Ori or Gabriel?
2. What dimensions/growth phase do you think you operate on? What about the majority of those around you? What positives and negatives do you see and do they align with the book?
3. While at the Point, they talk about a lot of issues facing the world, including desertification, conflict, etc. What do you see as the biggest issues plaguing the world today?
4. If you could choose between containing greed, ego, war, hate, which would you choose?
5. Have you seen or experienced a great deal of division among people today? What do you think drives it? What can be done?
6. Have you lost someone close to you? Like Malik lost Callie. Did it inspire you or change your course in anyway?
7. How connected do you feel to your roots? How has or does that impact you?
8. Do you often think about or try to interpret your dreams? Have there been any that have stayed with you for a long time?

9. Has fear of public perception or of failure stopped you from pursuing anything in your life?
10. If you were Magaly, at what point would you have bailed on that date, if at all? What's the strangest or most unexpected first date you've been on?

TURN THE PAGE FOR A SAMPLE OF
EMERGENT LIGHT,
BOOK 3 OF *THE REWIRED SERIES*

EXCERPT: AWAKENED WITH PURPOSE

The white flash of light was so bright it awakened Malik, compelling him to open his eyes. The crashing thunder that followed seemed to echo through the house. Malik turned his head to watch the rain out the window. Beyond the beads of rain trickling down the pane, he saw another succession of lightning bolt flashes, all quickly followed by thunder so close that each roar shook his home. Nursing a baby had caused his wife, Magaly, to become a light sleeper. Malik turned to see if she was awake, but her side of the bed was empty and still made. *Did she fall asleep in the nursery again?* Malik wondered, pulling himself out of bed and heading upstairs to relieve her.

Malik moved through the dark, barely feeling his own steps as he made his way up the stairs and down the hallway. Almost too quickly, he found himself in a bedroom that was both incredibly familiar and strange. The room had the same feeling of warmth, love, and familiarity as that of their son Aries, but something was different. Another flash of lightning illuminated the room enough for Malik to see he was not in his son's nursery. Instead, he was back in his childhood home, the one from before his parents' divorce.

Malik stood in what used to be his dad's upstairs office. It, however, was not how he remembered it. There was now a dresser next to the door, a bed along the opposite wall, and a rocking chair facing the window. The chair looked just like the one his grandmother had gifted them for the birth of their elder son, Noah.

"How did this get here?" Malik said softly.

The chair glided back and forth, as if someone were rocking in it. Malik reached out and spun the chair around, expecting to find Noah there, as he often did at home. The hair on Malik's arms raised when he realized no one was there.

Oddly, Malik did not feel scared; he felt more aware. His attention was pulled to the window overlooking the backyard. He glanced down at the old tree stump he used to play on when he was a boy. Several people were standing nearby in the glow of the full moon, untouched by the rain. Scenes he could scarcely identify passed before his eyes, yet he knew they were significant. In a moment, it was over; the faces and places washed away like watercolor paint swirling down a drain. His mom, his grandma, and Magaly were the only faces that remained.

Then farther back in the trees, he saw the familiar fair skin, dark hair, and thin frame of an old friend. "Callie," he whispered. To his surprise, she met his gaze.

Malik backed away from the window. "This has to be a dream."

"It is, and it isn't." Callie's voice came from behind him, startling him.

Malik wanted to turn and look at her, but he hesitated, recalling her request the last time he saw her alive. Callie wanted him to remember her from the before times, not the end times.

"No need to look away," he heard Callie say.

Malik turned to see his friend as she was when they were teenagers. She was healthy; her smile was vibrant. That same smile had been a ray of hope in some dark times. Even a beautiful life has its dark times. The house trembled as he felt the weight of those heavy feelings pulling on him.

"You can release those feelings." Callie gave him a nod of assurance. "Believe it or not, this is a wonderful dream."

"What do you mean?"

"Don't worry, you'll see."

"I'll see what?"

Callie took a few steps closer. "Do you remember the last thing I told you?"

Malik's mind pulled him back to the hospital room, where he sat holding his oldest friend's hand. He felt another wave of sadness until Callie's voice brought him back.

"No," Callie said, "not that. Remember what I said."

"That you know why all of this is happening, why everything is happening?"

"That's right," she said with a smile. "Everything happens for a reason. You'll get to see more of that reason soon."

"Am I dying?" Malik asked.

Callie's eyebrows shot up in surprise, and she quickly replied, "No, no!" She then seemed to consider the idea, shrugged her shoulders, and said, "Well, the old you maybe."

"What do you mean, the old me?"

She shook her head. "Never mind that. Listen," her voice was steady and focused, "what you and Magaly are doing for those boys is amazing. You've found it."

"Found what?"

Callie smiled and mouthed something that Malik could not hear.

"What?" He leaned closer. Callie's mouth was moving as though she were saying something, but Malik couldn't hear anything. The only sound was a loud, high-pitched whine. It sounded like a swarm of mosquitoes. He glanced up and around, feeling as if they were upon him, but he saw nothing. His first instinct was to swat, but his arms wouldn't cooperate.

"I can't hear you," Malik tried to shout, but he couldn't even hear his own voice.

He looked out the window for the source of the noise and caught sight again of his mom and grandma holding hands. A sense of calm came over him, and his muscles relaxed. The sound had reached a peak and was now softening to a dull buzz. Malik closed his eyes and inhaled deeply. Once he fully exhaled, the quiet returned. He opened his eyes and saw Callie still standing there, assessing him.

"What?" Malik asked, but she didn't answer. Before Malik could repeat himself, he heard a loud voice coming from the walls of the house. "Wake up!"

Malik jerked awake, his eyes darting around the room. He was back in his bedroom with the full moon's rays beaming through the window. Magaly was peacefully sleeping next to him, her head turned toward the baby monitor on her nightstand, her curls cascading across her satin pillow cover.

And then he heard it: "Daaadaaa."

ABOUT THE AUTHOR

Alexander had an active imagination his whole life, but it wasn't until the birth of his son that he began putting the stories in his mind on paper. He wanted to be an example for his son of someone pursuing his passion, dreaming big, and taking chances.

Alexander loves people, their stories, and their backgrounds as well as what shapes them, how they think, and what they dream about. He has a passion for learning and is known by most as an intensely curious person who eagerly soaks up anything and everything he can.

Deeply Rooted Dreams is Alexander's second novel and the sequel to *The Recruiter.* For more about him and his works, visit alexandermukte.com.